Moonscape AND OTHER STORIES

MOONSCAPE

AND OTHER STORIES

by **Mika Waltari**

Translated by Naomi Walford

G. P. PUTNAM'S SONS

NEW YORK

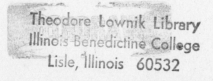

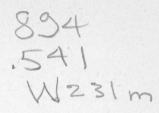

CONTENTS

Moonscape

1

An absurd little narrow-gauge railway ran from
the station to the village, which had now grown into a
market town. Compared with the frightening, snorting
great trains of the grown-ups, this little engine with its
miniature coaches all of different colors was comfortingly
reminiscent of a child's toy. In the big train I had felt oppressed and uneasy, afraid of losing my suitcase or of going
past the right station. The fear had been very real and in-
trusive, and it was with relief that I climbed into one of
the green toy coaches, sat down on a handsomely perfo-
rated wooden bench and stowed my suitcase between my
feet. After all my anxieties I felt I had reached my goal.

The little train suited me; its size was reassuring, and
when with a piercing whistle the engine jerked the coaches
into motion I felt pride on its account. The line was familiar to me; I knew where I had to get out and was sure
of being able to find my way. But I had never made this
journey alone before. Hitherto I'd been a child; now I was
twelve and traveling on my own, and among the underclothes, sandwiches and bathing trunks in my suitcase lay
Stevenson's *Treasure Island*, the most tremendously exciting book I had ever read.

The bathing trunks strengthened my sense of being no
longer a child. Hitherto it had never occurred to me to
wear such things, but in this little country town there was

a public bathing beach on the lake shore, and Mother told me I must wear them there. The moment she said this I realized the truth of it, and felt somehow estranged from her and from all the world, as if some protecting membrane had split and left me naked and afraid in an alien place. But this first confusion had long since passed and now I merely felt very grand in possessing bathing trunks, and also in having a suitcase of my own.

Barely three hours had passed since I had formally shaken hands with my mother on the platform in Helsinki, rigid with dread lest despite her promise she should disgrace me by kissing me good-bye in front of strangers. She had not done so, and these last three hours had swept me away from my former life—from safe, familiar things—into a solitude where I must fend for myself. This was a painful yet exhilarating feeling. Alone I had changed at the junction, and felt proud indeed to have found the right train without difficulty. The loneliness of that too big, too rapid express train had lain heavily upon me. Now that the ordeal was nearly over I straightened up, like a beetle which, having been frightened into shamming death, cautiously spreads its gauzy wings when the danger is past.

I leaned airily back, threw one leg over the other and looked out of the tiny window. The coach rocked pleasantly, the little engine hooted at every bend and a green and red spruce wood rushed by. Then appeared the outlying houses of the town, and the train drew up by an open space beyond which the ancient church, with its steep shingle roof, soared to the sky. Jackdaws were screeching round the steeple.

It was here I had to alight. No one had come to meet me, for my aunt was delicate and suffered from loss of breath, and my uncle disliked interrupting his work without good cause. I knew I should have no difficulty in finding the house, and at the thought that there was now no need for anyone to meet me I felt even more grown-up than before. I paused for a moment to look at the church, knowing that it was a noted feature of the place and was even pointed out to foreign visitors. Its walls were over three feet thick, and had huge stones built into them at such a height that no one knew how people living all those centuries ago had ever got them up there. Or so my aunt said, never forgetting to add that the bigger the stones they laid in the walls the bigger the sins for which they fancied they would be forgiven. Aunt made this remark with heavy irony, well knowing that it was by faith alone and not by works that mankind could attain salvation. Yet in thinking of those far-off days she would heave a gentle sigh and add indulgently, "Poor souls!"

The sight of the church aroused in me a strong feeling of repugnance, for already I could hear the minatory thunders of the organ; the paintings on the walls appeared to my mind's eye in dreadful detail, and again I felt the deadly boredom that had gripped me on every one of the countless Sundays I had spent there, when I was completely in the dark as to what it was all about. Such, again, was the prospect if I meant to spend the whole of August with my aunt, but I tried to persuade myself that those inevitable hours would now be easier to endure. I understood a certain amount by this time and had also begun to think.

I wandered along the dusty road that ran through the little town, looking in at the stationer's window and noting that a new house of stone had been built in the market square. The buildings were painted yellow or white as before and were surrounded by hedges of spruce or hawthorn, and in the gardens there were apple trees. At last I stood before the familiar house. I opened the discolored gate and walked cautiously up to the house along the edge of the sandy path so as not to spoil the wavy patterns made by the rake; Aunt was very particular about these. Quietly and warily I opened the outer door, for Aunt didn't like noise. A white rug striped with red lay on the gleaming, extremely slippery linoleum, and once more the eternal problem confronted me: should I walk on the rug or on the floor? For neither must be dirtied. But the familiar, Old World smell of the house drifted to me reassuringly: the scent of old furniture, clean linen, rusks, linoleum, and freshly roasted coffee. Aunt came towards me, temporarily dismissing all problems from her mind, and held out her big, bony, kindly hand.

"Well, here you are then, Joel," she said. "I'm glad to see you. How's your mother?"

I answered conscientiously all her questions about my mother, my home, and my journey. She showed me where I was to sleep, took the suitcase from me, and offered me a cup of coffee in the kitchen. Here was proof that she considered me full-grown; in the old days I had been given only hot water and cream.

Aunt sat with her chin resting in her hand, scrutinizing me with eyes that sparkled kindly in the big, lean face. When I had eaten four slices of wheaten bread and finished my coffee she glanced towards the door of the workshop and said hesitantly, "Maybe you should go and say how-do-you-do to your uncle."

It was clear that she was as nervous as I was of disturbing him. I therefore knocked cautiously, opened the door and amid the ticking of innumerable clocks walked across the spotless floor to where my uncle was sitting behind the counter. He let the watchmaker's glass drop from his wrinkled eye and turned to greet me. He wore his working coat, but with it a high starched collar and a gray silk tie.

His gray hair was combed carefully back and his scalp gleamed white between the sparse strands. His eyebrows were two wing-shaped tufts and the gray whiskers lent him an air of dignity. But his cheeks and chin, for all his grizzled age, had a sort of roundness and innocence about them, and I felt I had never seen so shy, modest, and kindly a face as my uncle's.

Nevertheless I was nervous as I gave him my hand, though I guessed he was no less so. He stammered and muttered to himself until I thought of giving him my mother's message of greeting. For this he was grateful, since it spared him having to find a topic of conversation; a task which he always found difficult. A black-haired apprentice stared at me from the other end of the table, and then openly stuck out his tongue at me. I was thunderstruck. For me, Uncle's workshop with its everlastingly ticking clocks was as solemn a place as church; especially when with all their clear, various voices they struck the hour together. One began and the rest followed in due order until the noise swelled to a tremendous din which gradually decreased, until only a few belated clocks struck their remaining strokes, half-scared it seemed at the sound of their own voices in a room that was to be silent for the next half hour.

My uncle was shy, though of course he would never own to it. But now that I was older my aunt let me see that she often smiled at him behind his back. It was when women came to the shop that he was most alarmed; at such times he often took refuge in the parlor and let the apprentice deal with them. Strangely enough it was this very shyness and reserve that had won him general esteem. Even the most garrulous restrained themselves in his presence, and although to me he never uttered a word of reproach, I held him in profound veneration, was always afraid of disturbing him, and did my utmost to be quiet when he was about.

When I came out into the kitchen again my aunt sighed with relief and said, "Uncle seems glad to see you." She had watched the greeting ceremony through the crack of the door, and years of experience had taught her to deduce my uncle's thoughts and feelings from his manner. She now looked at me hard as if at a loss what to do with me. "There's over an hour till dinner-time," she said. "You can go out and play till then."

She could have had no inkling of how deeply the word offended me. A person capable of traveling alone from Helsinki and changing trains all by himself had obviously left his playing days far behind him.

"I shall go and bathe," I remarked stiffly, and added, "I've got my bathing trunks."

This crushing remark silenced my aunt and made her look at me with new respect, or so I fancied. Proudly I set off with the trunks under my arm, and strolled through the town towards the beach.

2

Ah, those years of boyhood, when life is full and vivid and sleep comes as one's head touches the pillow—a sleep tranquil and profound! I was happy in that old house, although everything in it was painfully clean and one had to be constantly on one's guard against dirtying things or moving chairs and so on from their appointed places. I soon noticed that my aunt was easiest in her mind when I kept out of sight, and I availed myself of this to the full. She was a conscientious guardian, but had no chil-

dren of her own; to have a twelve-year-old boy on her
hands was as worrying as having a charge of dynamite in
the house. She would have liked to set me to work, for in
her eyes idleness was the mother of all vices; but since for
many years the routine of the household had run in
smooth and self-sufficient grooves it was hard to find anything for me to do. But she did hit on the idea of my
raking the sandy garden paths, and this I did gladly every
morning when dew was still sparkling on the grass and the
air was full of the freshness of approaching autumn. But
the wavy patterns I made never quite satisfied my aunt,
and she regarded the result of my work with pursed lips.

She also let me pick up unripe windfalls and take them
to the neighbor's pig, which ate them with relish and came
to look upon me as a friend. It was a massive, placid beast
with a glint of unexpected playfulness in its red-rimmed
eyes, and it liked nudging the toe of my sandal with its
snout. Discovering in it queerly human traits, I felt it was
wrong to feed and fatten it just for the sake of turning it
into Christmas ham. The idea depressed me, and I was
glad to bring it all the windfalls there were, since it set
such store by them.

But at this point my aunt's ingenuity gave out. Whenever she caught sight of me she began casting about for a
job for me to do, but so long as I was absent her conscience
slept; and so for the sake of her peace of mind I kept out
of the way as much as possible. On rainy days I took refuge in the bakehouse, which was very seldom used, and if
my aunt happened to look in to see what I was up to I
could always show her my arithmetic book and my Swedish
reader, as evidence of the many stiff holiday tasks to be
done before school began again. Uncle's apprentice lent
me a coverless, tattered copy of *The Three Musketeers,*
and for the first few rainy days I was blissfully happy.

When I began to yearn for more reading matter my aunt led me to Uncle's modest bookshelf. The black bindings of devotional works held no attraction for me, and the books on astronomy were too drearily reminiscent of school. Even my aunt realized that books of devotion did not make very exciting reading for a boy of my age; yet in her opinion training in temperance could never begin too early, and she therefore took down a thick book bound in green and handed it to me. It was called *Echoes from the Rostrum.*

I took it without enthusiasm and looked round the parlor. The boards were scrubbed white and on them lay white mats striped with red. The sofa, chairs, and table, ornamented with lathe-turned spheres and bobbins, were from St. Petersburg, where my uncle had trained. The seats were of red plush, though now in the summer they were hidden by neat blue-striped covers. It was in this room, in a narrow bed with brown wooden head- and footboards, that Uncle slept; but in its cleanliness and quiet the room felt quite uninhabited. One evening my aunt was distressed to find that I no longer repeated my evening prayer aloud, and she led me to the parlor door just as my uncle was going to bed. Through the door I could hear his high, clear, old man's voice saying his prayers, and Aunt said that if Uncle did this, I could. He used always to kneel, she said, but of recent years he had taken to saying his prayers in bed, lying on his back with his hands crossed on his chest. My aunt therefore felt she could not insist on my kneeling, but at least I must pray aloud.

I had to comply. Thenceforth I repeated "Look on me" as Mother liked me to, and then "God bless Aunt and Uncle and save the heathen and protect all sailors on the far seas," for Aunt considered this important. Knowing that she listened from her room every night, I occasionally added thanks for the cakes she had baked that day, mentioning that they had been specially good; and this did not displease her. She was always anxious to prove that little boys' prayers were noted in the highest quarters, and so whenever dinner had been really very meager I would summon up courage and express hopes concerning the next day's fare. Like most old people my aunt and uncle ate very little, though their food was always wholesome and good. Bread was cut in paper-thin slices and at dinner Uncle never took butter. My aunt realized that the Spartan diet decreed by him was unsuited to a growing boy, and she did her best to supplement it with snacks between meals. She also gave me money to buy fruit on market days, and I never had to account to her for it. One way and another my prayers were often answered most wonderfully, and my aunt was delighted. To me there was something frightening in this game between God, Aunt, and myself; but I supposed that on the Day of Judgment God, if he was God, would be merciful and forgive both Aunt and me.

In the strange vacuum of this house, where for years time had been at a standstill, my mind concerned itself more with God than was perhaps usual for boys of my age. Having read the astounding and unforgettable *Echoes from the Rostrum* I voluntarily added a further petition to my prayers: that God might protect all drunkards. For I was now fully alive to the terrors and temptations of drink. The book had been compiled by a noted orator and contained a vast collection of stories and anecdotes about the abuse of alcohol, some terrible, others ridiculous. Men beat their wives until they became permanent invalids, fathers flung their daughters into the fire, and the liquid waste from a whiskey distillery was so strong as to corrode the galoshes of passers-by. Small wonder that this robust world, described in so forthright a style, fascinated me as much as *Treasure Island* or *The Three Musketeers*.

Uncle was a good Christian and a blameless man, who had solved whatever problems life may have presented to him by withdrawing from the world, keeping his body and clothes clean, and avoiding all temptations. To counteract his sedentary hours in the workshop he went for a long walk every day at the same time and in all weathers. He may have fancied that he'd been neglecting me or that I was bored, for one day after dinner he coughed shyly and invited me to come with him. This was so extraordinary that my aunt was quite flustered; she made me change my clothes and put on shoes instead of sandals. Uncle was dressed in an impeccable white suit and an old Panama hat, and carried a walking stick with a silver crook.

Side by side we followed Uncle's usual route, first down to the shore, then along a woodland path and finally up on to the ridge. He must have felt every bit as embarrassed and ill-at-ease as I did, but he trudged bravely on, staring before him. I can still see his rounded, childish face and dreamy blue eyes. After a mile or so we reached a clearing in the woods and Uncle remarked, "They're going to bring a new electric cable along here."

He smiled, his whole face radiant with delight at having found something to say. Then we came upon a dead crow by the roadside. Uncle turned it over with his stick but had no comment to make. I would have liked to examine it more closely, but since Uncle found it unworthy of remark I refrained.

When we reached the top of the hill he paused by a grass-grown bank, stared at it for a long time and said, "This is where the Russian soldiers had their rifle range in the old days." Glancing at me quickly he jerked out, "The boys still dig up bullets here now and then."

It was the only hint he ever gave that his own sealed vacuum of a world could ever brush the borders of mine. We finished our walk along a route hallowed by a score of years—a route which Uncle had once chosen and never afterwards departed from—and as we walked I felt we were as far apart as if we'd been living on different planets. Yet this walk was for me so thrilling an experience that the memory of it and its countless vivid details remained with me for years, long after more eventful and superficially more interesting matters were forgotten. This walk, in the course of which my uncle uttered perhaps twenty shy words, still glows in my mind with the radiance of immortality.

The years of boyhood form a series of bright points between which all gray, sad, and hopeless things sink and vanish. At times, no doubt, I was unutterably bored, though I was perhaps unaware of it and merely supposed that that was how people always were.

Every Sunday we went to church. Uncle wore a dark suit and looked exceedingly uncomfortable as he walked along with short, slow steps, pausing now and then to allow Aunt to get her breath. As we approached the church door he had to raise his hat continually, and did so with modest dignity, his round face overspread with a shy, awkward smile. He was not himself again until he could subside into his usual place near the pulpit beside a mighty pillar, where he was hidden from the public gaze. Then he bent his head and clasped his hands in prayer. I had then two hours in which to contemplate the wall paintings and think of my own affairs.

I learned to know all the holy apostles and their emblems, for with each painting was a scroll inscribed in old-fashioned Gothic lettering. But my eyes turned for choice to the pictures in which something was happening, and there was no lack of them. Two especially seemed to vie with one another for pre-eminence. One portrayed a number of little sooty devils with long tails making up a huge fire with their tongs under some poor human wretches who seemed in agony. In the other an executioner had just struck off Saint Barbara's head; pale blood spurted in a broad jet from her neck into the air, while a wheel nearby suggested the immediate fate of the body. From the ground the saint's head regarded her still kneeling form in astonishment.

These pictures did not disturb me in the least, for I was only twelve and quite untouched by their imagery. Surprising things were going on in them, but they in no way concerned me and I could look at them as I would have looked at an exciting picture book, finding in them rich material for my imagination to work upon. They had as little to do with my innermost self as the sermon now echoing impressively beneath the vaulted roof. To me and perhaps to many of the grown people this echoing was what mattered; any possible meaning in the words was of secondary importance. Uncle listened with half-closed eyes, now and then sitting up straight to fix his attention. Aunt observed the congregation with keen interest, and from time to time stifled an incipient yawn. But when the service was over and, released from the clutches of the sermon and the weight of that ancient roof, we stepped out into the bright summer day, we all revived and felt extremely cheerful, as if cleansed from the week's misdeeds and in some way transfigured. At home the glorious smell of strong coffee filled the air. Aunt baked on Saturdays, and it was with light hearts that we sat down at the table.

Ah, those bright, immortal glimpses! The severed and astonished head of Saint Barbara on the wall of the church, the clean, sour taste of a red-flecked fallen apple, the au-

tumn freshness of mornings in the dewy garden that made
one's breast feel near to bursting; Athos, Porthos, and
Aramis in the flour-laden air of the bakehouse; but, above
all, one clear August day on the beach, when lightning
struck my heart.

The bathing beach was public. It had white sand and a
long jetty, and the water was clear. Close thickets of wil-
low and alder edged the shore on the landward side, and
behind them came the woods. At that time there were no
bathing huts, and bathers undressed in the thickets. There
was plenty of room for everyone, for the beach stretched
for several hundred yards. Sometimes with other boys,
though most often alone, I would undress, pull on my
swimming trunks and stride into the water; or I would tear
along the sand, roll in it, toss it about and laugh and
shout with the rest. It was a pristine joy, unmixed with
sad or troubling things.

But one day as I was making for home along the beach
I beheld a young girl in the sunshine near a clump of
willows. She had just come out of the water and was drawing off her wet bathing suit. Taking me for just a little boy
she didn't trouble to hide, and revealed her white body
unconcernedly. I was so taken aback that I stopped short
and gazed at her. She burst out laughing, waved the wet
bathing suit at me and shouted, "Hi, you there—what are
you staring at?"

I dashed away, stumbling in the deep sand and overcome with shame. But my eyes had been dazzled by the
sunlit, water-cool image. That lovely naked girl had smiled
at me, standing there so white, so wonderful, so outrage-
ously fair. I lost all consciousness of my surroundings and
as if blinded I trudged on, shaken to the core by what I
had seen; instinctively I felt that I had done something

shameful and ugly in staring at the naked girl, and yet I couldn't have said why it was so.

The lightning flash struck me to the heart, though I was still only a boy with a mind as limpid as a drop of dew. Never had I known either desire or pain, and human griefs were remote from me; yet from somewhere deep within me there sprang dazzling fantasies of nakedness and bliss and that incomparable ecstasy that can flood one's whole being with tumult. Outwardly I was exactly as before; inwardly something had changed, something had begun to grow. I wanted to forget it, to wipe it from my memory, for it troubled and saddened me. And perhaps I did forget it for long periods at a time, yet never entirely; it was there, though wrapped in darkness. That is why they stand out so clearly side by side in my memory: the cool, sunlit, naked figure and the alien darkness of my boy's mind.

For several days I searched, furtively and with a nagging conscience, for the face of the unknown girl among the other faces on the beach, and though I never saw her again I still remember her eyes and her smile and how she laughed at me. I loved her for having vouchsafed to me a glimpse of that sweet and terrible beauty—beauty that was even enhanced in my secret thoughts. But I feared her more than I loved her, for instinct told me that if Aunt and Uncle and perhaps even Mother had known of this they would have felt I'd done something disgraceful and forbidden—something too ugly for forgiveness. And so I was glad I never saw her again.

The day of my return to Helsinki was approaching when my aunt was visited by a delicate-looking woman who led a little girl by the hand. Though the girl was perhaps not much younger than myself she seemed to me a small child, for I had already identified myself with grown-ups. She had round, red cheeks and dark, inquisitive eyes. Two thick plaits hung down her back.

"This is Mir-yam," said my aunt. "Say how-do-you-do and take her out to play. She's starting school here this winter, and she's going to live with us."

The girl put her plump hand into mine and met my eyes fearlessly. I learned later that she had many brothers and was therefore not shy of boys.

"Come on, let's go out," she said, "so that Mummy can talk to Auntie."

I hadn't the least wish to play with her, chiefly because I thought I was too old. Her hair seemed to me much too black and thick and her cheeks too red, and I also considered that she was treating me over-familiarly. As soon as we were in the hall I took my hand away, and when we got outside I began kicking a stone across the yard without looking at her.

"My name's not Mir-yam but Mi-ri-am," she said, articulating very distinctly so that I might understand. I wondered how to get rid of her. For my aunt's sake I had to pay her some attention, and I led her resignedly to the well, which I thought the only thing worthy of notice on the place, for it was very dark and deep. She peered politely into it and said "Oo!"

With her brown eyes on me she shuddered as much from genuine fear as from the pleasure of being afraid. I looked at her with suspicion, feeling that she was overdoing it, and then reflected that girls probably always did. Picking up two green apples from the ground I said with the surliness of desperation, "Come and see the pig."

I took her to the neighbor's pig, to which I gave the apples. Miriam looked on politely and without a spark of interest. She was beginning to irritate me. She gazed into the distance and then with a quick glance at me she said suddenly, "I'm going to be a missionary when I grow up."

3

I believe a year or more went by before I saw my aunt again. It was during the Christmas holidays. I went there immediately after Christmas, and it seems to me now that during that time the weather was never cold, though snow lay on the ground. Yes, as I remember it, those Christmas holidays were strangely mild, and it is less the short, gray days that I recall than the soft, friendly lamps shining out from the houses at nightfall, and the airy dance of snowflakes within the radiance cast by the windows.

I had grown and was surlier than before, to mask my adolescent shyness. I gave abrupt, monosyllabic answers to the questions of grown people and avoided their eyes. I wore my best suit and long trousers to which I was not yet accustomed; they too seemed to have claims upon me. My general demeanor was intended to imply that I dwelt among my own thoughts, which were more important than silly questions and everyday doings. I may indeed have been meditating deep and significant things—who knows? If so they have long ago vanished from my memory. I must in any case have been a remarkably gloomy individual until I began to thaw out and adapt myself to the timeless atmosphere of the house, with its slow, gentle, infinitely melancholy ground bass: the ceaseless ticking of clocks in Uncle's workshop.

The moment I arrived Miriam rushed up to me, threw her arms round my neck and would no doubt have kissed me if I hadn't thrust her from me in confusion. Perhaps she had some right, as it had turned out that we were distantly related; her mother was second cousin to mine, or something of the sort. My aunt would have been able to explain the relationship exactly, and indeed did so, but I never bothered to listen. At that time nothing seemed to me sillier than long-drawn-out unravelings of family relationships. There were more important things to think about—the immortality of the soul, for instance, or that ingenious refrigeration plant at home with which one could make nitroglycerine.

Miriam had grown too and was lankier than before. Her face was no longer quite as round as when I first met her, but her hair was as black and thick, her plaits as long and shining. She rushed at me like a puppy that has been kept too long on the leash and is ready to romp with anyone. It must have been terribly discouraging when I pushed her away like that; she had been waiting for me, hoping for a playfellow. Perhaps she had imagined us both tumbling in the snow among the bare apple trees; for although this was the second winter she had attended school and lived with my aunt, she still failed to grasp that one must not trample on the fresh snowdrifts in the garden, or roll in them. The most we might do was to play in the snow in front of the bakehouse where we couldn't be seen from the road.

When Miriam realized that I was serious in my discouragement of her, her behavior instantly changed and she withdrew from me. In a moment she became grown-up and silent, staring past me into the distance with dark, dreaming eyes, and implying that her thoughts were miles away. If I asked her anything she would start, and apologize for not having heard what I said. My aunt watched her and confided to me that she was quite worried on her account.

"I never knew anyone so moody and fitful," she said. "She learns her lessons all right—she has to—but you can never tell what marks she'll get; she'll fail in one thing and be highly commended in the next. She fights with the boys at school, and sometimes she chatters and shouts and laughs so much that I'm afraid she'll get on Uncle's nerves. Then again she'll sulk for a week and refuse to eat. That's when she thinks she'd like to enter a convent and leave the vanities of the world behind her. Then all at once she'll turn to and prink and deck herself out like a gipsy, till it makes you sick to see her. Where can she have got it from? There's never been anything like it in our family. We're mostly even-tempered folk, like me and your mother. You can't spank her, either; she's too big for it. And now she wants to cut off her hair."

In spite of myself this exposition of feminine whims began to interest me.

"In Helsinki," I remarked, with the air of an initiate, "girls don't wear long plaits any more. Not that I've seen any. They're all either shingled or bobbed."

Aunt looked at me as if I had dropped a snake on her polished linoleum.

"What sort of heathen words are those you've picked up?" she demanded. "I'm disappointed in you. I thought you were a serious-minded boy. Don't you go putting silly ideas into the girl's head, that's all!"

I was cut to the quick.

"I don't know anything about it," I retorted with equal vehemence. "It's only what I've read in the paper and seen in the streets. Even Mother waves her hair."

"That's different," said my aunt irritably. "Your mother's a married woman. But it's not right for a young girl to wear her hair in sinful curls. And only fallen women cut off their hair."

Up to that time my knowledge of fallen women had been purely biblical.

"Let him who is without sin among you cast the first stone," I returned solemnly; and I meant it.

Aunt was silent and looked at me with quite a new expression in her face. For a long time she remained quiet; then she said almost humbly, "Perhaps you'll be a pastor one day, Joel." Supported by this glorious vision she was evidently ready to forgive much, and I deemed it wisest not to mention my determination to be a chemical engineer. This I had decided long ago. But I allowed Aunt to treat me as a priest-to-be, and even reveled in her changed attitude; though she still muttered to herself—in connection with being without sin—that never in her life had she so much as dreamed of cutting off her own hair.

As far as Miriam was concerned I might not have existed, and after a day or two this began to bother me. I saw that I'd snubbed her too heavily, and now tried to show a friendly interest. But she in her turn repulsed me. I was offended, and resolved to leave her to herself.

One mild, snow-dimmed evening the sewing club held a meeting at the Assembly Hall. The main feature was to be a lantern lecture by a missionary recently returned from Africa, though in Miriam's opinion it was her own performance that would be the star turn. She was to recite a poem; and she retired beforehand into the privacy of the bakehouse to practice. Just before we were due to leave she started a violent dispute with my aunt over a red silk bow which she wanted to wear in her hair and which Aunt thought unsuitable for a public gathering of so serious a nature. Miriam lost her temper and stamped, tears glistening in her alarmingly fiery eyes. Rushing up to me she screamed, "Look, Joel! Isn't it nice? Don't I look pretty with it? Tell me what *you* think."

I looked, and felt quite scared. She seemed all on fire, her mouth and eyes were wet, her cheeks burned and the red silk bow glowed in her black hair like a flame.

"I think it's very red," I replied cautiously.

"The girl can't stand up in front of a Christian gathering and recite a religious poem, all got up like a heathen monkey!" said Aunt decisively. "Sinful display and vanity's the short cut to hell."

In my mind's eye I beheld the road to hell lined with red silk bows, and it was a splendid sight. I should have liked to laugh the matter off with some conciliatory remark, but the emotional storm between the women was too violent to be allayed by an outsider. Only Aunt's religious zeal could quench Miriam's fire.

Uncle was dressed and ready and now tried to intervene, though this demanded a great effort from him.

"I wonder if anyone would really object to a plain bow like that in a little girl's hair?" he said with a nervous cough. "It'll hardly be noticed."

To so kind-hearted a man it was painful to see Miriam's tearful eyes, though he could not conceive how anyone could cry over such a trifle as a red silk bow.

Uncle was wrong. The bow was too big and too red for people not to notice it, and although I would have liked to help Miriam I sensed that she was fighting in a bad cause. My aunt wound up the dispute.

"She's getting to be a big girl now, and even if the bow did her no harm, the people there would blame us—blame you and me. We're responsible for her upbringing," she said.

"Then I'll stay away!" Miriam threatened. "I shan't come—I'll stay home. I shall go to bed." She frowned and blinked, and her lips quivered.

"Very well," said my aunt, relieved. "Stay at home,

then." It was evident that she had little faith in Miriam's ability to recite, and dreaded some mishap. This clinched the matter. Slowly, sighing deeply, Miriam removed the ribbon from her hair. But she was soon cheerful again, and although my aunt tried to hustle her she insisted on combing her hair once more, smoothing it down hard and plaiting it in two plaits which she tied with black ribbons. She also tore off the white lace collar that Aunt had given her to relieve the black dress. It was dreadful to see her with her hair tugged back tight enough to stretch the skin of her forehead, her little girl's figure in the ugly black frock, black woolen stockings and black boots. All that black made her face look pale. When she glanced at me she kept her eyes half-closed—then suddenly opened them to survey me, darkly, brilliantly, until she seemed to be all eyes.

Aunt muttered to herself, as if aware that in some obscure way she had suffered defeat. As we walked along to the Assembly Hall the bright lights from the windows shone out, and in the hall itself there was light everywhere. We hung up our outer garments or laid them on the wooden benches in the lobby.

Women smiled at each other in their best clothes, the hands of most of them still red from washing-up, but their toil-stiffened faces were relaxed and their harsh natures cushioned with Christian charity.

The hall smelled of varnish and mothballs. The President of the Sewing Club, who had startlingly large and white false teeth, welcomed the guest of honor who had come from so far away, and invoked the Lord's blessing on his labors in Africa. Then we sang and prayed, and with a tingling warmth in my body I felt myself becoming one with this reverently joyous company. I was ashamed of being so callous and stubborn and I determined to forgive all my enemies and repent of my sins. I also resolved to do better at school, to go oftener to church in Helsinki and to the YMCA meetings, which I had begun to neglect for secret visits to the cinema.

There were at least a couple of hundred people in the room. It was very hot. As Miriam's turn approached she gripped my hand as if seeking support. Her hand was moist from excitement. I tried to imagine how I should feel if compelled to step forward before this vast crowd to recite a poem, and was terrified on her account. Yet Miriam was not afraid; on the contrary she seemed to be reveling in the suspense. When her turn came and her name was announced, she wiped her palms with her embroidered handkerchief, squeezed it in one hand and walked slowly and composedly forward. Without hesitation she stepped up onto the rostrum, though the President of the Sewing Club had been content to speak modestly from beside it. Once there she curtsied, then turned her pale face upwards as if seeking guidance from the roof. The rash child had not taken the book with her, for she wanted to show that she knew the poem by heart.

It was a grandiose poem and it made a deep impression upon me and upon the rest of the audience. So far as I remember it concerned lions which ate Christians, and a little boy who would not deny his faith but repeated at the end of every verse: "I am a Christian!"

He—or rather Miriam—spoke these words timidly at first, then in defiance, then reverently and passionately until in the last verse the words swelled into a valiant, jubilant affirmation: "I am a Christian!" Aunt wept. Uncle wiped his forehead and nose with his neatly folded handkerchief. I too was deeply moved, and the President of the Sewing Club was said to have observed afterwards at the pastor's house that there was not a dry eye in the hall. Miriam's number was a triumphant success.

My own emotion sprang not from the poem alone but from Miriam, at whom I had stared open-mouthed throughout. In stepping onto the platform she had been transformed into someone quite different from the girl who had just been sitting beside me with her moist hand in mine; she became a strange being—a flame—whom I devoured with my eyes in stunned admiration. She grew as she declaimed; as a suppliant she raised her hands to mollify the merciless judges until her face shone with the rapture of a sure faith. I heard the roaring of the lions from the arena and felt giddy as I stared at her shining dark eyes. All applauded enthusiastically when she stepped down from the rostrum. She paused to curtsy with a radiant smile at the audience before returning to her place between my aunt and me.

The missionary was an overworked, careworn man in a shabby suit. He began his talk by asking a blessing on the young girl who had just given so moving a proof of her talents, and said he hoped she would ever continue to employ those gifts to the glory of God. He too could tell of lions: terrible live lions still lurking in the bush, lying in wait for preachers of the Word who sought to bring the glad tidings to the heathen. He spoke of children whose heartless mothers left them out to be devoured by wild beasts. He displayed skilfully made spears and shields as evidence of the blood lust of heathen peoples, as well as baskets and other domestic objects to show how these same peoples' interest could be diverted into peaceful channels once they embraced the Christian faith. Then he knocked on the floor with a rod and the lights were switched off. Colorful pictures flashed onto the screen and enlivened his accounts. His talk was in a practical vein and full of interest, without undue emphasis on his own work. Over and over again one theme was repeated: the harvest truly was plenteous but the laborers were few. What the mission station had so far achieved was but a drop in the ocean. He was much cast down and did not seem to feel that his life away in distant Africa was in any way praiseworthy.

But I could not listen to his lecture with proper attention, being far too deeply shaken by Miriam to receive further impressions until I had regained my balance. I wondered why I had never taken much notice of her before, staying as I had been in the same house, eating at the same table, and breathing the same polish-and-rusk-scented air. I was stone-blind, it seemed, and quite lacking in discrimination, since I had not prized her until everyone else had succumbed to her charm. I hadn't even noticed how beautiful she was—how radiant her face, how brilliant her eyes.

Miriam was restless too and fidgeted on her bench. She tried to whisper something to me, but Aunt, who was by now coming to her senses again, shook her by the arm and hissed at her not to disturb the missionary's lecture.

It wasn't until we were once more sitting round the tea table at home that we calmed down. Miriam had drunk in every word of praise that had been spoken of her, and my aunt was justly uneasy. She warned us against vainglory and at last forbade us to speak another word about the affair. We drank weak tea and ate paper-thin sandwiches. Twice my aunt had to get up and cut more bread, and she shook her head fearing lest Uncle should disapprove. But he didn't. On the contrary he passed a gentle hand over Miriam's hair with a dreamy look in his blue eyes. I fancy it was the boldest caress he had ever ventured upon, but he evidently felt impelled to express his fondness for her. I wasn't jealous; I thought it quite natural that all tokens of kindness and favor should be lavished on Miriam. I thought she was wonderful. I couldn't take my eyes off her and felt that I had never really seen her before.

Even now, when I smell wax polish or taste hot tea I see before me Miriam as she then was: a lanky girl in her teens with an oval face, dark eyes, and coal-black lashes. Perhaps she was beautiful even then.

After this we were no longer shy of each other. Miriam recited poems to me in the bakehouse, talked about school and confided her secrets. We talked incessantly together, yet with a certain wariness, weighing our thoughts and choosing our words. A hidden tension seemed to have developed between us, to which it seemed only some definite incident could put an end. This worried and puzzled me as if I'd been doing something wrong. But of these days—the days when we really came to know each other—I have nothing material to say. They melt like snowflakes on warm skin when I try to recall them.

I do remember however the mild moonlit evening when after a long interval my uncle brought his shining brass telescope into the yard again, fixed it to the tripod and let us look through it at the moon and the stars. The snow glimmered blue-white in the moonlight and the bare branches of the apple trees cast shadows across it. I gazed through the telescope at the moon's dead craters and dried-up seas, whose Latin names Uncle recited to me with shy pride.

But I wasn't thinking of Latin names. I was thinking of the boundlessness of space and the chill of eternity, of the moon's extinct volcanoes and rugged landscapes, of the motions of the stars that were beyond the reach of thought. A cold shiver ran down my spine when I saw myself as a mere speck of dust on the surface of an insignificant planet, born of nothing and vanishing into nothing. I thought as I surveyed the extinguished landscape of the moon: what do good and evil matter? My hope and fear, my suffering and pain would flicker out and be blown away like dust. In the time-reckoning of space a human life was but a second. As I scanned the sky through the glass, the notion of a personal God ruling the galaxies and their myriad worlds seemed senseless; and even if one could conceive of such a God it was unthinkable that he should concern himself with one silly little human life. Least of all could he bear any relation to the manlike god of the meetinghouses and churches, who had taken upon himself the form of a trinity and yet remained one and indivisible. No, the moon's dead landscape in the fathomless cold of the sky brought home to me the infinite foolishness of all human imaginings.

In his shy way my uncle began to betray a certain impatience, and we left him in peace to gaze at his stars and to make notes about them for some dim purpose of his own.

"Aunt, may Joel and I take an apple each?" Miriam begged when we were back in the house. Aunt's best apples lay carefully wrapped in paper and packed in shavings in a box in the shed. She hoarded them jealously for her guests, though now and then as a mark of extraordinary favor she would let us take one. Miriam did this without leave sometimes, when she was sent on some errand to the shed, though she knew that the box was not supposed to be opened except in her aunt's presence. But this time Aunt gave her the big rusty key, saying,

"Go and get them for yourselves—but only one each, mind."

My mouth was watering in advance as I thought of the juicy ripe fruit; my mouth watered, though my thoughts were still busy with the desolate crater-world of the moon.

Miriam lit the candle in a sooty lantern and we ran coatless from the bakehouse to the shed, the winter air cooling my hot cheeks. The shed was full of the scent of apples. I held the lantern; Miriam opened the box and after careful choosing picked out two. Then she said, "It's quite light in here," and blew out the candle. Through the open door the blue-white moonlight flooded into the dark shed. The smell of the smoking wick mingled with that of the fruit.

"You can have this one," she said, putting a big apple into my hand; in the cold air it carried the warmth of her hand to mine. We stood there with our apples. Miriam looked at me and her eyes glinted in the moonlight. My heart began thumping.

"Joel," she whispered very softly. I groped clumsily for her hand and held it in mine. Over and beyond space, galaxies and planets, I held her warm hand in mine amid the moonlight and the fragrance of ripe apples, while my heart thudded so violently that I could scarcely breathe. It was the first hint of emotional tumult I had ever felt, and perhaps I never again knew so pure a rapture. A moment only, and she withdrew her hand, picked up the lantern, and locked the door after us. But the touch was of eternity. I did not know, I never even dreamed that I was blindly in love with her. I had no desire to possess her, no thought that the contact might have lasted longer or led to more. I was blissful and thankful and not at all downcast by the knowledge that I must soon leave there, and might not see her again for a long time. Or perhaps in my heart, born of my sense of inferiority, lay the certainty that it was not for my sake she existed. And so I was merely grateful for that warm touch of her hand, and wished for nothing more.

On the last night of my Christmas holidays, when I was

already in bed, I heard her whispering and tittering with my aunt in the adjoining room. Then the door opened and she entered carrying a palm branch from some funeral wreath that Aunt had, and wearing a white nightdress embroidered at neck and sleeves in red. She glided forward in the light from the open door, waving the branch.

"I am Joel's guardian angel," she chanted solemnly. Behind her my aunt laughed dryly and said, "What'll the child think of next?" But she was not displeased.

Miriam glided up and down the room on bare feet, until with a sudden glance round at her aunt she rushed over to my bed. "Good night, Joel," she whispered, and bending down she pressed her cool, tightly closed young lips against my mouth. Her little breast touched my elbow and I trembled where I lay—trembled with ecstasy but also with guilt because I could feel that she was naked under her nightdress. Then she returned with dancing steps the way she had come, and Aunt, drawing her from the room, wished me good night and closed the door. I lay quivering in the darkness, still feeling the touch of her cool young mouth on mine. Perhaps it was a sin, I thought. Perhaps it was a dreadful sin, because it was so wonderful and made me so hot all over. But now I thought I understood how it was that people could fall into sin and yet have no fear of hell-fire.

4

Years passed before I saw her again, and for long periods I forgot all about her. I went through my own adolescence with my senses in a ferment. On rare occasions my aunt came to Helsinki to see the doctor, and would then stay with us. In my home surroundings she seemed less formidable and inflexible than in her own old house. Her face was growing thinner and yellower. In the evenings she sat in a basket chair conversing monosyllabically with Mother and smoking asthma cigarettes which she bought at the chemist's to relieve her breathlessness. I went my own way and saw little of her. I gathered only that she was worrying over Miriam and felt anxious about her future. The schoolteachers said that Miriam was gifted but lazy. At school she had taken part in fairy-tale plays, and once she had secretly run off to see a touring theatrical company that was appearing at the Assembly Hall. There was also a local amateur dramatic society, and Miriam had begged and pleaded to be allowed to join. But Aunt said that it would be over her dead body. The theater was sinful and actors immoral. The one exception was perhaps the National Theater which was said to have some fairly respectable people in its employ, though even here Aunt had her doubts.

I asked her to give my love to Miriam, and then forgot them both.

During my last summer at school I was sent as our representative to an interscholastic sports meet which was to be held that year at the little town where my aunt lived. Miriam's mother was dead by then and her brothers and sisters scattered about the country among relatives. Aunt and Uncle had undertaken Miriam's guardianship and she now lived permanently with them. To chase foolish and harmful notions from her head my aunt kept her hard at work. Aunt herself was now so frail that she could no longer manage housework, and Miriam had to sweep, dust, wash up, and help with the cooking. She was a tall, dark, sulky-looking girl with short hair when I saw her again. She was as strange to me as if I had never met her before.

At school dances I had admired the self-assured, self-willed girls who used powder and lipstick. I had won a certain reputation as an athlete and many of them took notice of me. Compared with them Miriam, with her dark shabby dress and smooth short hair, was very insignificant. I was deeply disappointed.

The house had shrunk and was much lower than I remembered; my aunt was fragile and my uncle's workshop absurdly old-fashioned; the apple trees were moss-grown and the grass in the garden uncared-for. I marveled that I could ever have been happy in this cramped house, whose ancient smell now seemed to me stale and stifling. And at first my former admiration for Miriam was equally incomprehensible, and I felt glum as I remembered my delight at hearing that the sports were to be held in this town.

Uncle and Miriam came to watch the sports. I came in third in the hundred meters, but in the high jump I was nowhere. This annoyed me, though no one had expected me to win points in this event. I took no further interest in the contests, and to conceal my sense of failure I made the excuse to Uncle that I'd been studying too hard to spare time for proper training. On the evening of the second day came the prize giving, followed by a farewell party. This was held in the school hall and we had permission to dance until midnight.

Miriam was drying dishes in the kitchen when I asked her to come. She hadn't expected this, and her eyes widened and shone. But she turned away her head at once and her face grew sulky and hard again. "I've got nothing to wear," she said curtly.

"Miriam doesn't dance," my aunt hastened to put in. Miriam flashed her a look of blazing wrath but said nothing, and went on furiously wiping the meat platter.

"I shan't dance either," I remarked, to please Aunt, who was convinced that dancing was a short cut to hell.

"That's right, Joel," she said approvingly. "You're a good boy, and perhaps one day you'll be a pastor. Miriam may go with you, so long as you come home in good time."

"I don't want to!" cried Miriam in a rage. Her lips began to quiver and she dashed out of the room.

"She's always like that," said my aunt despairingly. "What is one to do with her? Now she'll cry and sulk all the evening. Don't follow her, she may hit you. She bit my hand once when I had to give her a slap."

But I was sorry for Miriam, and went after her into the next room. She was sitting crying with her face in her hands, trying to stifle her sobs so that they should not be heard. I put my hand on her shoulder but she shook it off. Then, wiping her eyes with her clenched fists, she turned and looked at me defiantly. Her eyes and face were wet and swollen. She looked very ugly.

"Why do you pester me?" she cried. "You don't care about me—nobody does. You only asked me out of politeness."

"I didn't!" I assured her, and believed it myself. "If you won't come I shan't go. We can just walk about if you can't dance."

"But I haven't got a dress," she cried in despair. Yet her eyes had begun to shine again.

"Who has?" I said. "And what does it matter? It's summer."

"You're a boy—you don't understand these things," she said cuttingly. "All right, then—we'll go, just to annoy Aunt."

Her checked summer dress was certainly nothing to boast of, nor her cheap coral necklace. But she was young and slender, with straight, beautiful legs. Her little breasts swelled defiantly beneath the stuff of her dress. Now that her sulkiness was gone there was something challenging in her dark face—in her whole being. My aunt surveyed her disapprovingly and pulled at her dress; she was plainly racking her brains to find some way of dressing Miriam so that she shouldn't look indecent.

"You've grown awfully pretty, Miriam," I said impulsively when at last we had passed through the creaking door and out onto the white road. We both drew a deep breath.

"Don't talk rubbish," she snapped. "You're just teasing me." But she glanced down at her dress, stretched out her leg in its cotton stocking and said in a melting voice, "Do you really mean it? Have I?"

"Yes, really you have," I assured her. "What do clothes matter? You'd be prettier than anyone here if you hadn't any on at all." I was bold enough to say such things now, and my guess was right: she was not offended.

"That may be," she said in a matter-of-fact tone. "You ought to see me like that, Joel. That's something Aunt can't spoil."

I dared not meet her eyes. From some dark corner of my mind sprang the enchanted memory of the naked girl as she bent to take off her wet bathing suit. My heart thumped and I felt embarrassed, as if under cover of a joke we had touched on dangerous topics.

For form's sake some sort of program had been thrown together for the final gathering. It bored us both. I went up to receive my third prize and my share of the applause. Dancing began immediately after the prize giving, and I surveyed the local girls with a critical eye.

"Shall we go out?" I asked Miriam casually. I wanted to be alone with her.

"No, let's watch for a bit longer—just for a little," she

said quickly, laying her hand on my arm. As she watched the dancers sliding their feet over the wax-smooth floor her face seemed to come alive. Her whole being absorbed the dance music, quickening, yearning, opening like a parched flower in the rain. Unconsciously she squeezed my arm.

"I'm sure you can dance," I said. "Shall we try?"

She shook her head. "I daren't," she said. "Aunt would get to hear of it. There are too many people here who know her, and that kind of thing always gets round." She gave me a long look and added stoutly, "But you dance if you want to."

But for me dancing did not hold the same enchantment, so I drew her arm under mine and we remained there side by side. It was a summer evening and still fairly light. Indoors the lamps with their tissue-paper shades cast a soft glow over the darkening room. Through the open window I could smell meadowsweet. We stood side by side, her body swaying almost imperceptibly in time to the music, and at every touch of hers I felt a sweet, stabbing pain.

"Let's go," I said.

"Yes, let's," she answered, and we pushed our way past the dancers to the door. A few girls nodded to her and looked inquisitively at me. She carried her head proudly and barely returned the greetings.

It was lighter outside than in the hall. We strolled silently along the white road and out of the little town, while the wheedling, languishing music died gradually away to silence behind us.

"Shall we go to the ravine?" I suggested. She made no answer. Her face was once more hard and defiant, looking in the deepening dusk like polished stone. The scent of the woods hung heavy about us and from far out on the water came the chuffing of a tugboat.

We went to the ravine and halted on the narrow bridge to lean against the rail and stare down into the black water. Bare rock walls rose steeply on either side, and the sky above them showed like a narrow, colorless crack of light. I put my arms round her and drew her to me. She made no resistance, but stared past me into the darkness. I kissed her lips; they were soft and cool and unresponsive.

"What's the matter with you?" I asked, releasing her. The longing, the sense of light intoxication that I had felt since leaving the hall suddenly went, leaving me heavy-hearted. She burst into tears and pressed her face to her hands that were still clutching the rail, in a vain attempt to control her sobs. She had to have her cry out, and I felt guilty.

"Were you angry," I asked, touching her shyly, "because I kissed you?"

"No, no, no!" she sobbed vehemently, shaking her head. "It was wonderful—too wonderful to be true." And turning suddenly she threw her arms round my neck, pressed her body to mine and kissed me wildly time after time until my face was wet with her tears. "I can't stand it any longer, Joel," she said fiercely. "I shall go mad, or die. Aunt and Uncle are dead already and they want to kill me too. Every time I come into the house out of the fresh air it's like going into a mortuary. And I have to live there, Joel—day after day I have to live there and feel that everything real and alive in me is sinful and wrong and damned. I die a little bit every day; I'm getting ugly and wicked and hard. And there's nowhere I can run away to."

I stroked her hair and her shoulders; I wiped the tears from her cheeks and the corners of her eyes with my finger tips. I was confused, unhappy, and deeply agitated.

"Do you hate them so terribly?" I said. "They're simply trying to do their best for you. You're only sixteen."

"You don't understand, Joel," she said. It was difficult for her to speak and to find words; she beat her breast with her fists as if to force out the rebellious phrases. "You can't understand. I know—I can feel there's something more in me than just *me*. I must *be* something, Joel. But I'm too young. They'll make me die before I can get free. They're killing what's in me—and when they've done that there'll be no point in being free at all. Don't you see, Joel, they want to make me like they are themselves? That's murder."

"They only want to do what's best for you," I repeated. "They're good people, both of them. There are far worse people than that in the world."

She was still sobbing a little and staring down into the water; then she quieted down and became her cold self again.

"Let's get away from here," she said. "Someone might see us. Besides, I'm afraid of that water. It never freezes even in winter. Often I've come here meaning to jump in. But the water's black and cold—it would be horrible to suffocate, to feel it in your throat, choking you. I don't expect I shall ever manage to do it; but sometimes it helps to come here and stare down at the black water. It makes it easier—easier to give in."

She drew me away from the bridge, jumped a ditch and began climbing uphill between the dark firs. I followed her. She flung herself down on the moss near a sand pit, and I sat down beside her. The evening had grown cool, yet the earth still felt warm to my hands after the heat of the day.

"Let's talk sensibly," I said. "Of course you have a hard time of it, I can see that. But you have to give in. They're keeping you, paying for your schooling; they've got the right to ask something in return."

"Oh, yes! I'm an orphan, poor, penniless, and homeless.

That's what you mean, isn't it? But does that give dead people any right to force me to become like themselves? They're good Christians, I know that—there's nothing wicked about them. They even smile—quite often, when things go right for them. They're merciful. But they live only for heaven. I live on earth."

"It's a problem all right," I said, feeling very helpless.

"I live on earth," she repeated, "but they make me feel like a thief. I have to steal any scrap of happiness I get. I'm not even allowed to read poetry because it might put ideas into my head. It's nothing but school and lessons, housework and laundry, prayers and Bible reading, sewing club and church. If they keep on long enough I may get to feel that that's how it ought to be—that it's right to live only for heaven. Just think—when I was a child I thought I'd like to be a missionary! Now Aunt says I shall be a harlot."

She began to laugh and threw herself back on the moss so that her dress slipped up above her knees, and clasped her hands behind her head. "Remember, Joel," she said in a little while, very softly, "you were the first boy I ever kissed."

"Do you remember the apples?" I asked, "And the landscape on the moon?"

She smiled, and in smiling was still a child. Then she raised herself a little and drew down my head. We said nothing more. I kissed her lips and her warm neck, and pressed her to me. She flushed and grew warm and breathed unevenly. With clumsy fingers I undid two buttons of her frock, slipped my hand beneath it and caressed her breast. Never had I done such a thing before. It was sweet and terrible. With my mouth to hers I touched her breast—the naked breast of a young girl—for the first time.

"Miriam," I whispered, "Oh, Miriam!"

"Joel!" Her breath was on my face. "Oh, Joel!" She might have let me do what I would with her, if I had tried and not been afraid. As it was we sat up, with burning faces; her fingers trembled as she buttoned up her dress.

"Joel," she said, "we must always be friends."

It seemed up to me to say something.

"But Miriam, I love you," I assured her. No doubt I believed what I said; I was only seventeen.

"Oh, no you don't," she said wisely enough. "Perhaps we're rather fond of each other, but that's not love."

"Then it's wrong," I said.

"What of it?" she said defiantly. "It did me a lot of good. I feel much better now."

"Do you let just anybody do that?" I exclaimed viciously, and the rapture within me turned to jealousy. She started and stared at me.

"Beast!" she cried, and gave me a stinging box on the ear. Abashed at first I rubbed my cheek; then I grew angry. The blow had hurt.

"I'm sorry," she whispered presently. "I didn't mean it, Joel." She took my head in her hands, kissed me lightly on the cheek and pressed my face to her warm breast. "You know nothing about me if you can say such horrible things. I don't say I couldn't get like that. Perhaps that's why I was so angry, because I know I might. But I won't— I won't." She said this fearfully, pressing my head to her breast. "Boys have tried to kiss me sometimes," she went on. "In school and out of it. But I never let them. I know the boys here too well for that. They're stupid and bumptious, or else they're cowards. They never forget I'm an orphan living with an aunt. I can't stand them! You're more of a stranger, you see, Joel; I don't know you in the same way and that makes you more exciting. If I saw you every day I should probably feel quite differently about you. But you—you must be used to doing what you like, with whom you like." She released my head and looked at me searchingly.

"M'm, well—" I said awkwardly, unwilling to appear quite inexperienced.

"Shame, Joel! If Aunt knew—am I—am I as pretty as the others?"

"Prettier," I assured her warmly. "Prettier than anyone." My voice trembled and with the tips of my fingers I touched her breast lightly through her frock. "I shall never forget, Miriam."

"It's getting dark," she said, and rising she shook off the bits of moss sticking to her dress. "Aunt will be cross if we come home late. Have I got it all off?"

I felt quite worldly-wise as I brushed the dry moss from her back.

We returned to the road. The woods were very quiet. Somewhere in the distance a dog barked. I felt warm and very happy. Soon we saw houses, and friendly lights shone from their windows; then from the evening dark we stepped into the dim lobby and then into the lighted room that smelled of floor polish and freshly ironed linen. We drank hot tea and ate thin, thin sandwiches. Aunt regarded us searchingly, her big waxen face resting in her hand.

"Have you made up your mind what you're going to study, Joel?" she asked. "You'll be graduating next year."

"I haven't decided," I answered sulkily.

"I," said Miriam, staring at Aunt with a look of wide-eyed innocence, "I'm going to be a deaconess."

I choked over my tea. Filled with a sweet longing I gazed at the curve of her breast under the checked frock, and exulted in being now a man of the world. Next day I left. I should have liked to write to Miriam, but I couldn't, as Aunt opened and read all her letters.

5

A man's development is by no means a smooth, continuous process, but occurs in fits and starts surprising to the subject. Many apparently trifling matters pile up in the subconscious, and not until we're faced with the necessity for some action or decision is their influence felt; we may then behave in a way very different from what we or others expect. In youth these leaps are more violent; the swing of the pendulum is swifter then, and its arc wider. Youth darts from one extreme to the other, so it was perhaps not very surprising that I began to study theology.

The only scale by which we can measure the sin and misery of man is man himself. To a moral person striving after virtue the smallest deviation from the path is a more crushing defeat than the regular misdeeds of a hardened offender. It is not so much the act itself that counts as the traces it leaves in us. My faults as I think of them now were trifling enough; it was because I had led a sheltered life in a blameless home that my reaction to them was so violent. I fancied I had plumbed the depths. I fell a prey to frightful depression, and instinct told me that with the best will in the world, no man can attain to virtue by his own unaided powers.

Who was I to rebel against a faith in which thousands better and wiser than myself acknowledged their lowliness? I humbled myself too, and found spiritual satisfaction in so doing. After the death of my father, his best friend—an eminent theologian—offered my family his help, and he easily persuaded me that I should lose nothing by studying divinity. I could always change my subject if I found it was not in me to become a faithful servant of the Church; while on the other hand the knowledge thereby acquired might help to dispel my religious doubts, so typical of youth. The feeling that my own shortcomings rendered me unfit to teach others was no more than seemly in a young man, and proof of his humility. My mother was the only one who distrusted my sudden resolve. My aunt and uncle wrote to say that they would pray for me fervently now that I was fulfilling their dearest wish, and that if necessary Uncle would contribute towards the cost of my training.

I was too impulsive and self-willed to submit to the dry curriculum without a struggle. Perhaps I had graduated too young. I suffered, doubted, and rebelled a great deal that first winter.

In the spring a disaster happened to Miriam: she was expelled from school. She had been absent from lessons without leave and forged my aunt's and uncle's names on the sickness report. She had been seen dancing in public rooms which school children were forbidden to enter, she had smoked cigarettes, and struck a schoolmaster who had punished her. She had lost her good name and fame in the town.

I was horrified to hear this catalogue of crimes, but my sympathies were all with Miriam. I assumed that much of the story had been exaggerated, as so often happens in a small town. Miriam was certainly not bad at heart. In a way Aunt was of the same opinion, and when next she came to Helsinki she owned that she might have been too strict with the girl. And though she never minimized Miriam's sins, yet when further accusations and slanders began to pile up against her she opposed them and defended her. Miriam herself wanted to take a secretarial course, and Aunt agreed that it would be better for her to leave the place for a time.

Next autumn, therefore, Miriam came to Helsinki. She boarded with friends of my mother's, a strictly religious family, and visited us very seldom. She looked shy and scared when she did come, and always avoided saying anything about her work. She was afraid of me; I was to enter the Church, and that was enough to make me appear an enemy in her eyes, and likely to betray her. I didn't understand this then, and was inconsolable at having lost her friendship. But since the sight of her overwhelmed me with feelings most unsuitable for a young divinity student, I too felt it best that we shouldn't meet too often.

I was passing through a critical phase. Inwardly I rebelled against the mold into which I was to be poured. I was too young and hot-blooded for a penitent. I was too frank with my fellow students about my faults and failings and too sardonic in my criticism of the articles of faith. One day the churchman I have mentioned rang me up in a state of indignation to demand that I should call upon him at once. By the time I arrived he had calmed down a little, and perhaps was warned by my air of stubborn defiance not to broach the matter too brusquely. He began in quite a conciliating manner by saying that we all had our faults and that it was natural for a young man to run off the rails occasionally. But, he said, ugly things were being said of me in the theological faculty, and a friend of his among the professors had given him a hint of this, so that he might warn me before it became necessary to take disciplinary action.

"You're a clever boy, Joel," he said, "and you know what I'm getting at. Gossip is gossip and we needn't pay too much attention to it; but there's no smoke without fire. Weak people are always ready to slander strong ones, and you'll harm yourself and your calling if you give rise to scandal. If at times we can't help sinning, at least we shouldn't do it in public."

He was mild and human now as he took the glasses from his nose and rubbed his tired eyes. "Why, bless my soul," he said, "the flesh is weak and man imperfect; we all know that. If you must get drunk, then do it privately. If you must have recourse to loose women, at least don't be seen in the street with them. There are other places. God forgives but men don't. Always remember that."

He can't have realized how enraged I was. He meant well, and it was needless for me to explain or defend myself. Seeing me still inflexible he said sorrowfully, "Let us pray together for you."

After what he had just said this seemed to me sacrilege; but he was an old man and when he knelt down at one end of the sofa I knelt opposite him. Reverently and earnestly he besought the Almighty to guard me from temptation and forgive my sins. I did not pray. I watched him, and as he was praying I saw him pull his watch from his waistcoat pocket and give it a quick glance; he was in a hurry to get to some meeting. All else I might have forgiven him, but not this. My aggressiveness left me, and I felt empty and cold. So severe is youth in its blindness.

As I made my way home the windowpanes were blazing in the early spring sunset. Then the street lamps were lit and a green shimmer crept into the air, while the icy street crackled under my feet. I felt empty, lonely, and disconsolate. Yet like a dizzying wave there rolled towards me a feeling of release which I dared not acknowledge. On the following day I resigned from the theological college and applied to the military authorities for permission to

do my military service at once. This would give me time
to consider what to do next.

It was of course not this small incident alone which
decided me; it merely precipitated matters. The real causes
had long been accumulating within me. I had read church
history; I had read of iconoclasm, of council and synods,
of religious wars. The history of the Church now appeared
to me enveloped in the reek of the martyr's pyre—in the
steam rising from the lifeblood of millions. I was horror-
stricken at the evil wrought by those who strove for nothing but the general good. Religion said "Either—or—"; but
this was a message of fanaticism and intolerance to all
mankind. I came to loathe intolerance, not perceiving that
this loathing contained within itself a glowing core of
bigotry.

My mother had met Miriam by chance in the street and
invited her to dinner. "The girl's got thinner," she said.
"She looks ill. Perhaps she doesn't get enough to eat where
she lives. And by the way, what was she doing out in the
middle of the day? Why wasn't she at the school?"

Miriam was indeed pale and thin, and there was a hard
look in her eyes. She dressed differently and I thought her
even more beautiful than before. When the meal was over
I invited her into my room, offered her a cigarette and
took one myself, as a token of peace and reconciliation.

"Well, well—and you a divinity student!" she said ironically, but she lit the cigarette and drew the smoke greedily
into her lungs.

"I'm no divinity student," I said laughing. "You can
talk to me like a human being again. Let's be friends,
Miriam."

At first she didn't believe me. Then she laughed with
delight, ran to me and hugged me like a sister. I took her
by both arms and fixed my eyes on hers. "What were you

doing, strolling about the town in the middle of the day?"
I asked. "Aren't you supposed to be at the secretarial college? Mother was too tactful to ask questions."

She reddened slowly, looked away and sat down, throwing one leg over the other with an air of defiance. Then
she took a lipstick out of her bag and began carefully
making up her mouth, smoothing out the red with
her finger tips. Then she powdered her face. Finally she
stretched out her leg, surveyed her darned stocking and
said casually, "I'd give anything for a new pair of silk
ones." Only then did she look at me. "Can you keep a
secret, Joel?" she asked.

When I assured her that I could she told me without
preamble that throughout the winter she'd been attending a private dramatic school. She had had an audition and
been accepted, and had never even tried to enter a secretarial college.

"I'm going on the stage," she said. "Hell or no hell, I'm
going on the stage." But she was plainly terrified.

"Aunt and Uncle will have heart attacks when they hear
of it," she said lightly, little guessing how near she came
to the truth. I wondered how on earth she'd been able to
keep her secret for so long. Yet it was not really surprising.
The family she boarded with were only concerned to see
that she left for work punctually, returned punctually, and
did not stay out too late at night.

"I've 'walked on' at the theater once or twice," she told
me. "One can make a little money that way. I told the
people I lodge with that I'm coaching a private pupil in
mathematics, for the Intermediate exam, and that as he's
at his job all day he has to study at night. They believed
me when I showed them the money. It brings me in
twenty-five marks a day. Of course I haven't had any lines
to speak yet, but perhaps next year—"

Her greatest difficulty was in studying parts, for she dared not speak them aloud in her own room; and so she began coming to me when Mother was out. Sometimes I kissed her, but she had more experience now and slipped neatly from my arms when I grew too amorous. Now and then she asked me to lend her money and I gladly gave her the little sums she wanted, though I knew she had no intention of repaying them. "It's more respectable to ask for a loan than for a gift," she said with a teasing look. I saw that she was willing to discharge her debt somehow, nevertheless, so I bent down and kissed her. She responded readily, then pushed me firmly away.

"You're selling yourself, you slut," I remarked. "You'll come to a bad end."

"Who knows what's good and what's bad?" she demanded. "I'm too poor to stand on my dignity. Paw me about if it amuses you; others have." She grew somber and for the first time alluded to her expulsion. "There was the schoolmaster—but what would have been the good of saying anything? No one would have believed me—and even if they had, I'd have gotten the blame just the same. I was wicked and bad and abandoned, wasn't I? Aunt harped on it until I came to believe it myself. But I'm not really so very bad yet, Joel."

There was not the same candor between us as before. My caresses came to have a staleness about them of which I was sorrowfully aware. When she had gone I felt sweaty and sick. I probably didn't love her. We had only one thing in common which neither could have had with anyone else: we were friends. Yet I felt somehow shabby in my relation to her, perhaps merely because of my physical reaction: the backwash of a desire that found no outlet. I wanted her, but could not bring myself to exploit her in cold blood; she was surely not as bad as that. Nothing came of it, therefore, but a drab, provocative game between us.

One day she took me to have coffee with her at Morkku's, the restaurant in the basement of the National Theater, where supers and dramatic students used to gather after rehearsal to talk and feel professional. Miriam, intent on showing me that she was already a part of this world, led me confidently through a number of dark corridors, addressed a well-known actor by his Christian name just for my benefit, and introduced me to her colleagues. They talked of nothing but theaters, parts, plays, and big scenes, and were alarmingly severe in their judgments. It appeared from what they said that the theater in this country was at its last gasp, and only new blood and new leadership could save it.

I felt like a fish out of water, but Miriam seemed fired with new life and became a stranger to me, talking and discussing with fervent enthusiasm. I was conscious of slipping further and further away from her, and when we left the theater with a crowd of others I said good-bye at once and went my way, though she called after me. I was jealous, no doubt, and also envious of her because she was so sure of herself and her calling. Yet I failed to understand just why I felt so resentful and out of humor.

Soon afterwards I began my military service, and was posted to the field artillery in a distant part of the country.

6

The following autumn, when I was at the Reserve Officers' School at Hamina, I saw in the paper that my uncle had died, and on the same day I received a letter from my mother asking me to get leave and represent her at the funeral next Sunday. Like all youngsters I was thoroughly selfish, and after the first shock I felt nothing but delight at getting a bit of extra leave and escaping for a couple of days from the strict monotony of the officers' school. Not until I was in the train and memory began to melt the ice of selfishness did I feel sorrow. I remembered once more my uncle's kindly, childish face and gray whiskers, the everlasting tick of clocks in his workshop, the telescope in the mild winter night and the dead landscape of the moon. It was strange that he should have been the one to die. Aunt had always been the more fragile and delicate of the two, and I had vaguely thought of Uncle surviving indefinitely.

A crowd of distant relatives came to the funeral and many of them spent the night in the house. My aunt seemed to have straightened up to her full height, and her thin, waxen face was serene; only her eyes had an odd, bewildered look in them. Everything in the house was spotlessly clean, polished and worn to smoothness; huge quantities of bread had been baked and the smell of this and of coffee overcame that of floor polish and camphor. Miriam, white-faced and in mourning, helped her aunt with the serving. Her eyelids were red; she had been crying. I hadn't expected this, but I supposed it to be merely another manifestation of her impulsive nature. However, the longer I remained there and absorbed the atmosphere of that house of mourning, the more oppressed did I become and the more keenly was I aware of some unspoken menace looming over us.

No one spoke to Miriam, but many watched her furtively. She appeared taller than before, and moved stiffly, unnaturally, through the rooms. She met no one's eye, not even mine.

I found it hard to stifle my curiosity, and as soon as I had a chance I asked an old cousin in a whisper how Uncle had died. He whispered back that one morning when Uncle was sitting at his work he turned sick and giddy, and went to lie down. Two hours later, as he had not reappeared, his assistant went into the parlor to see how he was and found him lying on his back on the bed with his hands crossed on his breast. At first he thought the old man was asleep; then he noticed that his eyes and mouth were open, and drawing nearer found that Uncle was no longer breathing.

"What a peaceful death," I commented, relieved.

"Maybe," said the cousin, glancing at me as if wondering how much I knew. Then a malicious, almost gloating expression came over his face as he whispered meaningly, "Ask Miriam!" and I realized that something dreadful must have happened before he died.

Later Aunt took me to the parlor to see my uncle, and shut the door after us so that no one else should come in. The room was as it had always been and as I remembered it from childhood. There were the black chairs, the sofa with its dark red cover, the white-scrubbed floor, and on the ceiling the clouds and figures painted in thin reds and blues. But the room was full of flowers and the once so strictly closed windows now stood open to let the cold air of late autumn stream in. Nevertheless I was aware of the sickly smell of death.

Uncle lay in his black coffin. His face was grayish white and his hands were crossed on his breast. The hint of a shyly apologetic smile lay on his lips, as if he were regretting the commotion and trouble he had caused. The gray whiskers were white now, but even in death there lingered something of childish innocence and shy reserve about him. I was a little boy again in that big room, and burning

tears forced their way to my eyes. I was mourning not for
my uncle but for the futility and transience of life. I
mourned for myself, for the little boy who had gone forever and had been succeeded by a cold, selfish man, in
whom decay had even now set in.

My aunt passed her thin, shaking hand over Uncle's
forehead and said, "Miriam killed him." Then she broke
out into violent sobbing. She had controlled herself too
long in front of other people, and now the tears had to
come. I would have liked to take her in my arms and comfort her, but I was far too shocked by what she had said;
and besides, even as a child I had never been demonstra-
tive with her.

"You mustn't talk like that," I said harshly, in spite of
myself. It was distressing and embarrassing to see an old
woman weep so uncontrollably.

Aunt took out a handkerchief and wiped her eyes, and
then leaning on the table she moved to a chair, sat down
and looked at me. "It's true," she said vehemently.
"Miriam killed him." And she told me the story.

Certain kind people had felt it their duty to tell them
that Miriam, far from attending any secretarial college in
Helsinki, had joined a drama school and was going about
with all sorts of disreputable people. But Uncle could not
bring himself to believe it. "Miriam would never lie to us
like that," he said. "People are just being malicious." But
Aunt had insisted on sending for Miriam at once so that
she might give an account of herself. The girl was surly
and obstinate when she arrived, and there had been a
scene. Aunt lost her temper and so did Miriam: she threatened and defied them and screamed outrageous things. In
the middle of it all Uncle went out. This was late at night.
The next morning he got up as usual, drank his hot water

and cream with a lump of sugar in it and went to his work. The rest I had already heard.

"You see, Joel, he couldn't survive the shock. Not only that Miriam had deliberately deceived us—lied to us. Up to the very last he trusted her and liked her. It was that that broke his heart."

I found something touchingly unworldly in the fact that after this painful discovery my uncle had chosen to die rather than accept life as it was. Being outside it all I could look upon it from a bystander's point of view, and see what was petty and even ridiculous in the affair. What was so tragic in a talented girl's preferring the stage to an office? Yet a tragedy it had been.

I saw this when I tried to speak to Miriam.

"Don't come near me," she snapped. "I'm unclean." And I don't know that I should have made things any better by speaking up for her in front of them all and declaring that she was not responsible for her uncle's death. No one would have listened to me—no one would even have answered; at the most they would have withdrawn from me too, with shocked and disapproving glances. This was the worst part of it: no one spoke out. No one addressed Miriam directly; they just let her feel how much they despised and hated her. It was no doubt the wisest—and the worst—thing they could do, for if they had clothed their accusations in words they would have become enmeshed in a tangle of explanations which must have shaken their belief in Miriam's guilt.

They may really have thought that Miriam was wicked, cruel and rotten to the core; but as we stood by the grave I reflected that they were being even more cruel. Those who stepped forward after the committal to sprinkle earth on the coffin thrust Miriam aside, and took away the trowel when she put out her hand for it. The grave was

filled in, and wreaths laid on the mound. Miriam was the
only one who brought no flowers. I knew she had no
money, but had assumed that Aunt would get a wreath
for her. Yet she stood her ground by the graveside, knowing that all the others disapproved of her being there.
Tall and straight in her light-colored, shabby raincoat
and black dress, her eyes dark with sorrow and defiance,
she stood close to the grave as if defending her right to
be there, if only in acknowledgment of all the kindness
that Uncle had shown her while alive. If she blamed herself it was because far from pleasing him she had brought
him only trouble and anxiety. Perhaps it was for this
reason that she wanted to drain the bitter cup of shame,
slander, and censure to the dregs.

But I thought not only of her. I thought of Uncle and
my own childhood. I thought of the darkness of the grave.
I looked at the church, lofty and massive with its black
shingle roof, which loomed over the churchyard, the
stones in its thick walls bound with iron-hard mortar;
stones which long ages ago people had dragged there in
expiation of their sins. Every stone in those somber walls
represented a sin, whether large or small. Men had built
a house for God with their sins. The jackdaws, those
strange church-birds that had so frightened me as a child,
screeched round the steeple. It was late autumn. Rain was
beginning to fall and people started drifting away from
the newly filled grave.

As we returned in scattered groups from the churchyard I thought of all the fine things that had been said of
my uncle at his graveside: some uttered in sonorous,
preaching tones, with unnatural solemnity; some whin-
ingly and mournfully; some loudly and some almost inaudibly, through lips that quivered. These phrases were
no doubt sincere, when stripped of the flourishes which a

man's pettiness and vanity are apt to add in the presence of an audience. Uncle had been all that they said: a fervent Christian, a man of irreproachable character, benevolent, good to the poor, modest and simple in his ways. Yet the phrases told us nothing of the real man, only of such qualities as might have been superficially observed by anyone. His true self had gone beyond recall and no one now could touch his secrets. I only knew that in his kindness of heart and his ingenuousness he had been the best man I ever knew.

The chilly autumn rain ran down my face and my uniform cloak was sodden. I was deeply conscious as I walked along of how solitary each one of us is—how not even our closest friends can know us. Miriam I forgot completely.

A crowd gathered at the house for coffee, and later my aunt provided a meal for the relatives. She had a great deal to see to personally, despite her many helpers. The atmosphere began to lighten; one or two people even smiled and there was no whispering now. Some of the younger guests, myself among them, stood by the door of the bakehouse, under the eaves, and smoked. Stimulated by the coffee we talked freely, and when someone happened to mention the word "will" I was suddenly curious. If I'd thought about the matter at all it was to suppose that Aunt would inherit everything; yet when I suggested this there were vehement protests. My uncle died childless, so my aunt would get only half and the rest would be divided among the brothers and sisters or their children. I thought there would probably be little to divide among so many; nevertheless I began to feel a pleasant anticipation, for if that were so I should be one of the legatees. There were others who maintained that Uncle must have made a will in favor of my aunt.

We went inside again and my aunt came up to me.

"Where's Miriam?" she asked urgently, as if fearing that the girl was up to some mischief. I began searching through the rooms. Miriam had helped with serving the meal but was now nowhere to be seen. On the bookshelf in the parlor I saw a black book in which I remembered Uncle making notes about the movements of the planets. It had never before occurred to me to touch it, but now I picked it up and opened it. It contained various data, the signs of the planets and their degrees, but there was also other matter written in Uncle's round, painstaking script.

"God is infinite, eternal and everywhere present," I read. "How can a feeble human brain endure such knowledge? I can but bow in humility before Him. God is in the infinity of the heavens and in my own frail sinful heart. It is a sign and a pledge of the certainty of salvation."

I shut the book abruptly with a feeling of distaste, as when touching underclothes that someone else has just taken off. Remembering Miriam I continued my interrupted search, but she was nowhere to be found. At last I stood on the threshold of the outer door and looked out over the yard. It was still raining. I saw footmarks in a flower bed, and a few frostbitten asters that had stood before the stricken house were now gone. At once I knew where Miriam was. I put on my cloak and went quickly to the churchyard. It was growing dark and in a couple of hours I must catch my train if I was to be in Hamina the following morning.

Miriam was sitting on a fallen tombstone in the rain. Her face was somber, her hat and light raincoat soaked. She was staring at the wreaths on the grave among which she had thrust the withered, blackened asters from the garden. I stood unable to utter a word. Her rigid stare frightened me, and it crossed my mind that she meant to do herself some harm. But presently she looked at me and said harshly, "Give me a cigarette."

It was most unseemly to smoke beside a newly filled grave, and she no doubt suggested it out of defiance and for the sake of doing something outrageous. My soaked cap felt heavy on my head and rain dripped from its peak. I lit a cigarette for her and one for myself. She tried to protect hers from the rain with her hollowed hand, but it soon got wet and went out. She trod on it and scraped wet sand over it with her foot.

"Come home now," I said. "You'll be drenched."

She shook her head violently. "So much the better," she snapped. "If I get wet and fall ill and die you'll all be rid of me. But I shan't die—just to spite them I shan't die." She dug her foot into the sand again and added, "You needn't think I've come here to repent. I'm only saying good-bye to Uncle. I suppose I ought to crawl on my knees and cry, 'Forgive me, dear, dear Uncle.' But the dead don't hear anything. It's no use repenting; I'd rather fight back."

She stood up abruptly and shook her fist at the dark walls of the church. "There's no God!" she shrieked above the rain. "There's no heaven and no hell. There's only the earth and the people on it. It's enough—enough—enough! Everything else is lies, to frighten children and weaklings with."

I seized her clenched hand and forced it down. She was shaking all over and staring wildly in front of her.

"Shut up, you fool," I said. "What do we know about God, you and I? Stop screaming."

"You're afraid too," she said scornfully. "To hell with it—be a damned soul, like me! It's wonderful being damned and seeing it in everybody's face. But I *will* be something, if I roast for it, just to spite them."

She was still very young. That was why she shouted and stormed. Experienced people never shout; they keep their knowledge to themselves. They are wary and avoid upsetting those about them. Arguing in matters of religion is useless, since no one ever really convinces anyone else. Yet he who holds his tongue condones, and is as guilty of evil as any who in the name of religion bring the evil about. I felt suddenly tired and disgusted. Miriam, I reflected, was first and foremost an actress, with a weakness for large gestures, loud cries, and emotional outbursts.

"Shut up," I said. "You're putting it on. You don't know what you're talking about; you're just scared and unhappy and lonely. But it won't help to scream about it. Everybody feels like that, deep inside. One person goes to church, another drinks, a third does social work. But it's all an illusion; no one can ever get away from his own loneliness and fear."

She fell silent and her black eyes gazed at me through the dusk. "I've been wounded, deep inside me," she said, "and all the blood in me is running out. That's why I scream."

"Wounds aren't healed that way," I answered. "Only children cry. Grown-up people hold their tongues; they're ashamed of their wounds."

I felt myself getting colder, wearier, and emptier as I stood there in the wet sand in my wet cloak. The autumn evening was growing dark, and lights were being lit in the houses. No human being could ever help another, I felt.

"I might have loved you, Miriam," I said, "but I have too much sense. Forgive me, you love nobody but yourself."

She was on the point of retorting, but checked herself.

"No, no," she replied presently. "Even that's not true. I only love the things in me that are good." She began half-walking, half-running in front of me along the sandy path. When we arrived home I had only just time to say a hasty good-bye to Aunt and grab my suitcase. Once in the train I was overwhelmed by a sense of having behaved meanly and foolishly throughout my visit.

7

Those nearest Miriam might conceivably have come to forgive her for her uncle's death, but what they could not seem to forgive was that he had left her half his estate. Uncle had certainly been her guardian since her parents' death, and for many years she had lived like a daughter in his house; yet she was only a distant connection and would have had no right to any of his property if my uncle had died intestate. I was not there when the storm broke; I was marching along the muddy roads of Hamina with slung rifle, on the way back from a morning training exercise, but I can well picture the excitement and indignation of those concerned.

Pride of possession, greed, and a sense of personal injury can goad people to even worse deeds than those born of moral prejudice. For several weeks the disappointed relatives discussed in all seriousness whether they could bring an action against Miriam on the grounds of her having been the cause of Uncle's death, and thereby deprive her of her legacy. The lawyers had the greatest difficulty in persuading them that they hadn't a chance of bringing such a case to court. I fancy they were never quite convinced, and considered that a gross injustice was being done them under cover of some legal technicality.

When the contents of the will became known and the first shock was over, they reflected with relief that Miriam would never accept the legacy. They believed all possible evil of her; they considered her depraved, callous, sinful, practically a murderess, but even she, they thought, could not be so shameless as to take the dead man's money. And it is possible that Miriam, being young and proud, would have been willing to renounce it in their favor, but this she had no power to do, as she was still a minor. She was tied to the legacy, and even if in other circumstances she would and could have forgotten all that had happened, this fact now made it impossible.

When all was said and done the legacy was not a large one, for although in his time Uncle had had quite a comfortable sum in the bank, his savings had been lost in the inflation that followed the First World War. The house was old and dilapidated, and only the land it stood on was valuable, the town having by this time developed into an industrial center of some importance. But since by the terms of the will Aunt was to have the house for her lifetime, the property could not yet be sold. Uncle's assistant, who had run the shop for many years, was glad to buy the business and rent the premises; but by the time the few modest bequests had been paid out—to the missionary society, the church-workers' league, the peace society, and the YMCA—there was little money left.

Nevertheless the relatives continued to feel that they had been grievously defrauded and would have nothing further to do with Miriam. Immediately after the funeral she returned to Helsinki and continued her theatrical training as if nothing had happened. My aunt had no wish to meddle in her affairs or exercise any control over her. Miriam was now and forever to be numbered with the lost. My aunt, old, lonely and ill, consoled herself with the thought that one day Miriam would have to suffer for all her wickedness. No doubt the Almighty had his own stern plans for her and she was not going to interfere.

Neither my aunt nor Miriam were much in my thoughts at that time. Soldiering suited me. I liked the early rising, the strenuous training and the strict discipline. I took up athletics again. The vacuum left in me since the day I burst my spiritual bonds I sought to fill with outward, physical self-discipline. I began to shun alcohol; its clouded exaltation was harmful to anyone who wanted to keep fit. Now that the emotional stresses of first youth were past I felt coolly adult, and my will power hardened.

When on leave in Helsinki I would sometimes try to get Miriam on the telephone, but she was never there. Not until the beginning of summer did I succeed. She agreed to meet me and we went out to a restaurant. While we were waiting for the meal she had a whisky. She was better dressed and in my opinion more beautiful than ever, though with her dark hair and eyes and somber face she had a wild, restless, almost menacing appearance. Her cheeks had narrowed, her mouth was too heavily made up and there were dark shadows round her eyes. Her hand shook as she held the glass.

"You saw it in the papers, of course," she remarked.

At first I didn't know what she meant. "About the student production?" I asked. Her press notices had struck me as decidedly poor for one who was regarded as one of the most talented pupils in the school, but I hadn't been unduly concerned. I thought she had probably deserved higher praise; she had been so impulsive, so vital and glowing in her enthusiasm for the stage, but as I had never had the chance of seeing her act I was reluctant to express

an opinion. Then too, no doubt the critics were elderly
and cautious and afraid of overstatement.

"I was a flop," she said, "an utter flop. I was hopeless.
I couldn't have believed it. I expected to make a hit—
everybody thought I would. But when it came to the point
I couldn't move, I couldn't speak, and I forgot my lines.
It was ghastly."

She finished her drink and ordered another, and then
sat staring in front of her. "Ghastly," she repeated. "When
I got in front of those footlights and felt those hundreds
of eyes on me I was scared. I don't mean I was frightened
of the stage, or even of the audience. I think I was afraid
of myself. You won't understand, of course, but I was
suddenly alone somewhere in the cold and the dark and
Uncle was lying on his back with his hands crossed on his
chest, saying his prayers. I didn't know what I was doing.
We'd been rehearsing the play all the winter and yet I
couldn't remember my lines. It was like a spell. As soon
as I left the stage I woke up again, and I felt hot all over
with shame. I knew I could act. But on the stage—no."

"It'll pass," I told her. "You're not fully trained yet.
Keep at it and you'll learn. You're tired and nervous; you
ought to go away this summer—go into the country and
rest, and get some bathing. And not drink so much."

"Joel the preacher," she remarked. "What are you going to do when you've finished your military service?"

"I shall study again. Probably Oriental languages."

"*Oriental?* But why?" she asked in surprise. "You were
going to be a chemist."

"Well, I'm not now," I answered. "I couldn't tell you
why. I just feel an urge to study Oriental languages. Perhaps because they're of no practical value to anyone. I
think we shall soon have more than enough of practical

things. In the meantime I shall enter a language-mon-astery."

She regarded me with new interest, and I saw that she was striving to find some explanation for the change in me. She played with the food on her plate but ate nothing.

"But that won't get you anywhere," she said mystified. "Will it even help you to a job?"

"I shall live in poverty," I told her. "The fewer one's needs the happier one is and the less one has to lose, in a superficial sense. I shall be content with a roof over my head and my daily bread, and liberty to read Sanskrit in peace and quiet."

"You're joking," she said, looking at me suspiciously.

"There's a grain of truth in every joke," I said. I was suddenly overcome by a feeling of despair. "Miriam, can't you see—we're all living in hell nowadays. People torture themselves for power and success and fame and money. They wrap their minds in fog to forget, and rush about trying to have a good time. And meanwhile everything round us is dissolving; nothing that we see can last. We've taken too big a step too suddenly and lost our balance. The time will come when I shall be glad to be poor and alone, without fame or ambition. Why shouldn't I study hieroglyphics and cuneiform rather than chemical formulas which will destroy the world?"

"You're being far too profound, Joel," she said, but she looked at me with greater interest than before. Her breast rose under the red dress and she breathed uneasily. "There's that little devil of a theologian hiding in you somewhere and giving you no peace. Oh, how I hate that theologian! You ought to *live!*"

How empty and tawdry that word "live" sounded to me even then, in the sense in which she used it.

"What does that mean?" I demanded. "Every rapture

has its hang-over, and leaves us that much emptier, harder, more dead. The purest intoxication is that of expectancy, but intoxication is still only intoxication, however pure."

She was hurt and said dryly,

"Anybody would think you knew it all. Don't pretend, Joel! It's only sour grapes."

"What do you know of my life?" I retorted, flaring up like a sulky schoolboy. "What do you think of this:

'Rapturous is the game in its beginnings,
Hesitant-sweet, yet turns the night to fire.
Sweeter resistance, when a thief forestalls you
Stealing, ere you have won, your heart's desire.' "

She repeated a few of these words and said with a sneer, "Did you write that yourself?" But her manner changed and she seemed to lose something of her assurance.

"And if I did?" I asked roughly.

"You're right in a way," she said. "You mustn't be too eager, or too easy. You have to pay for it. I made that mistake—I thought it was all part of the game. I thought it was freedom—I thought I could do what I liked with my own body. But one's body gets dulled with too much freedom and won't listen any more; it has to be tormented and chastised with desire before it wakes up—and that's too exhausting. A little of that and it seems better to go numb and simply use the body as a means of barter."

"How much do you charge?" I asked.

"It all depends," she replied tranquilly. "A job, a good part perhaps. Just now I'd settle for a fur coat. Some accept rabbit fur and others hold out for mink. I suspect any woman in a fur coat, Joel. I don't think a young actress ought ever to wear a really good one if she cares about her reputation. I don't bother about mine. I lost it long ago at school."

"Most of them get married," I remarked.

She spread out her hands affectedly and cried, "Ah, but I have my work, my career. I live only for the theater." She put out her cold, flat hand and laid it on mine. "Would you marry me, Joel?" she said.

I considered the question from various angles. "Hardly," I answered. "I don't think we'd suit each other."

She withdrew her hand, smiled, and sighed in affected disappointment, but there was something more than affectation in that sigh. I looked at her sharply. She was desperate, tormented through and through; I was merely torturing her without being able to help.

"But you'd like to have me, wouldn't you?" she persisted, putting a note of hope into her voice.

"Why not? It depends on the price."

Out of the gray past there floated a picture: a ravine, a bridge, and black water. My mouth went dry. She was another person now, and so was I. Gone was that pure passion, forever; a cloudy fever was all that was left to us.

"What I really need is a new hat," she said reflectively. "That would do. After all, we're old acquaintances, aren't we? It would be just a friendly gesture." She looked at me and added, "Or would it?"

My calm had left me. I was all on fire. She was joking, of course, but the joke had a grain of sour truth. I needed all my strength of mind to steel myself against the temptation that her mere presence was for me.

"Do you despise yourself as much as that?" I asked. Her dark, brilliant eyes were upon me.

"Yes," she answered. "As much as that."

I paid. We walked through the streets of Helsinki that spring evening, and I saw her home. There was a green shimmer in the dusk. The lights of clanking trams blinked as they passed us. At her door we paused.

"I'll see you again, Miriam," I said. She offered me her lips and I kissed her. Her lips were warm but her eyes still brilliant and expressionless.

"There's no one in," she said. "You can come up if you like."

To this day I don't know why I refused. It was probably just as well, though my going with her would hardly have changed anything. It is sometimes said, rather cynically, that in old age we regret all the opportunities we've let slip. But I believe that resistance fires our minds and goads us to action. Satisfaction means surfeit; it holds us in the groove of habit until we give in and settle down in the dreary prison of the body.

On my way home I experienced one of those rare glimpses of eternity that sometimes come to us. I saw myself and Miriam as I believed we really were, underneath all our talk and fooling and cynicism. We stood on a hilltop and before us lay the boundless plains of life in all their heart-searching beauty. We might choose: should it be the jungle or the lofty peaks? The jungle was perhaps as brilliant and as purposeless as the bleakness of the heights. She chose the jungle, I the hills; and to each of us the goal appeared equal in loveliness. Should we recognize each other when next we met?

8

She soon took a job at a small provincial theater far up in northern Finland. As soon as I was released from military service I began studying Oriental languages at the university. Once she sent me a couple of notices from the local paper and a photograph of herself in the part she had played in some operetta. But neither of us wrote to the other. I gathered from her press notices that people liked her for her youth and beauty and verve. A year or two later she had the chance of making a trial appearance at the Folk Theater, but at that time I was attached as photographer to a scientific expedition in Palestine and couldn't go to see her.

My stay abroad confirmed me in the belief that the world was going full tilt to hell. Hatred, violence, and fanaticism prevailed everywhere, leaving no room for tolerance—not even for passionless scientific research. More determinedly therefore did I withdraw into myself and my studies on my return home. Miriam had had no luck with her trial performance and had not been engaged by any of the theaters in Helsinki. However, a film director gave her a small part. She did well in it, left the theater, and took a more permanent job in films. Photographs of her began to appear in the magazines; she was even on the cover of one of them. I bought a copy of it at a newspaper kiosk, noticing at the same time that the posters carried announcements of the Munich negotiations.

A little later when I was on my way home I saw her in the street, at the corner by Fazer's. She was dressed in a conspicuously expensive fur coat and was surrounded by a crowd of people, all talking and laughing. I didn't think she had noticed me, but she shouted, "Hello Joel! Aren't you going to speak to me?" and waving good-bye to her friends came over and took my arm. Many of the passersby recognized her and turned to look at us. This public attention was not at all to my taste and I cautiously withdrew my arm.

"You're famous now—congratulations!" I said, very conscious of my tight, shabby overcoat beside her splendid furs.

She leaned over, put her mouth to my ear and whispered with a roguish smile directed at the people round us, "Go to hell!" like a cheap little tart from the suburbs. I jumped, fearing that someone might have heard her, but laughed in spite of myself.

"I was a flop on the stage," she said. "A film's tacked together shot by shot, and I've got a good film face. Shot by shot I can remember my lines, but on the stage I forget them. It's my nerves that are wrong; I just never come to life in the theater. But I'm not picture-postcard enough for the real star parts. My specialty's romping in the hay. I'm good there; have you noticed?"

"I don't often go to the cinema," I said, clutching my shabby leather brief case more firmly under my arm.

"How delightful men are!" she remarked gaily. "They like things made easy. When they've seen me in film after film as a sultry farm-wench or a floozie they think that's what I am. I do better with them than any of the stars. What do you think of my coat?"

"Films seem to pay better than Arabic," I observed.

"And you? I saw in the paper that you've been photographing ancient archives in Palestine. What did you think of the Arab girls?"

"The belly-dance is an astounding result of physical training," I told her, "a triumph of evolution hardly to be surpassed—even by you."

"Is that supposed to be sarcasm?" she demanded. "Are you still jealous?"

"Of you? No fear."

"When are you going to come to life? Still waters run deep, you know. I hate to think what you might turn into."

"I've just begun to learn how to live," I said. "It's a slow, troublesome business, but I may pull it off. I'm learning to live without fear so as to die without fear. Perhaps it's of no more value than the belly-dance, but it suits me."

She was in a hurry and had no time for more than a wave and a "be seeing you" before she darted into the offices of a film company. Her face remained before my mind's eye long afterwards: beautiful, tempestuous, wayward. But I wished her well. I hoped she would meet some rich man who would marry her before she became too badly scorched by spotlights, restaurants, alcohol, and the lust for pleasure. She had no place in my life any more. I had lost her for good now; I had lost her from my heart of hearts. Yet I still went on tearing her photographs out of the papers and putting them away in my drawer among my travel notes, with my revolver as paperweight. I never put them in an album as I meant to.

The atmospheric pressure of years discharged itself in a storm that resounded all over the world. When war came I was spiritually ready to join up; readier than many others who, enthusiastic, ardent, and immature, went into battle and, terror and cold notwithstanding, fell with their eyes still alight with dreams. For me it was merely the outcome of what I had long seen coming to the bursting point; an inevitable outcome, the world being what it was. I went too, without hesitation and without pain; if I was haunted by a sense of bitterness it was a bitterness whose causes had buried themselves too deep for me to be aware of them.

My fellow officers in the reserve made fun of my studies, but their laughter was friendly. During the winter, war there was little enough to joke about. We fought at Taipale and Miriam sent me a parcel and a big photograph of herself, assuring me in the accompanying letter that it was she who had knitted the woolen socks. Her picture was pinned up on the wall of the dugout, and became stained and smudged by many secret kisses in which an infinity of youthful thirst for life was pent up. And there it was left, like so many of my companions, when the hour struck for our return home.

During the interval between wars I completed my language courses and qualified, and then went straight on to prepare a thesis for the graduate examination, obtaining a scholarship reserved for young research workers. This was the only financial help my work had yet brought me. My mother died and my sister's family took over the flat, though one room was left at my disposal. I didn't need it long, however, for war began again—another war, longer and fiercer and grayer year by year, until for me and my generation war became a more normal way of life than peace. Internal disputes in the command, and envy borne of promotion and distinction, began to poison the air. When on leave we got drunk and amused ourselves with tarts and errant schoolgirls. Perhaps this was only one side of it, but it was an important, hardening side. The radiance of our dreams faded, life darkened and I grew numb from a sense of futility. The men drank and fought with the Germans, ran after girls and contracted war marriages as freely as their officers. When my arm was smashed at Rukajärvi and afterwards amputated, I came to after the anesthetic with a sense of guilty relief. I did not have to die! Now I could return home with a clear conscience, plunge into my books again and await what was to come.

While I was convalescent Miriam used to come and go for walks with me. I was a wounded officer from the front, my uniform was shabby, my face thin and brown and my chest covered with medal-ribbons. I was something to show off in restaurants, where people smoked Red Cross cigarettes bought on the black market, and businessmen, in the flush of new prosperity, stood "black" meat all round, with German champagne and tinned delicacies. Far from being outraged by all this, I thoroughly enjoyed everything that was offered me; it was all part of war and would never change while there was such a thing in the world. The dead beneath their flat crosses did not complain, and the survivors thought only of how much they could grab from life, dismissing all thought for the morrow. When my sister boasted gaily of how she had been first in the queue and had managed to get something which many others there had to go without, it was exactly the same as when drunken businessmen boasted about the millions they made by illegal trading and spent haphazardly on pictures, carpets, furs, and girls. All this seemed to me a way of life doomed to destruction: the death throes of a race caught in its own prison and suffering from an inflamed craving for life—a result of the war. Why should I criticize or condemn? The spasms of a sick and wounded man are ugly to watch, but he can't be blamed for them.

I tried to resume my work and to collect material for my thesis, but much of the intellectual passion which originally spurred me on in my apparently pointless task had evaporated in the clutch of fear and compulsion. I slept badly and had nightmares about the front line. Now that I was free to continue my life I was seized by the wildest terror every time I heard the air-raid sirens. Outwardly I was under control, but every nerve in me quivered. It was absurd, futile, that having escaped the fighting I might yet be killed by a bomb or a collapsing wall. I had tried to learn to live without fear so as to die without fear, but that idea had been an empty fantasy. Though my mind seemed to master my miserably quaking body, the victory was illusory. At the moment when danger threatened I could control myself, but as soon as it was past I shrank into a panting, sweating rag of humanity.

I knew quite well that this was the result of shock, loss of blood, and the amputation, but the knowledge brought no comfort. It was alarming and humiliating to have to acknowledge the power that the body exerts over the mind. I tried to drill myself, so as to avoid sympathy and manage without help. But my inner wound was worse than the bodily disability, as I found when I used to be awakened in the night by my own shrieks of terror. I took to staying awake and wandering about the streets. Finally I took to drinking again when Miriam asked me out to a restaurant with her usual crowd, and we went on to some party afterwards. One night I met a woman who thought it would be exciting to go to bed with a disabled officer. I went with her when she asked me, but when I left her I couldn't even remember her name. This sort of thing did me no good; it only aggravated the state I was in.

Once after an air-raid night in February as I lay uneasily dozing in the middle of the day my sister came and called me to the telephone. It was Miriam.

"Aunt's ill," she told me. "They've just telephoned me. Can you go and see her?"

"Why don't you go?" I asked. "Are you scared?"

"I'm needed on the set," she answered. "They want to finish shooting the picture before the next raid."

"Heroes, heroes everywhere. Any other news?"

"My windows have been smashed for the third time and the bedclothes are full of glass splinters. Otherwise nothing."

"How disagreeable for your boy friends—they'll have to bring their own sheets. Yes, I'll go and see Aunt. It's safer here than there. This bombing's getting me down."

"You leave my friends out of it!" she said sharply. "Anyhow I'm going to be married."

"Poor chap. Who is it? The producer?"

"Better still: the backer." She told me his name and I knew then that her future was secure financially. Moreover she could stay in films if she still wanted a career.

"Many congratulations! Shall I tell Aunt and set her mind at rest about you?" But to this Miriam made no reply.

I went. My aunt had been bedridden for over a year and her room had the musty smell of illness and medicines. She gave me her gray-white hand and the thin fingers trembled when I took it in mine. "It was good of you to come, Joel," she said. "I'll soon be going now, very soon. And I shall be glad to leave this world of suffering and sorrow."

I spoke to her of my sister's family, of the shortage of goods, of the general belief that the war would end well if we could only hold out, and also of Miriam. She listened eagerly to what I had to say about Miriam. I told her how hard-working she was, how ready to go up to the front line and entertain the troops and how she visited the wounded in hospital, and I mentioned the woolen socks she had knitted for me. Aunt gave a pale smile when she heard this.

"Maybe there's hope for her," she said. "Even she may be humble one day."

Aunt still had all her mental faculties, though her body was powerless. Her gray eyes shone large and transparent in her thin face. She tired quickly; the medicines slurred her speech and made her forget things she had been told, but as far as I could judge she might live on indefinitely. The nurse assured me that she would, once she had recovered from the attack which had induced them to get in touch with Miriam. The house was still very neat and clean; her aged servant saw to that. I stayed there all that spring. One evening in February I stood out in the yard watching a steady glow in the sky far to the south. Helsinki was suffering another all-night raid. I had no wish to return there.

My aunt slipped further and further into the next world and no longer cared to think about or comment on this one. She often prayed aloud, and the nurse read to her from devotional books until she fell into the light sleep of old and ailing people. Her servant admired me because I was a war hero, and she collected food from the wealthy farms in the neighborhood so that I lived better here than in the town. On clear evenings I took Uncle's telescope out into the yard and looked at the sky. And I reflected that if events continued at their present headlong rate, our world would soon differ little if at all from the dead crater-landscape of the moon.

The world must be changed, I thought, but for that to happen man must change. Faith alone can change him, but faith also often means injustice, intolerance, and the persecution of those who think otherwise, whether about the things of the spirit or about our earthly future. Faith is the soil in which the seeds of intolerance and destruction thrive. But a man who strips all dreams and fantasies from his emotional life becomes sterile and cold. Man is incurable; he makes the same mistakes over and over again and bequeaths his dreams to his children, to whom in turn they can bring only disaster. Increase of knowledge means increase of sorrow, but faith springs from emotion and can sow murder. Basic human nature will never change, only the relationship between man and man. So there was nothing to be done, I felt, but to resort to the old methods that had been tried a thousand times: to draw up plans and define frontiers, to cast new molds and force us into them not as individuals but as statistics; to build up states, systems, and communities which at least guarantee the continuity of the race until the next clash of faiths blows the world to pieces.

I started, and wondered whether I'd become a misanthrope. Perhaps I did hate all those who in their stubborn conviction that they were right were ready for their faith's sake to hurl others to destruction. I loathed force, I loathed intolerance, but man I did not loathe. Yet I hoped wryly that I might be forgiven if, after what I'd been through, I couldn't bring myself to love him very intensely. Man was a disturbing phenomenon, with his everlasting dreams, failings and errors, but in himself he was scarcely worthy of love. So I thought as I contemplated the world about me.

But the March sun shone as ever on the unbroken snow-crust of the garden where the mossy apple trees cast blue shadows. In April the eaves glittered with water drops and the widened sky heralded the coming of spring. The sun still shone though the earth was full of anguish and want, though death ravaged the towns and smoke billowed from charred ruins. My mood softened and I relented, thinking that perhaps after all man was worth loving, just because he erred so wildly and continuously, just because he thought himself and his ideas so desperately important, and because he matured only to pass away and leave no trace behind.

When summer came I went back to Helsinki, and Aunt pursued her feeble, panting life. I worked. Miriam married. And the front collapsed, at Näset.

9

From her husband's first wife Miriam gained a fine house. The husband was about fifty and had been twice divorced. He was a self-assertive man of business with many commercial interests; he had bought up the film company when it got into difficulties, since by devious means he had acquired a large stock of unused film. It was in this way that he met Miriam. He was not disagreeable, but he was hard; he knew precisely what he wanted, talked in commanding tones and never listened to what other people said. He succeeded in making me, for one, feel a failure. He had acquired Miriam as he acquired fine wines or Oriental rugs, for the adornment of his house. He was ruthless and caustic with his subordinates.

"You've picked a winner," I observed to Miriam, looking about me from a comfortable armchair.

"Oh," she said indifferently, "the best things have been moved out of reach of bombs. There's nothing here of much value. Besides—" and here she gave me a significant look "—I've learned to hold my own—in everything."

"You're lucky," I said sincerely. "You've got all you ever dreamed of. You're famous, your photograph's in all the papers, the critics make a fuss over you, you earn a lot of money, you have a beautiful house and a handsome husband, and no doubt you'll have children too, in time. And you can hold your own—in everything. Very few people do as well for themselves as that."

"How long do you think it'll last?" she murmured. "But after all why shouldn't it? My husband's a businessman, he's not involved in politics and he's not too rich.

We can always move to Sweden if it gets too difficult to live here."

She wiped a fine apple with a paper napkin, held it for a moment thoughtfully and then handed it to me. I split it in half and said, "Damn it, look at that—it's all maggoty."

"Exactly, Joel, exactly. It always is."

She gave me her hand in tacit understanding, and for a moment of ineffable melancholy I saw again the moon-lit shed and the apple which, on that mild winter evening long ago, had carried the warmth of her hand to mine. I seemed to smell those apples, and the reeking lampwick, but neither of us was a child now.

"There'll be peace soon," she said. "My husband says so, and he always knows what's going to happen. Then life will begin again."

"A maggoty life, but life anyway," I said, and went.

Aunt died in August and at her own wish the funeral was a very quiet one. At the end of August Miriam took me with her to go through the papers and shut up the house. Her husband drove us there on his way to Tampere. The servant had covered the furniture in dust-sheets and packed up all the things that Aunt wanted distributed among the relatives. The rooms still smelled of wax and polish, linen and camphor. The workshop was empty, as the business had long since been transferred to more modern premises in town.

In the empty parlor I turned the pages of Uncle's note-book. "May I keep this in memory of him?" I asked.

"Take what you like," she said, and so I took also that sensational book of my childhood, *Echoes from the Rostrum,* and Uncle's telescope and tripod.

"My husband bought the shares of the other relations

in the house and gave it to me," said Miriam. "Aunt got badly into debt during her illness. My husband paid a stiff price, but he said it was worth it. The land's valuable. I probably shan't sell it yet." She was talking merely for the sake of talking, looking restlessly about her meanwhile, as if floor and walls were saying things to her which she would rather not hear.

The old servant had prepared a simple meal. The bread was cut in paper-thin slices. As we ate Miriam stared at me fixedly, but we talked little. There was something gloomy and oppressive in the atmosphere of that old house. When we had finished Miriam gave the servant leave to choose some clothes and other things for herself.

When the old woman thanked her with conscientious sobs Miriam said impatiently, "Don't bother about washing the dishes. I'll see to that. Go home and take the key with you, and come in here once or twice a week to clean until I decide what to do with the house."

The woman departed with her boxes and her bundles. Her home was on the outskirts of the town and she was now planning to retire there and live on her savings. Miriam put water on to heat in the kitchen, took off her rings and began washing up.

"You'll spoil the polish on your nails," I said.

"I must do it just once more," she answered. "This is how it used to be, day after day, year after year. Would it have been better—? I must think."

I sat on a stool and watched this mature, lovely woman in her plain black dress, washing up by the stove where the linoleum was worn through; yet I seemed to be seeing her as she once was: a tall, defiant, sulky girl with blazing eyes.

"We'll have some tea later," she said, drawing her arm

across her hot face. "Then we'll go. Can you smell anything?"

Tobacco had blunted my sense of smell, but with the cool of evening I noticed it: a pleasant, infinitely delicate fragrance. I went into the dining room and the hall. It was there too, though where it came from I couldn't be sure. We hadn't smelled it when we arrived. There was something uncanny about it.

"I can't think what it can be," I said when I went back to Miriam.

"Switch on the light, it's getting dark," she said. The same eerie feeling had assailed us both, and the scent grew stronger every minute.

With my one hand I put the dishes away in the cupboard as Miriam dried them. Once or twice when I took them from the table my hand touched hers. I knew exactly where everything belonged. In some queer way life seemed to have gone back to what it once was long ago. Only Aunt and Uncle were missing. And the indescribably sweet, unearthly fragrance intensified about us.

"I can't stand this, Joel," cried Miriam suddenly, flinging down the cloth. "What is it? Come on, let's go and look. We must find out what it is or I shall go mad."

The uncanny scent now filled the whole house. We turned lights on in the dark rooms, we peered into the cellar, we even went to the bakehouse. But the smell was strongest in the parlor where the furniture was stacked in the middle of the room under dust-sheets. I lifted one of the sheets and saw the worn black chairs with their carven flourishes. It was not from there that the scent came.

Miriam had gone over to a window that was covered by a paper shade. "Come and look, Joel!" she cried suddenly, in a voice tremulous with startled wonder. I joined her.

On the sill of the south window stood a forgotten cactus plant on which a creamy-yellow flower as big as a baby's head was unfolding. From it a sticky fluid dripped onto the sill.

"Aunt's Queen of the Night," said Miriam, staring as if bewitched at this phantasmal flower. "She had it for more than thirty years and never saw it bloom." There was a moment's silence, and then with a quick look at me she whispered fearfully, "Why now? Why should it flower for us?"

I quivered inwardly, but remarked sensibly enough that if people had been waiting thirty years for it to flower it was high time it did so. Perhaps it had been left on the sill by mistake, and been exposed to the burning rays of the August sun; perhaps it had been watered irregularly. Many circumstances might have combined to make it bloom just now.

We stood there enveloped in that penetrating, intoxicating fragrance. Trembling, Miriam looked at me and I put my one arm round her.

"It blooms only once, just for a night, and then fades and never flowers again," she said, her gleaming dark eyes upon me. "It's a miracle. And that it should be today! Why for us?" she repeated.

I kissed her. She had not put on any lipstick and her lips felt dry and shrunken. She moistened them with the tip of her tongue.

"Why did you do that, Joel?" she asked.

"I don't know. It was bound to happen sometime."

"Put out the light," she said. But when I went over to the door she ran after me and clung to me. "Hold me!" she gasped. "Don't leave me alone. I'm frightened—I've never been so frightened before." When the light was out our eyes soon grew accustomed to the darkness. The windows glimmered red in the last glow of sunset. We stood in the dark with our breath on each other's faces, and with all our senses we inhaled the strange fragrance of the cactus.

"Would you like to stay on here, Joel?" she asked. "The house is mine and there's some furniture left. It may be years before the place can be rebuilt. You're short of money and you could live cheaply here—and for as long as you like so far as I'm concerned."

The same idea had occurred dimly to me. "I might get a job at the grammar school," I said reflectively. "And I could write. I should be near enough to the Helsinki libraries if I want to go on with my scientific work. And I've got Uncle's telescope too."

Only now as I said this did I become aware of a hitherto unconscious desire: to run away. It was flight; and too often had I yielded to the impulse of blind flight. I was forever seeking a shell in which to hide, to stop developing, to stay where I was because it was easiest, to let the future pour over me like a tidal wave.

Miriam's mouth sought mine; with trembling fingers she took my hand and carried it to her breast. "Can you hear it beating?" she asked with a nervous laugh. I quivered from head to foot as I felt her breast under my hand. "It's the only way," she whispered. "Otherwise I should imagine there was something else—otherwise I should go mad."

"Nonsense," I said. "Why do you work yourself up like this? It's no use." But I didn't withdraw from her, and my voice caught in my throat as I went on, "It's no use. I've tried often enough and I know." The unearthly scent surrounded us, seemingly stronger, more swooning for the darkness. She laughed coolly and stroked my neck with

her finger tips. "There are no impotent men, only un-
skilled women, don't you think?" Her caressing hand
made my skin shrink as if with cold, but she didn't understand what I meant.

"There's also spiritual impotence," I said thickly.
"That's worse than the other kind. Believe me, it's too
late for us to try."

But she was no longer listening. Pressing her body to
mine she whispered, "Do you feel it?" My wretched body
trembled against hers, but still I tried to say, "Miriam, it
would be better if I might keep at least the illusion of
you. It's terrible to live without illusions." But it was no
good. I wanted her and could no longer escape what had
to be.

That night I held her in my arm in the narrow iron
bed in which I had slept as a boy—the bed beside which
she had bent to kiss me good night with her young, tightly
closed lips, that evening when she had played the angel.
She was no angel now, nor I a little boy on whose heart
was imprinted the image of a young girl's naked body.
Desperately we goaded and spurred our jaded senses, yet
with every moment I grew colder and emptier within. It
was cold pleasure which left my heart untouched. She began to weep with short, jerky sobs, inconsolable as a child
crying alone in the dark. I stroked her shoulders and
breathed the unearthly fragrance that still hung about us.
This caress was sincere, worth more than all the rest. With
me she was a disappointed woman, and I too was disappointed. We could bring no real solace to each other with
our bodies. When I caressed her it was like caressing any
smooth, soft, lifeless surface, such was our estrangement.

"It was by our own choice," I said. "The fault is ours
alone. If life is burned out for us we can't blame anyone

else. You were selfish, and I was even more so. There lies the fault."

She was just another human being, one who had ruined her own life; and my void was as terrible as hers. The night we lay together on that uncomfortable iron bedstead was the loneliest, most terrible night of my life.

"What a frightful bed," she said next morning. "I'm black and blue all over." We looked coldly and searchingly at each other, as if to detect the smallest hint of tenderness or compassion through which we might attack one another. But we were both empty, both cold. In the parlor we glanced fleetingly at the cactus-flower. It had closed again and was withering. Miriam pinched it off calmly, dropped it and wiped her fingers on her handkerchief. "Ugh, how sticky it is," she said. "And what an awful smell. It's given me quite a headache."

It was then I knew, from the steely tone in her voice, that we were dead; more so than Aunt and Uncle were. We could feel neither remorse nor shame nor hope. My own development, always a matter of fits and starts, had brought me to an absolute zero from which there was no place to go. Or so I believed then.

And I thought that in some ways it was better so; that this was the way to meet the future now looming over me, without dreams and without hope, tranquilly, taking each day as it came. This foundation for my life was desolate, as desolate as the landscape of the moon, but it was solid. Something might be built upon it, if ever something could be born in me which would put an end to my selfishness.

"You're very quiet, Joel," said Miriam impatiently, looking at me with hard, dark eyes. "Why don't you say something?" She was beautiful with her smooth face and heavily painted mouth. I looked at her as I would look at a rare butterfly, mounted on a pin in a glass case.

"Why talk just for the sake of talking?" I asked. "We have nothing more to say to each other."

Soon afterwards I celebrated my thirtieth birthday. I had run away from life long enough. Now I would live and wait for the world to change.

An Island of Ice

1

The sunlight was slanting between the trunks of the pines when the girl came out of the wood and caught sight of the lonely shack among the birches. It was not far from the station, but she had to pause here for breath. She was panting a little and as she stood looking at the house she wiped away beads of sweat from her temples.

The shack was dilapidated, and paint was peeling from walls and window frames. A broken pane was patched with a bit of cardboard streaked with oil paint. The plot was enclosed by a tumble-down barbed-wire fence, and the gate had long ago been kicked from its hinges and left to rot against one of the posts. The flower beds emerging from the snow were moss-grown, and there was mildew on the gooseberry bushes.

But the late afternoon sun shone brightly, and among the wet brown leaves on the littered ground the hepaticas made vivid flecks of violet. The girl continued along the path to the house, noticed a rubbish heap close by stacked with empty bottles, and entered, carefully avoiding one of the wooden steps, which was broken. Most of the small glass panes in the outer door had been knocked out, and inside someone had left a muddy bicycle without troubling to wipe up the wheel tracks. The girl sniffed the musty dirty smell of the place, looked in vain for a bell and knocked cautiously on the inner door. Hearing voices she opened it and walked boldly in, doing her best to conceal her disappointment.

What she had heard was true, then, for all she saw bore witness to slackness and decay. "Why must they always be such awful people?" she wondered.

The room was large and the bright evening sun made it seem light. The acrid smell of turpentine and oil paints, the aroma of stew, and the stench of dirty clothes wafted to meet the girl as she paused in the doorway. A man was sitting at the table eating; he was stocky and gray-haired with unnaturally long and powerful arms. He was in his shirt sleeves and wore dirty boots. The girl recognized him, though he had aged a great deal since any photograph of him had been published. His face had become deeply furrowed, and seemed to her to have coarsened. Opposite him at the table sat a white-haired old gypsy-man with a gay scarf round his neck. Between them a sooty saucepan stood on a newspaper. The bottle of *brännvin* was half empty, and they were drinking it out of odd cups, one without a handle. As the girl came in both men turned and looked at her.

"Good evening," she said. "I'm sorry to disturb you. I'll wait till you've finished."

"No need," said the man; he poured out more liquor for himself and took a gulp. "I'm not selling anything."

"And I couldn't buy it if you were," answered the girl smiling, though what she most longed to do was to run away. "I wanted to see you."

"I'm not buying anything either," said the man. "I'm not ordering anything and I'm not putting my name on any of your damn lists. You needn't wait."

"I should like to talk to you," said the girl. "I'll wait outside." She left the room quickly, shutting the door behind her, and after a moment's hesitation she sat down on the steps and lit a cigarette to stiffen her courage, though she was strictly forbidden to smoke. The rough reception had hurt her, but she waited resolutely, finishing her cigarette and staring at the violet flecks of the hepaticas to avoid looking at all the junk that lay about.

"Good heavens, how stupid and childish I am to be put off by these external things," she reflected. "After all, he was something, once."

Yet with the best will in the world she could find nothing to admire in the unshaven man who sat drinking spirits from a broken cup in company with an old gypsy, with a newspaper for tablecloth.

"He's gone all to pieces," she thought. "I shan't get much here; I ought never to have come."

Nevertheless she waited. When she had finished her cigarette she put her thin arms round her knees and stared into the sunset until her eyes smarted. Disappointment cut at her heart.

2

At last the doors opened and the gypsy came out, wearing a sheepskin coat and carrying a bundle under his arm. The man followed him out to the steps and pretended not to see the girl sitting there.

"Have a good trip!" he shouted after his visitor. "Hope you can get to the train, you old scoundrel!"

"Ay, ay—with the help of God," returned the gypsy piously, and staggered off down the path leading into the wood. The man watched him go, and then glared angrily at the girl.

"What the devil have you come here for?" he demanded. "All I ask is to be left in peace with no one to bother me."

"I've come to talk to you, damn you!" the girl replied. "I can swear too." She looked at the man with distaste. He smelled strongly of spirits and frowziness. She went on, "I'm studying at the university, and I'm going to write about you for the History of Art exam."

"Good God!" he exclaimed, in genuine amazement. "Would I do for a thesis? I don't believe it. You have to be buried for at least fifty years before you're any good to the professors. They're necrophiles, the lot of them."

But he was no longer hostile; there was even the hint of a smile on his face, and the girl fancied he was pleased despite his pretended indifference. "Come in," he said. "You'll be cold out there." He nodded in the direction taken by the old gypsy and added, "I've had him here as a model for a while."

As they passed through the smelly lobby the girl could not resist a sarcastic little dig: "So you do still paint, then."

The man started slightly, but made no reply, and in silence they entered the big room. He went over to where a large canvas was leaning against the wall, and turned it round. Its colors blazed out so wildly that the girl gasped.

"The light's bad," he said; he shifted the painting and going back to stand beside the girl he surveyed it searchingly and critically. "What do you think of it?" The bluster had left his voice. As she didn't answer he added quickly, "I don't think it's too bad."

The old gypsy looked at them from the canvas; he wore his ragged sheepskin, but his scarf was brilliant. He held both hands outstretched, fingers crooked, and his face was lit with a passionate hunger for life. The background glowed red, and every brushstroke was vibratingly alive. The girl stared at the picture, breathing deeply, and there were red patches on her cheeks.

"What do you think of it?" the man repeated.

"It's fearful!" she whispered, unable to take her eyes away. The room seemed to rock round her; she was rapt, dazzled, absorbed in the ecstasy shouting at her from the canvas. "It's glorious," she gasped, and looked at him with a warm, radiant smile. "I never knew you could paint like that. You've never done it before. There's nothing in any of the collections to touch it."

"It's still wet," the man said, going over to test the paint with his black-edged thumbnail. "It may look a bit crude now, but the colors will harmonize better when they're dry." He looked at the girl and couldn't restrain a broad smile. "I painted the old chap three times. I picked him up a couple of months ago at the station. He was sitting on the steps blind drunk and dying, and the train had gone without him. It was pneumonia. I brought him home on the pung and looked after him. I even got a doctor. Otherwise the cold would have finished him."

He glanced at the girl who was listening with parted lips, and a shadow crossed his face. He turned away and said with deliberate harshness, "There was no philanthropy about it. I wanted to paint him as I'd seen him, sitting on the station steps blue with cold. Why the hell would I have dragged him back here otherwise? I had to hang on to him like mad when he got better and the snow melted; his gypsy blood was driving him out on to the road again. Still, I managed to paint him three times."

He smiled to himself. "He made damn-good soup. He slept there by the stove; that's why there's such a stink in here. Three times he pinched my watch, but he gave it back when I tackled him about it. And before he left I went through his bundle and found a whole lot of my shirts and underpants and things. 'Ay,' he said. 'Good job you took that stuff back. It would have been bad for my soul to steal from you—but you see you can't help it when you're a born thief.' Yes, I painted him three times."

The man avoided the girl's bright eyes, and going over to the table he poured *brännvin* into his cup and drank it. "Cranes flew over the house today," he said. "And when he heard their call not even *brännvin* could keep him here. Funny he could hear them; he's half deaf. But now I've got the picture done and I can drink in peace. You don't drink, of course."

It was a statement, not a question. But the girl answered, "Pour me out some. It must be dull for you to drink alone."

Again the man started in surprise, but took another cup from the cupboard, looked at it dubiously and murmured, "I wonder whether there's a single clean cup in the house. And there's only *brännvin*—I haven't drunk anything else for years—it's the cheapest way of getting tight."

"Pour it out," she said. "I was in the war too."

"In the war—a kid like you?" he remarked good humoredly. He filled a cup and the girl sipped the spirits with a wry face. "Will you show me the other two canvases?" she asked. "I should love to see them."

The man withdrew abruptly into his shell again, and with a suspicious look at the girl he went over and turned the old gypsy to the wall. "There's nothing worth showing," he said. "It was only by accident you saw this one; it just happened to be out." He looked at her as if wanting her to go; his face reddened and then in a sudden burst of anger he shouted, "What the hell does a mother's darling like you know about pictures? What business have you got to come here? You needn't write about me—I don't want anybody to write about me. I want to be left in peace to paint, so long as my hands can do it. You can write later, when I'm dead. You can write what you bloody well like then, and cash in on the corpse. You could never understand me anyway."

The girl sat down on the bench by the table, took another defiant sip of the *brännvin* and looked in amusement at the stamping, gesticulating man. "Art is the only thing I live for," she said. "Since the war I've had nothing else. Art's the only thing that's real—it's more real than life."

"Art's tripe!" he roared. "Go to hell."

"Does being a genius hurt so much?" she wondered. "He's got no skin—he's flayed. That's why he's afraid of me." But aloud she said, "When I first saw your pictures I went hot all over; I could hardly breathe. I was angry—almost furious—at first. I was immature then, and I felt as if you'd picked up a fistful of blood and filth and thrown it at me. But you were right. I had to come back again and again and look at them. I've seen all there are in the galleries and private collections. I always wanted to write about you sometime, when I'd learned how to write. I imagined myself kneeling to you if I ever met you. Childish, wasn't it? Then I heard that you'd drunk yourself silly and couldn't paint any more. When I was ill and had to start taking care of my lungs I remembered that the climate here's supposed to be good. I want to stay for a bit and work at my thesis, if you'll help me."

The man stood silently looking at her. Twilight was deepening in the room, and in the twilight the girl looked paler than before. "Are you ill?" he asked.

"A bit," she admitted, and shrugged her thin shoulders. "But it won't hinder my work, if you'll help me."

"You can see for yourself what I'm like," he said. "What they say's quite true: I'm a disreputable old drunk. But I haven't stopped painting—that part was a lie."

"I don't think what the rest think. I believe you measure things by a different scale from other people—things like right and wrong and ugliness and beauty. It's not for me to give an opinion of your work, but I think the gypsy's good. I think it's the best thing you've ever done."

The man grinned and rubbed his stubbly chin. "Have you seen 'Hanged Man' too?" he asked dryly.

The girl remembered and shuddered, and she avoided his searching look. "Yes, I've seen it," she answered. "No one can ever have painted death with such frightful finality. Not in this country, anyhow."

"Do you remember his feet—just his feet?" he asked, staring straight through her. His anger returned and he flung out his arm. "No taste, no style, no subtlety, they say. Subtlety! They can take it and stuff it—"

"And your language is every bit as crude!" the girl flared up. "Why shout at *me?* I'm only trying to understand. I want to understand you as well as I possibly can. I'm only drinking your horrible *brännvin* to show you I'm trying to understand. Don't you yell at me."

The man recovered himself and stared at her. "I haven't asked for your understanding," he said lamely. There was perhaps apology in the tone, though not in the words.

"Why do you always choose such ghastly subjects? Just dirt and blood. You can't see anything fine even in death. When you look at the 'Hanged Man' you can smell the stench of the corpse."

"Really?" said the man, his face lighting up. "I suppose you'd rather I painted nice, tidy, pretty pictures. Why? Other people can do that. Besides, it isn't I who choose the subjects; the subjects choose me. I don't ask 'what' and

'why' and 'is it worth it'? But of course I've done landscapes too. Damn it, I once painted a bunch of hepaticas
in a white cup."

"Show me," she said.

"Perhaps I will," he muttered, staring at her. He poured
out more *brännvin* and tossed it back so violently that he
spilled some on himself. Then he sat down as if he were
dead tired. "If you've seen 'Hanged Man,' " he said with
an effort, "get out of here before I hurt you. A kid like
you. Can't you see it's myself I painted in him? And it's
the same with the gypsy—that's me too. I'm a wolf. Why do
you visit my lair of your own accord?"

The girl took off her gray beret and smoothed her dark
hair. "Perhaps I'm Little Red Ridinghood," she said.
"Perhaps I've come to rescue my grandmother, if there's
anything left of her."

The man burst out laughing. "You think you're a match
for me, do you?" he said. "You're mad. Out of your mind."

The girl smiled. "That's what the professor said when
I told him I wanted to write about you."

This softened him a little and he spoke more gently.
"Listen, child; I might help you. Sometime I'll tell you
all I can, but now you must go away. You don't understand. I don't drink all the time; when I'm painting I
don't drink at all. I drink in the winter when it's dark
and one can't paint and it's hard to sleep. But now I've
painted the gypsy, after three weeks' work, and I'm as
empty as an old shoe. I've just got to drink or I'll go to
pieces. Body and soul scream for alcohol. After that I'll
start with a clean canvas. Come again tomorrow, the day
after tomorrow, in a week's time—how should I know?
But you must go now—you oughtn't to see me like this.
No one ought to. Believe me, I hate you to see me like
this. In a week's time I may have sobered up. Come again

if you must—otherwise stay away. I'm better alone. I'm not a misanthrope, but I like people best from a distance."

The girl rose hesitantly, and as the man stood up she said, "I'd like to see the painting of the hepaticas before I go."

The man swore and switched on the ceiling light. Its bleakness made them both look dead. The man's hair was long and dirty gray, his features drawn and etched with lines of vice, dirt, and suffering. He strode ill-temperedly into the adjoining room and returned with a small canvas, locking the door guardedly after him. Then he tossed the painting onto a chair; but he loved his work too much to remain surly. He was compelled to stand and gaze at it, anxiously critical, searching for faults and weaknesses, gnawed inwardly by the relentless desire for perfection. All this the girl could feel.

"It's just a trifle," he said, though there was great gentleness in his voice. "But I may have hit off something with that purple. An impossible color anyway."

The girl looked at the flowers in the grayish white bowl, unable to speak for the lump in her throat. The little canvas was austere and touching in its beauty, with form and color purified to agelessness. Just a few specks of violet, and the gray-white poverty of the bowl; yet in this slight painting a breath of eternity had been caught and held.

"There is no other heaven," said the man, turning his sunken face to hers. She nodded, smarting with held-back tears. "I'm over-sensitive," she told herself crossly. "Sniveling like a schoolgirl as soon as I see anything beautiful! It must be because I'm ill." Aloud she said nothing; she drew a little handkerchief from her sleeve and twisted it absently round her thin fingers. The man took away the picture and locked it up again in the next room. "His treasure chamber," she thought. "Pandora's box. Perhaps it'll be Pandora's box for me too. What do I care? What do I care about anything? I'm going to die soon."

"We'll meet again, then," she said. "I'll come another time if I may. I've got a skeleton list of your works, and I'd like to complete it. For your sake it's important that it should be as full as possible. And I've got any amount to ask you."

The man neither answered nor held out his hand; he was standing with hunched shoulders by the table, staring at the floor. His shadow loomed large on the wall behind him. The girl went out into the gathering dusk and drew in deep breaths of the cool spring air. "Perhaps this is my last spring," she thought, her heart sore with the craving for beauty. But she thrust aside her own sensibility, saying, "That's nonsense. I'm going to get better."

That night as she lay in her narrow bed beneath a downy blanket, she drew the thermometer from her armpit and found that the mercury had climbed far higher than it should. She lay looking at the colorful, unopened books on her bedside table; they were like strange birds from foreign lands, and their colors were love calls. But she didn't open them. She lay on her back with the light on, thinking of hepaticas, of war, of death.

3

The next afternoon she went back to the house, but now the doors were locked and no one answered her knocking. She sat for a time on the steps and then went home again.

The next day her landlady told her that the painter had

got into a brawl in a village café, smashed a window, and landed in jail. "He's a shocking man," she said. "And he uses such frightful language. No decent people even say good morning to him any more. It's a pity he can't be made to leave the place, but he owns that shack."

That day the girl made no attempt to meet him. She stayed in her room reading history of art and looking at colored plates. The third day she once more took the path to the shack. Sharp spring rain was falling. The moss was wet and the gold of the pine trunks was dimmed. When she knocked and walked in the man sat up angrily in his dingy bed. He was fully dressed with muddy boots on, and he had drawn the bedclothes over himself, for it was cold in the room. The fire hadn't been lit for a couple of days. The table was cluttered with dirty crockery and in opening the door the girl knocked over an empty bottle and sent it rolling across the floor. The man's face was flushed and puffy, and his eyes wavered as he groped for a half-empty bottle that stood by the foot of his bed. He raised it to his mouth and drank from it in deep draughts.

"You're making yourself ill," she said. With a gesture of impatience she snatched the cap from her head and sat down. Bright drops fell on the floor from her raincoat, and her pale face was white. The room stank of spirits and vomit.

The man looked at her, groping in his drink-corroded mind for her image. "At least eat something," she said. "That'll help."

He picked up a gnawed bit of hard bread that he had in bed with him and began chewing it, still staring at the girl. His eyes were as gray as rain and their pupils had shrunk to insensitive dots. "I'm seeing him in his deepest degradation," she thought. "But what does it matter? He's still the man who painted the hepaticas and the gypsy.

What I'm looking at is just the outer husk, and I oughtn't
to let it worry me."

"You little fool!" the man stammered suddenly, with a
fatuous laugh and threw the bread away. Leaning on bed
and table he rose and reeled forward towards her, groping
for her with his hands. The sour smell of stale alcohol
came from his open mouth, and the girl started back and
stood up. "Will he remember this in the morning?" she
wondered.

She stiffened but did not retreat when he put his slack
arms round her. "Fool," he repeated, and pressed his wet,
rough mouth on her cheek. She twisted her head away and
held her breath.

"Shall I hit him?" she thought. "But what good's that?
He doesn't know what he's doing. And there's no fun in
hitting people."

The man pressed his horrible mouth against her cold
lips. "A woman was married to him for twenty years," she
reflected. "How could she do it? How could she stand it?"

He held her arm tightly and paused to look at her.
"What are you fooling about like this for?" he said bru-
tally. "Get those clothes off; I want to see you naked. Take
them off and get into bed." Releasing her he went back
and sat on the edge of the bed, took a gulp from the bottle
and looked at her challengingly.

"Not today," the girl returned, shaking her head
slightly. "There's no point in it; you wouldn't remember
anything about it in the morning. And besides it's cold in
here." Her own answer made her laugh, and her icy wrath
melted away. "Why should I be angry with him?" she
thought. "It doesn't matter what happens to me—it's entirely unimportant compared with the hepaticas. He said
there was no heaven but that—and this room must be the

only hell. If I can be a drop of water in a parched throat, then why not? But not today."

"You mustn't harm yourself like this," she said aloud. "Eat something and get better. And you might wash, too. I'll come back tomorrow, at four o'clock."

The man gave no sign of having understood. The girl put on her beret again and buttoned up her coat. From the bag she carried slung over her shoulder she took pen and paper and wrote: "I'll come at four P.M. tomorrow." She laid the paper on the table and shoved the dirty dishes to one side. But just as she was leaving she hesitated, walked over to him on light feet and gently stroked his rough hair and his cheeks. She felt as if she were stroking a sick, ill-tempered animal. "I'll be seeing you," she said. He sat limply, staring after her with bloodshot eyes.

Once out on the path she wanted to laugh again. "That note will shake him when he comes to," she thought. "He'll curse and puzzle himself silly about what might have happened. What a fool I am to laugh—there's nothing to laugh at in his wretchedness. But I do think he's child-ish—a childish old man." She moistened her handkerchief in the moss and wiped her mouth clean. The sour smell of spirits still pricked her nostrils; she sneezed and blew her nose.

Just after four the next day she returned. As soon as she glimpsed the shack through the trees she could see that it was no longer dead. Smoke was rising from the chimney and a window was open. When she entered she saw that the floor had been scrubbed and that a red sleigh-rug had been spread over the bed. The man was sitting at the table with a clean shirt on. He had even shaved, and in doing so had cut his chin. His hands shook and there were beads of sweat on his forehead.

This time he returned the girl's greeting. "Good day

to you," he said. "You've come then. And you were here
yesterday. I must have been terribly drunk."

"You're alive anyway," the girl said smiling. Her eyes
were very bright and her cheeks pink.

"I've lit the fire in the bath-house," he told her. "I had
a bath earlier in the day, but I shall have another this evening. My heart's weak and it won't stand a proper steam
bath these days. I had a woman come up from the village
to clean things here. How are you?"

"Very well, thank you."

He avoided her eye and moved his shaking hands uneasily on the table. "I hope I didn't do anything to offend
you yesterday," he went on. "When one's drunk one
doesn't think what one's doing."

"No, you didn't offend me at all. You only wanted to
kiss me. And you asked me to undress and get into bed
with you."

He sighed and stared at the floor. "Hell," he said, "I'm
sorry. But I'm glad it was no worse. And me nearly sixty
—I might be your grandfather."

"And I don't think I'm your type anyway," she said
smiling. "I'm too thin. You only paint fat women. Big
thighs and bulging breasts. That's what you like."

"A farm wench who's calved twice," said the man.
"When one sees something like that it's as if all nature
were rolling over one. It's not a question of beauty or
ugliness."

"May I make a note of that? I should love to see the
professor's face when he reads it." She took out a pad and a
pen, and when she had finished writing she said, "Tell me
something about your life."

"What is there to tell?" he said, and closed up again.

"Of course I know all that's in the encyclopedias and the

artists' directory," she said. "But that's not much. When did you begin to paint?"

"I've painted all my life. I painted before I could read, with chalks and water colors." He waved his hand defensively. "Words, words! I have no words to explain what it meant to me. Sometimes it was like a sort of pain—a frightful depression or sickness—a sense that there was something more in me than just myself, but that I couldn't get it out. I had a home once, with dinner services and tablecloths and all that. And two children. And I painted. I painted prettily and smoothly. Hell, even the museum bought some of the things. That's what started me drinking. I used to look at my pictures and think: what's the matter with them? What the devil's the good of painting like that? I had to get away. I went to Spain and lived there for two years—right up to the First World War. That gave me a good shaking-up: the mountains, the roads, the burning light, the red soil. I painted a few pictures too, but they didn't take on over here. When I had no money for paints I lived in a mud hut; I worked with peasants in the fields and with dockers on the wharves. It was some tourist who saw me then and talked about it at home afterwards. I'd gone to pieces, he said. I only painted when I was drunk. When war came I went home. I wanted to paint, God damn it! Nothing else, just paint."

"But you didn't paint anything for years."

"No, it all stopped. I couldn't paint any more. I was no good even to myself. You've no idea how ghastly that was. Not a moment's peace—colors burning into me, and I couldn't put them down. And war everywhere. The old world smashing up. They said I was changed, brutalized. And at home the everlasting nagging—change your collar, shave, there are people coming to dinner. God Almighty, what had that to do with me? Or it was the rent, the electricity, the gas bill, the school fees. How did all that concern me? I did try, you know. But the internal pressure built up and up, and I drank. I used to drink for days on end."

The man fell silent and looked sideways at the girl. "I'm only telling you all this to try and make you understand," he said. "If it's hell to paint, it's far worse hell to thrash about and not be able to. When one's painting one can sometimes feel as if there were some meaning to life; otherwise what is there to do but drink? And it's then that life starts creaking at the joints. I told my wife that she must choose: she must either be with me or without me. We sold things, we economized—and at last the deadlock dissolved. At last I was working again, but in quite a different way. It wasn't easy any more. It was a struggle—it was one long battle. One long defeat, seen in the light of what I wanted to paint. The 'Beggar Boy' dates from that time, if you remember him. That was me, too. I was the beggar— I was begging for just a crumb from heaven. But I was no good for exhibitions any more; my work was 'brutal and repulsive.' That was the time. It lasted ten years."

"Yet it was then you made your name," the girl said.

"Madman was the name they gave me. Even my children were told by their mother that I was a boor, a soak, an abandoned wretch. But it's wrong to blame her. It was probably my fault. When a woman's trying to preserve the last vestiges of outward respectability and her husband keeps smashing it all up, no amount of tenderness or angelic patience will help. What happens? She invites decent, cultured people to the house—he disappears. Or for once, perhaps, they're both invited out somewhere—and he's drunk. But think of it from the man's point of view. Say I'm painting again—say I'd really got something at last. That would be the moment when dinner was ready and getting cold, or something had to be paid for at the shop, or some other nonsense. What can a man do but curse and lose his temper? So loneliness grew up round me—but the lonelier I was, the better I painted. That was the price I had to pay—and no price would have been too high. I preferred to swap affection and companionship for the fondling of a whore—friends and good company for a drinking den in the harbor. From their point of view people were right when they said I'd gone to pieces. But it was then I painted the dockers and the tar boilers."

"And then you were divorced," said the girl.

"I was locked up for a few weeks," he said. "And when I came out we parted for good. It was the best thing to do. The children had grown up. I send her a picture every year. At first she sold them all for the price of the frame. Now she's wiser; she's waiting till I'm dead. I wonder if you've understood anything of what I've been saying."

"It's possible," the girl said. "You loved her."

"Of course I loved her!" he cried, flaring up. "There's never been any other woman in my life. The others were just whores. But she didn't understand me, whether I was painting or in bed with her. I couldn't have stood it for twenty years if I hadn't loved her. And the children too. But it was all for the best: to paint seriously one's got to be alone. From loneliness to greater loneliness. It's the only way. I jettisoned all the ballast. Alcohol is good fuel. Alcohol burns away superfluity until only nakedness remains. There's nothing of value in life but the naked human being. That's what I paint, when I paint. Myself, in fact."

The girl wrote for a few moments. "From loneliness to greater loneliness," she repeated to herself, and looked about at the bare room.

"It entails frightful suffering," the man went on. "Nothing's more cruel than art. It strips a man to poverty and leaves him not a moment's peace of mind. He can never be satisfied with himself. He must always be in doubt, always uncertain; and drink's all part of it. I'm mean and greedy, as I expect you know—but only so as to be able to paint. Nothing else matters to me. I live on an island with nothing round me but the cold ocean, and only wrecks drift to my shores. And yet I love life—and so I paint. They call me brutal and drink-sodden, but don't think of that; think only of what I've been able to achieve."

The sunlight was slanting through the window. The man walked quickly to the door of the next room, unlocked it, and this time left it open. He brought out two canvases, set them against the wall and went back for more.

"I haven't shown these to anyone," he said. "They were done during the last three years. It's safest not to let them be seen, or my creditors would pinch them. I want to keep them for life, to help me believe in myself; to persuade myself, during my phases of emptiness, that one day I shall paint again."

The girl looked at the pictures as he went on, "The worst thing about it is that I never know beforehand whether I'm going to be able to paint or not. Sometimes when I'm at my worst I try to force myself—I struggle on day after day, toiling and sweating, but nothing comes of it. Nothing's gained by force, and I have to scrap it all. Then at last the order comes and a tremendous power pours from my hand. Then there's nothing I can't do—it all comes easily, in a sort of frenzy. I've learned to accept this, and be humble. In the winter I borrow books from the library. Biographies mostly, and travel books. I sit here quite passively and trouble nobody, so long as nobody troubles me. That's if I'm not drunk, of course. When I am, I do racket round a bit, though not often; mostly I lock myself in and soak in private!"

But the girl was no longer listening. She was looking at the paintings. She saw the corpse-yellow hands of a dying gypsy, and the serenity of his sunken face. She saw a berry-picker and a woman in a blue dress. She saw a naked figure that seemed to have been carved with a knife, so austerely that not a spark of sensuality remained. She looked at one picture after another and thought, "I'm not worthy to see all this. I can't stand his loneliness; it crushes me."

But the man said, "Sometimes even these die to me and I can't believe in them. It's as if I went blind inside. There's no agony like it; but I've *got* to believe. That's all that keeps me going. And sometimes I shout, 'Thank you, Earth, for giving me life—thank you for letting me paint, for nobody else has ever painted like me.'" He glanced at the girl and his voice turned hoarse: "Because by God that's true! No one has ever done anything like it. I have no rivals in this country; if I compete it's with the whole world. Once one has crossed the last threshold there are no frontiers. Only the round earth, and man."

He looked at the girl again and raised his voice. It broke and was full of self-mockery. "Write it all down, and give 'em something to laugh at. I don't care a damn for you or your opinions. You know now that I'm even crazier than you thought."

But she was gazing at the pictures, staggered by the shock of them. In looking at them she considered neither form nor color as she usually did, so formidable was the power with which these paintings were flung onto the canvas. It was as if by some titanic effort they had been torn from a matrix of reality—a reality stronger and more savage than the common kind. As she beheld them the protective veils of everyday reality fell away; yet the loss of them caused her a searing pain. "It's only because I'm ill," she thought. "It makes me uncritical. He's putting a spell on me."

Aloud she said, "Thank you for showing them to me. I don't know whether I'm worthy of so great a gift."

He touched his canvases with tenderness. His nature was at rest. His face aged even while she watched it, as the spitting flame of self-assertion flickered and died. "How I do talk," he remarked sheepishly. "Of course you understand that none of this is true in itself. Words only skim the surface; it's like blocking out the first shapes on a canvas with charcoal. That's why it's so hopeless to talk to other people. I should like you to forget what I've said. One stroke of a brush can tell you more about me than all my chatter."

He remained absent-mindedly staring at the berry-picker; his hand quivered before the painting and seemed to be groping. "I don't even ask for comprehension any more," he said very humbly. "True understanding can't be expected after one has crossed all those thresholds into solitude. A man like me is bound to be condemned by everyday standards. I have banished myself from human goodness. I still have a will towards it, but goodness is a thing I can only paint; I can't realize it in my own life." He gave the girl a bitter look. "I said I loved my wife and children. It was not true. I loved only myself. All I got I threw into the balance—love, goodness, home, hope, and kindness—until it tipped the scale."

Slowly he began taking the pictures back into the other room, and having done so he locked the door again. The girl sank down on a shabby stool and stared at the floor. She was sweating all over; she felt as if she had made an immense physical effort and was exhausted. The man stood in front of her, looking down at her bent head.

"Why am I talking like this to you?" he said. "A kid like you—and to think you were serving in the war, too! But my humility's just a hang-over, believe me. One gets a headache, you know, on the morning after; one feels like throwing a bridge across to some other fellow mortal."

He sat down and began filling a blackened pipe, still watching the girl who sat staring at the floor as before. The hint of a smile appeared in his rugged face. "People live their lives tied to work and knowledge and habit," he said. "From childhood they spin threads round themselves and wrap themselves up more and more tightly until they're nothing but cocoons. When they're completely rigid and can't draw a single breath of fresh air—when a single new idea hurts them—then they lay their burdens on their unfortunate children and send them packing—out into the same wilderness, with the same bonds. I was never like this. The whole of my life has been a loosening of threads and ties. A bound person stiffens quickly, yet every thread one loosens causes pain. Threads of habit cut right into the flesh and when they're torn away leave their trace in blood. But now at last I'm free in my solitude; flayed and wounded though I may be, I'm free, and I'm myself."

He lit his pipe and pulled a sour face as the smoke reached the spirit-parched membranes of nose and throat. "Art is the loneliest battle, and it is fought against the whole world," he said. "Once you've crossed the first thresholds you can't go back and ask advice. You have nothing but your own eye and your own feeling to rely on, and you can only pray to God that reason will stand the strain. Applause must be resisted as firmly as abuse. Even good advice is just another set of snares. You must have the courage to make mistakes, over and over again—

but there's always a pack of wolves at your heels, and that's why I don't exhibit any more. I can't stand the snarling and snapping. That'll show you how thin-skinned I am. And if I won recognition, what good would it be to me now? It wouldn't help me in the slightest; it would merely lead me astray. The only true verdict is that of my own life—and even that sometimes fails me, so that on my worst days all I want is a length of good strong rope with a running noose at the end of it. And when I die I shall be just as unsure of myself as I am now; I shall never know whether I was right, whether I was anything out of the ordinary, or whether it was all a mirage born of solitude. What does the flesh matter, or alcohol, bad language, or unscrubbed floors? There's only despair. Art, my little one, is constant despair. It demands a tough body and a satanic endurance. That's why so many die early. That's why so many choose the easier way—so-called success. But true success lies within oneself, not outside."

He laid down his pipe and looked in surprise at the girl's bent head. He went slowly to the stove and thrust in a few logs, then filled a coffeepot with water and put it on to heat. While he busied himself with these things she wiped her face with the back of her hand, and then furtively taking a little mirror from her bag she dabbed the corners of her eyes with her handkerchief. "I must be in pretty poor shape to snivel like this," she reflected. "Am I doing it on his account or mine?"

She remembered an old dog she had seen in the village— a dog that can never have been well treated. For even now —old, toothless, blind and rusty-coated—it could only growl and snap at the hand outstretched to pat it. "Life is a desolate thing," she thought. "I've grown up more now, with this madman, than in all my student days. I'm cultivating two flowers in my heart. One's beauty, and the other's death. Perhaps they're the same flower, though I never realized it before."

4

The man spread a cloth on the table and put out two cups. He poured sugar into a bowl and brought the coffeepot over to the table. "You shall have some coffee since you're going to write about my work," he said. "Others have come here with the same idea, you know. One of them wanted one of my pictures in return for his trouble. Another even brought a photographer with him. I told them to go to hell."

The girl drank the hot coffee eagerly. "It's awful to think you've got all your paintings here, in a wooden house," she said. "A fire could destroy the lot—" she paused "—especially as you drink."

He stared in front of him. "You forget that they'll disappear anyhow in time," he said. "Factory-made colors don't last; they lose their brilliance—they alter with time and the life goes out of them. In ten years they'll be tamer, in fifty they won't look the same at all. In a hundred years these paintings will be ripe for the dustbin. When I was younger I didn't know that. I wouldn't have believed it if I'd been told. I know now. But what does it matter so long as I've painted them?"

The girl didn't understand, and was dismayed. "Do you mean that pictures die too?" she asked.

"Nothing in the world lasts. Even pictures die. The paintings of our time die just as people do, though their lives may be a little longer. But why should we let that worry us? What can it matter to me if future generations understand my pictures better than this one does?"

"But—" the girl objected lamely. She felt as if the ground had dropped from beneath her feet and she was suddenly gazing down into vacancy. "What's the good of anything, then? Why paint at all? What's the use?"

The man looked at her with a sad smile, and his eyes held no comfort. "There, you see? You'll never understand," he said gently. "I've crossed a frontier, and on my side of it the question of survival and nonsurvival, of vanishing or living, hasn't the same importance. It just doesn't matter. The main thing is that I have painted— that I shall paint so long as my eyes last out. That's what art is." He took the girl's thin hand in his, stroked her soft palm with his thumb and looked at her pink nails. "A hand," he said softly. "Do you remember 'Fishwife'? There I tried to paint human hands—gnarled, sore, smarting hands. The endlessness of human labor and its appalling futility. But who understood?"

He released her hand, but she smiled timidly at him. "You can hold it if you like," she said. "It feels nice—now you're sober." He blushed and looked down at the table. "When you were drunk you kissed me, too," she added.

He brushed her hand roughly aside and a malignant look returned to his gray eyes. "So that's what you want!" he said wrathfully. "Is that the hook I'm to wriggle on? But my guts and jaws are so lacerated that ordinary hooks won't hold."

The girl was dismayed. "I only meant I wanted to show you some small kindness," she said shyly. "You've let me see your pictures, you've talked to me. I thought perhaps you didn't dislike me." She struggled to find the right words. "I felt that after what you've given me there's little enough I can do in return—except perhaps just be near you. I've nothing else to give."

"A kid like you," he said, looking at her with deep distaste. "And as thin as a rake. I don't like your eyes either—they're far too much alive. Don't turn them on me, it only makes me angry. What is it you do want, for Christ's sake? I don't like pussycats. It's much simpler to take a tart to bed if one's cold; all they want is money and drink. That's honest at least."

"Oh, what a beast you are!" Her lips were trembling. "And cruel, too." She wiped her eyes and blew her nose. "Why must you always be so suspicious? I only meant that my own life has been wasted. I've never been able to give anyone anything. When the war began again there was a boy of my own age; he wanted me. He said it would be easier to die if he had me first. I suppose that's what all men say. I'm just stupid—I believe everything I'm told. It made it no easier for him to die—it made it harder. He was weak and he overstayed his leave, so they sent him to the front with the shock troops. He'd have found dying easier if I'd been unkind to him. He was killed at Sordavala. And I don't even know whether I loved him. It's all so long ago. And when I was in the war myself someone wanted me; it seemed such a little thing. I thought why shouldn't I if it makes life better for him? I've never valued myself very much, you see; only other people. I thought perhaps you might like me, as you're old and lonely and unhappy. Just the presence of someone else— no more than that. Perhaps I myself need to be near someone—I'm so afraid of dying. When I saw your pictures I felt braver, and I thought that perhaps there was no death—not in the way I'd thought."

The man looked at her incredulously. "You must be out of your mind," he said.

The girl's vehement speech had started her coughing; she coughed and coughed, her mouth drawn sideways in pain, and tears trickled down her cheeks. In spite of himself the man laid his hand on her shoulder, and he felt her trembling. "You seem to be really ill," he said. "And your hands are much too hot." She made no reply and simply pressed her face to his rough sleeve and clung to him, as if she had been near drowning in emptiness and had at last caught hold of something real.

"You're still so young," the man said comfortingly. "You'll get well. One oughtn't to feel so desperate at your age—nor so helpless. One oughtn't to let oneself be dirtied."

The girl drew herself up and cried hotly, "Nothing that happens to people can dirty them. They dirty themselves. I'm not hard. I'm not pitiless. I'm clean; I'm candid."

The man stroked her hair with fingers that were swollen at the joints. "I've talked too much," he said. "I didn't know you were so sensitive; you oughtn't to be too sensitive. If you are, you have to set about getting toughened. You have to roll in the muck-heaps of the world. It's better. I've done that. Fire will lick us clean afterwards and burn away the dirt."

Pausing, he stared at her and his face turned gray. He cleared the table and put the coffeepot back on the stove, stroking the girl's shoulder clumsily as he passed. "I'd be a swine to touch you," he said. "You oughtn't to have come here. I oughtn't to have shown you the berry-picker; you can't take it. You ought to write about stained glass. Church windows." He chatted away as if to a little dog.

"Can't you understand?" the girl whispered in desperation. "I must have some purpose in my life, or I shall have lived in vain. I may not be able to write as I want to; I haven't much talent. But if I can be a friend to you—if

I can win a tiny place inside you—my life may have been worth while. You can do what no one else can, and in you I should come back to life. My stupid, empty life would have meaning. Only to touch you, to be near you. It would endure longer than anything else I've done or thought."

"Rubbish, little girl," he said: there was both compassion and self-mockery in his tone. "Run along home now before it gets dark. You ought to stay in bed when you're so ill." He went up to her, and putting his hands under her elbows he lifted her to her feet, looked into her eyes and shook his gray head. Her body felt so frail and helpless in his arms; he could feel her ribs and the warmth of her body. "This too!" he marveled. "First the gypsy and the hepaticas and the cranes. Now you." He bent his head and kissed her cheeks and neck gently, as if he were holding something infinitely precious. She closed her eyes and lifted her face. Her eyelids above their short black lashes looked childishly wrinkled as she held them tight shut. He kissed her lightly on her fevered lips; there was nothing brutal about him now. Indeed, there was a simple wondering tenderness in his touch. For a moment he held the girl in his arms. "Go now," he said softly. "I want to be alone."

As the girl went towards the door he took his pipe from the table as a defense against the greed of his hands. His throat burned from his drinking, and his stomach felt dead. The girl walked along the path through the dusk. Once she turned and waved to the lit window, smiling. The rippling of brooks rang in her ears, though there were no brooks in the moss among the pines.

5

When she awoke next morning she felt dry and hot and her heart smarted from feverish dreams. She drank a glass of water and took her temperature; it was alarmingly high. "I won't go back to the sanatorium," she thought. "I don't want my ribs cut away and my lungs squeezed up." She rose, but her knees failed her and she was giddy. She spent three days in bed, waiting for her temperature to drop; and as she lay she passed her hands slowly over waist and hips and over the points of her breasts beneath the flimsy nightgown. "I get thinner every day, however much I try to eat," she thought. "Soon there'll be nothing left worth having."

Lying there under the light blanket she thought of the paintings she had seen. She could recall every detail of them, and they blazed before her mind's eye. "There's no other heaven," she said to herself, remembering the flowers in their grayish-white bowl. And the man's fingers, swollen at the joints, as they touched her ribs. "Ugly, brutal, dirty," she thought, "but he fills me to the brim. He fills me and makes me happy. Completely happy. Madness! He might be my grandfather. Good Lord, surely I can't be in love with him? Ridiculous!"

For three days she lay in bed, homesick for the ruinous shack, the neglected garden, for the smell of paint and turpentine in that chilly room. By the time she was up and about again the last of the snow had melted from the hillsides. But as she followed the path through the glowing pine trunks she was very much afraid. Afraid of events, words, contacts. Everything in her quaked with fear.

"Well, so there you are at last," the man said irritably

as she walked in. "I've been waiting for you." He had stretched a new canvas and set it up on the easel. "Keep your beret on but take off your jacket," he said. "You've kept me waiting; I remembered your face. I must paint you to be rid of you. I can get rid of anything if I paint it." He squeezed colors from their tubes and chose a brush.

The girl sat on a stool with her hands in her lap, while the man scrutinized her with keen, rapid glances. " 'Girl in a gray cap,' " he said. "I don't like your eyes—I loathe brown. I can never bring it to life. Turn your head a bit so that I get the line of the jaw. I only need the cap and the jaw-line and the eyes; I don't want any more." He shifted the easel a little and began to paint. The girl sat without daring to move.

For an hour, two hours, she sat there, wide-eyed, with her hands in her lap, until the sense of unreality became so strong that she was compelled to pass her hand over her face. She didn't feel the cold. Her immobility made her neck and side ache.

The man was painting. His eyes bored into her until she felt as if they had sucked out her whole essence and spat it back onto the canvas. She was being emptied, emptied, until thought fell silent in her brain, her fingers grew cold and her heartbeats fainter. At last the man's movements became slower; more and more often he stood still staring at the canvas, and virtue went out of him. At last he laid aside palette and brushes, unscrewed the painting from the easel and set it up on a bench against the wall.

From the canvas a girl looked out at her: a girl in a gray cap, whose brown eyes were filled with pain. There was the jaw-line, fined to the bone, and the narrow neck; she was staring straight at death. "Do I look like that already?" she asked herself in dismay. She rose stiffly, and noticed that she was so cold that her teeth chattered. Knife-edged waves of fever cut through her body.

"You've painted me," she said in a voice of awe. "Now I shall never die. When I'm dead people will still be able to see what I was like—to see me as you saw me. More truly than anyone else ever saw me."

The room went black before her eyes and she steadied herself against the man's shoulder. But he never noticed it; he was staring at his painting with a look of stern scrutiny, to detect the faults. "The cap's good," he said. "It's the same gray as rain clouds in spring. The eyes, now. Perhaps that brown's alive, but we shan't know for certain till the paint's dry. I hope that shine won't go dead. They're human eyes all right."

The girl was still leaning against him. "In history of art books I've seen portraits of women who died long ago," she whispered. "They're still alive—they still smile. Perhaps in years to come someone will look at my portrait in the same way, and like me although I'm dead. It was very good of you to paint me."

"I painted you to be rid of you," the man replied roughly, still staring at the canvas. "Now I'm empty again; you've squeezed the strength from me. You've squeezed out desire and hope. Bed's the easiest place for two people to meet."

The girl moistened her feverish lips and tried to control her shivering. "I love you," she whispered.

"Nonsense," he said, with a brusque look at her. "You don't love me at all; you're simply afraid of dying." But he didn't thrust her away. "Did you get tired sitting? Lie down and rest; I've exhausted you."

The girl took one reeling step, and then the man lifted her in his arms and carried her over to the bed; she was very light and her head fell against his shoulder. She closed her eyes, and again he beheld the black curve of the short lashes against the childishly lined eyelid. He covered her up, but she pushed away the blankets. "Don't worry, there aren't any lice," said the man dryly. "Kick off your shoes; you'll be more comfortable." He pulled off her shoes and wrapped the blanket round her feet; then went over to the stove and thrust some logs into the dying embers.

"Don't go away," the girl pleaded. He came back, sat down heavily on the edge of the bed and rubbed her thin hands between his own.

"Why do you think you're going to die?" he demanded. "You're so young. Red cheeks and small breasts—long legs like a calf. You're only a child; of course you're not going to die."

Tears forced their way under her eyelids; she sighed and squeezed the man's hard hand between her moist palms. "One lung's been treated," she told him, "but it's spread to the other. All they can do now is to operate—and even that mightn't help—my heart's too weak to stand the anesthetic. I saw girls at the sanatorium who'd been operated on. I've had myocarditis, and I'd never come through it."

"A child," the man repeated to himself. "A little girl, with the whole of her life in front of her."

The girl opened her eyes and looked at him. "I'm not regretting that," she said. "My only regret is that I'm not a complete person. If I'm to die let's have no pretense— don't talk to me as if I were a dog. Talk as if you were talking to a human being." She clutched his hand and beneath the blanket her whole body went taut as she fought against another paroxysm of coughing. "Hold me," she said, "or I shall bleed all over your bed." The man raised her to a sitting position and held her firmly in his arms.

When the attack was over and she relaxed again he cov-

ered her carefully up to the chin and said, "Now you must
lie absolutely still. Sleep if you can, while I do some cooking. I'll make a pancake for us—I'm good at pancakes." He
scratched his gray chin as he looked at the girl. "As a rule
when I've finished a painting I go to the village for a meal,
and get tight," he said. "But I don't feel like that today.
Perhaps tomorrow, I don't know. Lie still now, and I'll
make a pancake."

The girl kept her eyes shut. The dirty blanket smelled
of bad tobacco; she pressed her fingers hard against it and
felt the man's presence with her whole body. She heard
him moving about the room and dozed off now and then,
but each time she woke with a start, bathed in sweat. A
fragrance reached her from the stove; a smell of childhood,
of war. She was melting inwardly with the love she felt.
But when the pancake was ready and the man began to
feed her she could only swallow a few mouthfuls.

"I'm poisoning your bed," she said, "and you'll have to
disinfect the forks and plates."

"Don't talk rubbish." He finished the rest of the pancake and felt for his pipe, then laid it down again. "Move
over," he said, and lying down beside the girl he drew the
blanket over himself. They lay beneath it and were warm.
The spring sun shone slanting through the window and
bathed everything in the room with a faint rosy light.

"I tried to paint you out of my system," the man said.
"It's not my fault if you wouldn't let me." He laid his
hand lightly on the girl's breast and turned to kiss her.

"Don't," said the girl. "It's only because you're sorry
for me. I don't want that." She drew away from him and
laid her hand restrainingly on his. "I don't want false
coin," she said, with tears in her voice.

"I'm old now," he said. "An old man compared with
you. People imagine we grow cooler with the years—that

our emotions grow cold and our senses blunted. But when we're old the slightest caress means more to us than the double handfuls of life we took when we were young. Why, my heart's swelling just from lying beside you."

But the girl's body was muted by fever; all she felt was a human presence. He sighed deeply and drew her towards him under the blanket. "Child, don't hunger for life; life burns our hands and sears the sight from our eyes as nothing else does. It's better to lie still—quite, quite still." He pressed the girl's face to his neck so as not to breathe his stale-tobacco breath on her. "That's right," he said. "Sleep if you can."

In his arms the girl drifted away from existence into sleep, the one reality. She smiled and sobbed in her dreams. When she woke the room was almost dark and her tears had made the man's neck quite wet. Raising her hand she stroked his bristly chin lightly in the dark. "Can't I do anything for you?" she whispered. "I would like to be as kind to you as you are to me." He didn't answer. The gray dusk of the spring night filled the room. She hesitated, the blood burning in her cheeks. "That time when you were drunk you told me to undress," she said softly.

The man twitched impatiently. "Don't be absurd," he said. "You're ill."

She kissed his cheek, felt for his mouth with her lips and kissed it longingly. "Does it matter?" she said. "My lungs are bleeding, and soon I shan't be able to breathe any more. Soon no one could want me. I might be more whole as a person if I could be good to at least someone. I should like it to be you."

"You're raving," he said roughly. "You're just a plain nuisance. What a girl! I was burned out years ago. I'm no good any more—I'm rotten. You wouldn't enjoy it. We're better as we are."

The girl was overwhelmed by so deep a sense of futility that again her eyes brimmed over. She didn't cry; the tears just poured, fast cooling, down her cheeks, past her ear and along her neck to the pillow. They stung her thin skin, but she didn't dry them. "I've lived for nothing," she thought, "and I shall die for nothing, and all that's left will be some brown and gray patches of paint on a coarse canvas. Orpheus fetched Eurydice from the underworld; no one will come for me when I'm there."

With fumbling hands she undid the press-studs of her blouse and the zip-fastener of her skirt, and her suspenders, touching with her finger tips her moistly smooth skin. "Dear God," she thought. "Only this is real—only this is life: a pale spring night in a cold room, a blanket smelling of tobacco, a bristly chin by my head. This is reality—the only reality. The taste of blood in my mouth, tears stinging my neck. In a few months there may be nothing left. Nothing. Just a brown pillar of smoke from the chimneys of the crematorium."

Trembling she pressed her mouth to his eyes, feeling the lids quiver against her lips; she groped for his hands and held them against her skin. "Touch me at least," she said. "I long for someone to touch me. Nothing else exists. Life holds no other comfort."

The man let his hand slide over her skin. "I thought I'd seen everything," he said, but his voice was gentle and his rough caress restrained and passionless. "Funny little creature," he whispered to himself. "Blue hepatica. Gray Cap—with the frightened eyes. Red Ridinghood, perhaps."

He whispered much tender nonsense in the dark, touching the girl as one would touch a flower. At last he said, "Isn't that enough? You're getting so hot. I'm only doing you harm." Her body quivered under his hand. He threw back the blanket, stood up, groped for his pipe and filled it, then went over to the stove and having thrown in a couple of logs he sat down to smoke. The wood caught, the firelight shone out over his face as he smoked and gazed into the flames.

"Tough threads," he said. "Strings and snares, cutting edges. Sharp teeth. That's all it is. It starts with such little things—you don't notice. Open the window. Scrub the floor. Put on a clean collar. Don't go there. Sit here. Touch me—and there's the snare round your throat. Your eyes are misty, the heat stifles you. A dog would be a better companion. Humans are dangerous; they can only be loved at a distance."

The girl sat up in bed. "You're tired of me already," she said in a dead voice, and began to straighten her clothes. Like a lingering tremor she felt the caress of that hand on her skin. "You want me to go and leave you in peace. All right, I'll go. I don't want to be in the way. It was silly of me to think I could bring any warmth to your loneliness. You're greedy."

"And you're a child who just doesn't see," said the man kindly, as he sat by the stove. "Poverty and greed aren't the same thing. I'm poorer than you. Even when you die you'll possess all the wealth of life in your eyes and your lovely body. Its fires and desires—its fears, sorrows, and its despair. An ocean flows through your body. I envy you."

The girl frowned and her hand paused at the fastening of her blouse.

"An ocean of blood and human warmth," the man said and knocked out his pipe against the stove. The sparks floated down to the darkness of the floor and vanished. "But I'm condemned to live on an island of ice. I've frozen stiff; only drink can warm me now—and that warmth is a delusion. It's death one drinks. And the ocean, the ocean—

if I dive into it, it simply spits me up on the ice again, like a bit of flotsam. I don't try any longer."

The girl got up off the bed and smoothed her skirt down over her hips. "Yes, I understand," she said. "We're talking about different things. Whatever we say we shall never meet. It's just glass clinking against glass—ice against ice. You're brooding over yourself, and I'm brooding over myself. Each of us suspects the other of being better off. Neither of us has any pity. How could we long for the near presence of someone else? It was a good thing you didn't take me. Neither of us can love—you've taught me that much. You've robbed me, and I'm empty. You're so wise and experienced."

The man didn't answer. The girl switched on the light, combed her hair, moistened her forefinger and passed it along her eyebrows. She looked angry. She snatched up her coat and threw it on; he didn't help her, but when with drooping head she started towards the door he rose, slipped the empty pipe into his pocket, took his hat from the peg and followed her out.

"You needn't come with me," said the girl coldly. "I can find the way quite well by myself. Don't trouble."

Beyond the dark wood a glimmer rose against the sky from the bleak street lights of the village. The man walked silently after the girl, who soon became breathless and had to slacken her pace. He took her hand and they walked side by side along the path, so that they brushed against each other at every step. The pine trunks loomed black in the gray night, and far away could be heard the quavering coo of wood pigeons.

"There's no need to come with me," the girl said again.

"I think perhaps you ought to go into the hospital," the man said hesitantly. "You certainly ought to see a doctor. Have an X-ray—something. That would be the most sensible thing to do. But I'm not your keeper. I've never known what's best for myself; that's why I am what I am."

"I'm not as ill as all that," she said crossly. "I lied to you. You turn back; I can get home by myself."

The man seemed to be laughing. "How do you know it's for your sake? I may be just on my way to the village to get *brännvin*. I know several dives where one can get a bottle at midnight, if necessary."

"Of course," the girl said. "I ought to have thought of that. I'm sorry. You'll want to have a proper drink after all the bother I've given you. You're quite right."

The dusk of the spring night faded under the crude light of the street lamps. They passed the druggist's and the red lamp of the police station. Near the railway station the girl stopped at a house with stone steps leading to the door. "This is where I live," she said; she took the key from the bag that hung from her shoulder and squeezed it hard in her hand.

He put his arm protectively round her and drew her towards him. She stiffened and resisted him, but relaxed again and with a half-sob raised her pale face to his. He kissed her several times on the mouth, gently and sadly.

"Good night, then," he said.

"Good night." She walked up the steps with her key held tightly in her hand. The man remained below in the half-darkness, his figure sharply outlined against the lamp-light. "Like a rusty sword," the girl thought. "A sword that's lain on the ground a long time." Aloud she said again, "Good night."

Towards morning, when it was getting light, she was wakened by the long whistle of a train, and she lay awake with her hands on the bedclothes. She felt her body as a fruit swelling with juice beneath the silky skin. "I've been a green fruit up to now," she thought. "I've simply believed everything I was told." She thought of the young man with the curly hair and good-humored eyes, but with hard, merciless limbs that had hurt her. "He was no happier for it," she thought. "He only wanted to live, just as a thousand others wanted to live. To go on as before. To bequeath their disillusionment to their children. But they had to die green. Death doesn't care whether one's green or ripe. But it hurts—it hurts so much to grow."

All that morning the train whistles sounded through her dreams. And her dreams were of departure, farewell, divorce, and pain.

6

When the girl was on her feet again she was no longer thinking about her thesis. She went into town and sat in the doctor's waiting room, as so often before. They looked up her case history and X-rayed her. "Well, well," said the doctor. "This doesn't look too good. You'd better go into the hospital at once; in a case like this we can get a bed at a moment's notice. Don't worry; we shall just have to cut a couple of ribs and collapse the affected parts. In a month or two you'll be up again, I hope."

"Oh, this eternal, cruel optimism!" the girl thought. "Do they really think anyone believes them? It's only hope they keep alive with their smooth words."

"What about the anesthetic?" she asked.

"We'll give you a local," he answered cheerfully. "That's best for the patient; we've had excellent results." He radiated confidence, like a slaughterer fingering a fatted calf.

"Am I sure to get better?" she asked, looking at him sadly. He became impatient.

"Well, of course, one can never be certain beforehand," he said. "You've already been in the sanatorium, and it would be wrong to pretend that this isn't a serious business. You know better. Some get over it in a week, while others have to stay in bed for months. But it's all we can do."

"You can't force me to agree to an operation," she said. But she knew that her wishes would not be consulted. The hospital had its own methods of persuasion.

"You'd be very unwise not to agree to it," the doctor returned, tapping the table impatiently with his pen. There were many patients in the waiting room.

"You mean I'd die. But I shall die anyway, even if you operate. I couldn't stand it."

"You never know with this disease," he returned. "New methods are being discovered and tried out all the time. With a good climate and a regular life some people recover by themselves. Everything depends on the patient's powers of resistance. But from the experience I've had, I should say an operation is your only chance. You'll regret it if you don't have it now, while there's still time."

"I shall have to think about it," said the girl, and fled. Instead of going home she went straight to the station and bought a ticket back. The damp air of the town tore at her lungs, and she found it difficult to breathe.

"It was silly of me to come," she thought. "It was childish to expect a definite answer. He had to speak as he did. So I'm going to die. But I knew that already."

She looked out through the carriage window at the shining, newly plowed land, and at the flocks of birds on the telephone wires, and felt dizzily free. "The evil in my chest is real, my hands are real, the plowed fields are real," she reflected. "But I'm already unreal. I am an un-reality of imperishable dreams." She smiled suddenly. She laughed aloud. "Perhaps I shan't die," she thought gaily. "Perhaps this is all nonsense and I shall wake up quite well and ashamed of these ideas."

As the train thundered on she remembered the hepaticas and the girl in the gray cap, the gypsy, and the fishwife. Those deliberate, fierce, febrile colors glowed within her. "Only art is real," she thought. "Only color, torn violently and painfully from reality, and form which is more than reality. Enduring, incredible, overwhelming. That must be why I love him."

But the journey was too much for her. When at last she found herself safely in her room she began coughing. Pain stabbed like a red-hot knife; blood welled from her mouth and stained the downy blanket. Exhausted, half-suffocated, she lay on her bed unable to move. "There now," she thought. "The doctor's experience and advice can reach me even here. Hepaticas in dirty snow at the foot of the slopes. Spring."

When she had recovered she undressed and went to bed again, took her medicine and lay quiet. "I'm still alive," she thought. "I do want to live a bit longer. There's no point in it, but I do want to see the sun shining on the trunks of the pines. I want to hear the chaffinch. And I want to see *him* again."

She had great trouble in washing her blanket so as to conceal what had happened; the slightest movement wearied her, yet stubbornly and with frequent pauses to rest, she cleaned and tidied the room. She sat still and hummed to herself, and when she looked in the glass her brown eyes were soft and bright. "I seem to be all eyes," she thought. "That was how he painted me. But now my eyes aren't afraid any more. There's something greater than fear inside me. I'm a fruit ready to split. I shall split from abundance of life." Her clothes were sticking to her body, and her hands and feet were cold. "If I die I shall die wildly, ecstatically, like the colors on his canvases." But this was not true, and she knew it. And when she slept her dreams were shot through with those plaintive whistles from the trains.

The days glided radiantly by. Her curtain floated in the fresh breeze, and from the tree outside the chaffinch's notes seemed to be ringing from beneath some glorious vaulted roof. The evenings were blue. "Perhaps he's painting again," she thought tenderly as she lay in bed. "Or perhaps he's drinking and has forgotten me. But I'll play a trick on him. I shall die in his arms. That'll surprise him, for all his frosty intelligence." She smiled and her eyes shone. "He's too hard on himself, so I'll die in his arms, if I get the chance; it'll give him something to think about."

One day she received a parcel done up in dirty brown paper. She opened it and the hepaticas reached out towards her hands, immortal in their gray-white bowl. She pinned up the canvas with drawing pins at the foot of her bed, and lay looking at it. "There's no other heaven," she said to herself. "When you come to think of it, he's not having much fun either. But he can wait; it seems to soften him." Yet she knew she would have run straight through the wood to his house, if she'd had the strength. "What an idiot he was not to come himself," she thought indignantly. "What do I want with his pictures? It's his loneliness I want to break into, so that he minds when I die."

Smiling, radiant, bright-eyed with fever she lay impatiently waiting, while the immortal violet of those woodland flowers glowed for her in the grayish white bowl. "There's no death," she thought, "there's no death. I shall live on in his paintings when I'm dead—in every brush-stroke. But how childish and vain it is of me to imagine such a thing." Every night the whistles of locomotives forced their way into her dreams.

7

Not until two weeks had passed did she venture to get up. Her fever had left her, and she enjoyed her food again. Spring was by now far advanced; the twigs of the birches were turning red, and by the roadside coltsfoot and green grass were piercing the soil. People were busy digging in their gardens, and the girl felt pleasantly giddy as she took it all in. "I've never seen things so clearly before," she thought, "and colors have never been so bright. Never was there such a clear day or such freshness in the air. Only a child can see things as keenly as this. Perhaps death is making a child of me again."

Panting, with sweat moistening the hair at her temples she followed the path, and the trunks of the pines glowed about her once more, tall and stately. While yet some distance away she could see the man; he was digging up his rubbish-strewn garden within the barbed-wire fence. He had his back to the path and was thrusting impatiently with his foot to drive the spade into the soil. The girl went up to him on light feet. "Good morning," she said smiling. "Thank you for the hepaticas."

The man drove the spade into the ground and left it, then turned slowly towards the girl. "It's you at last, is it?" he remarked crossly. "I'd begun to miss you." He wiped his earthy hand on his trousers and held it out to her without meeting her eyes.

"You've begun on the garden, then—and not before it was time. It's like a rubbish heap."

"One does funny things when one's bored," he said. "One can't think all the time, after all. Come in."

He let the girl go first and followed heavily in his muddy boots. As soon as she entered the light room the girl took off her cap and turned towards him, pressed against him and put her arms about his shoulders. "So you've missed me already," she whispered. "Were you bored without me, really?" She raised her smiling face to his and he bent reluctantly to kiss her.

"Infant," he said, and kissed her with his cracked lips. "To think a tiny little thing like you can turn everything upside down."

"My darling, my own one!" she said gaily. "I'm mad about you. I'm bursting with love, you ugly old man—you horrible, filthy old man. I'm in love with you, see?"

He pressed her harder against himself until she couldn't breathe, and she thrust the palm of her hand against his chest to get free. "Lord," she said, sniffing at his lapel. "I'm in love with just the smell of you: tobacco, turps, dried birchleaves, and stale alcohol. I'm mad—stark, staring mad—but you won't drive me away again, will you?"

He held her fast in his arms, staring over her head into the distance. At last he released her, and taking down a key from the wall he locked the door. "Undress, then," he said. "I can see it's the only way to be rid of you."

The girl looked at him doubtfully; she shivered a little and blushed. "You don't mean that," she said uncertainly. "You only want to paint me naked, as you've painted other people. I don't want that—I don't want that now."

The man fumbled at her clothes and began to undo her

blouse without meeting her eyes. The girl put her hand defensively on his. "Is it as easy as this?" she asked beseechingly. "Is there no more to it? Is this how it's done?"

The man held her hard with his other arm and pressed his mouth to her bare shoulder. She trembled. "It's you who make me mad," he mumbled. She lifted her body to his lips like a cup, thinking in a delirium, "Being *with* someone—hardness, tenderness, beauty—that's what it means." She shuddered and sighed, feeling as if her body were a young tree which in an instant burst out in a thousand blazing buds. Her body felt desire and yearning; and for a moment her happiness was complete.

Later she thought about herself again and about the man who lay panting so heavily beside her, shamelessly unbuttoned. "I ought to be disgusted—ashamed. I suppose it was beastly to let him take me." But she smiled to herself. "How natural and simple it all is. Why should I be ashamed? Why, when I'm content?" She stroked the man's stubborn forehead abstractedly, tracing its furrows and staring wide-eyed at the ceiling. "Now I'm his mistress," she thought. "That's what they call it in books. But that belongs to the last century. I'm his of my own free will, without asking for anything and without hoping. Death embracing solitude." But she tired of words and lay still without thinking, staring at the ceiling while the spring sunshine filled the room with its brightness.

The man moved and turned his head, and looked at her with a grim smile. "I bet you're thinking how to arrange a respectable old age for me," he said, "with people to dinner, a housekeeper, regular meals, new wallpaper, one-man shows, newspaper articles—that's what you're thinking about. 'How to grow old gracefully.' "

"I'm not thinking at all," the girl said, staring

bright-eyed at the ceiling. "I feel light. I'm happy. It wasn't perhaps what I expected, but it was good."

"I burn like green wood," he said. "I steam and smoke, but I do burn. I suppose it has to be like that. I glow when I paint, when I drink—even when I'm having a hang-over—and when I'm with you. Life is hell—sometimes a lovely hell. I've found you, only to lose you—that's how it always is. If you die I shall hang myself."

"Not you," said the girl soothingly. "You'll drink for a week—perhaps two. Then you'll start painting again and forget me. I know. But I don't care. I'm glad. My cheeks are burning with love, and my breasts. My whole body's gloriously on fire with love."

"Don't say things like that," he said. "It makes me feel a fool." He put out his hand. "Shall I paint you again, woman?" he asked, and squeezed. The girl cried out.

"No," she whispered. "Don't leave me."

Presently he said, "You must eat something, or you'll be worn out." But the girl shook her head and clung to him. She knew she was so replete that she could never swallow. "Don't get tired of me yet," she begged.

The man fell asleep. Evening drew on, and the bird outside fell silent. A gust of wind blew from the wood. The girl lay tremulous, feeling as if a flame were flickering lightly over her limbs. Her body was awake and longing. "Can love be as hopeless, as terrible as this?" she wondered. "It's better to die. I should never have the strength to live with him." Her heart wearied and weakened.

As darkness fell she was overpowered by her burden of loneliness. The man took her to himself again; they clung together, they kindled. The girl gasped from sick lungs, and sweat poured off her. He did not release her. They spoke no more.

At dawn the girl began to cough. She freed herself from his arms, sat up and held her hands against her breast, coughing. Once more the blood welled over her hands and onto the bedclothes. From outside came the jubilant trill of a chaffinch. The girl coughed and went on coughing, and the man put his arms round her jerking body. "I've killed you," he said, in a voice of terrible emptiness. She tried to shake her head but couldn't.

He went to fetch help from the village and the girl was carried out to the ambulance. She was already unconscious.

This time the man didn't go with her. He put a new canvas on the easel and began painting. But with every hour that passed he grew more restless. When evening came he took his hat and went into the village, walked past the druggist's and the police station and the stone steps. A couple of hundred yards further on he turned into an untidy yard and knocked at a door through the crack of which a light was showing. When he'd been given his bottle he put it straight to his mouth, and the spirit ran burning down into the frightful emptiness within him.

"I'm a swine," he said to himself, as he strayed through the darkness and sat down on the stone steps in the light of the streetlamp, bottle in hand. "I've killed her," he said to himself; he drank, and wiped his mouth on the back of his hand. "Three gypsies, hepaticas, the girl in the gray cap." He ran them off on his fingers as the fumes went to his head and he grew giddy. "Not bad. It's worth a proper drink." He emptied the bottle and smashed it to bits against the steps. Then he drew a shabby wallet from his pocket and counted his money, staggered back to the black-painted door and banged on it with his fists. "Three more," he said with a curse. He thrust the bottles into his pockets and with heavy, reeling steps set off for the shack, muttering and mumbling to himself all the way. People crossed to the other side of the road when they saw him.

Having hauled himself through the door, he lit the lamp, unlocked the door of the inner room and brought out the picture of the girl with the gray cap. He leaned the painting against the wall, moved the stool into the middle of the floor, sat down on it with a bottle within reach, and stared at the canvas. "So young—such a child," he said aloud. "But I didn't mean it, it wasn't on purpose —hell, I didn't mean to do it." He took a gulp or two from the bottle, went over to the bed and picked with his nail at the dried blood on the blanket. "Dirt and blood," he said laughing. "Just dirt and blood." But then he sank to his knees and buried his face in the bedcover.

When he had wept for a time he raised his head as if in surprise, wiped his eyes with his fists, and swore.

"How quickly this stuff's going to my head," he said. "It must be old age. I can't take it any more." He rose unsteadily, and drained the bottle to the last drop.

The Tie from Paris

1

As I walked downstairs I glanced at my watch and was glad to find that we'd finished lunch in good time; it was not yet three, and I could get to the bank, go through the papers and sign them before it closed. On the steps outside, daylight and fresh air swept over my face; my temples were still warm from good French brandy. I was sweating a little, and I could feel the sting of cigar smoke right down in my lungs.

Pausing for breath in front of a florist's I stared at some brilliant carnations in the window, and wondered vaguely whom I could send a bunch to, this fine autumn day. It was with a pang I realized that there was now no one. It would have been silly to send them home, for my wife would merely deduce that I'd been drinking brandy in the middle of the day. However, I was not yet such a fool as to drink anything but genuine cognac when for once it was to be had in this poor country of ours. I felt suddenly depressed, and disinclined to return to my dark office, where on cloudy days one had to switch on the light at noon, and where Järnefelt's portrait of my father-in-law stared at me from the wall with its slightly prominent eyes. He suffered from exophthalmic goiter—my father-in-law, that is; not Järnefelt.

Nevertheless I cut across the Esplanade in the direction of the bank, and the rich, melancholy foliage of the lime

137

trees cast its shade over my fevered head. I breathed deeply and walked with short, careful steps; yet I was soon breathless after that too abundant lunch. I was also assailed by an impotent, humiliating rage. Before lunch I had been to try on my new suit. The material was dark, discreet, and dignified, as befitted a man in my position. As a rule my wife chose the stuff for my suits, for she lacked confidence in my taste. But I'm hard to fit: my neck pokes forward as a result of too diligent desk work, and my stomach is not what it was before the war. The tailor had shifted his mirrors and turned me in such a way that I could get a view of my back. He stroked the soft material across my shoulders to show me how well the suit was cut, but all I saw was the back of my head. I hadn't seen it for years, and to make the unexpected discovery that one's going bald is an unpleasant experience for any man.

Unexpected is perhaps the wrong word, for I had known quite well that my hair was getting thin at the back. But my wife had often assured me that it was no more than thin, and the female barber whom I visited every Friday at 11:30 declared that one hardly noticed it. She was a pretty girl, with such a candid smile that I saw no more reason to doubt her than to doubt my wife. So now I stood transfixed, staring at the back of my head in the tailor's glass, with the resentful sense of having been fooled. That may be why I drank that extra glass of brandy at lunch: a man needs cheering up when he finds he has slipped from the indeterminate "prime of youth" into the calm of middle age.

I sighed heavily as I walked on beneath the shady splendor of the limes, aware that in that brief moment before my tailor's mirror I had taken a big step towards decay and dissolution. It was a damned unpleasant feeling; and just then Julle Cypress advanced along the Esplanade towards me, with loud and gleeful cries.

He wrung my hand and yelped, like a dog welcoming his master after a long absence. I was startled by his enthusiasm, and suspected for a moment that he wanted either to borrow money from me, or through me to draw a bill of exchange on the bank. If so, his errand was in vain, for during the very first months of my banking career my father-in-law had dashed the fond hopes of all my former friends. I was on the point of telling Julle this, but he spoke first.

"A drink!" he cried. "For heaven's sake come and have a drink. I've been to a perfectly appalling lunch—not a drop of anything, and we had to sit and listen to three dreary speeches about moral rearmament and reconstruction. This is the second time I've trudged up the Esplanade. You can't think how glad I am to see you, old man. Let me think—it must be seven years. . . . But you're just the same. You haven't changed a scrap. Same old Valter! How's your wife? And the boss? How many kids have you got now? My daughter graduated last spring."

Still chattering he shoved me through the door of Kämp's and never stopped until we had sat down in the almost deserted dining room and a sour-faced waiter had taken our order. I attempted a feeble protest:

"I must get back to the bank before half-past three; I've got a whole stack of bills of lading to go through, as well as the English mail."

He pretended not to hear. "Kämp's isn't what it was," he said, eyeing some strangers at a corner table.

"Nothing's what it was," I replied sententiously. "Ours is a poor country. We shall have to put our backs into it if we want to make any sort of recovery. And talking of that, I've simply got to get to the bank before four o'clock."

"Nonsense," said Julle coldly. "The bank won't fail just because you have a drink—and if it does, then it's high time. I had to walk up and down the Esplanade twice before I found anyone I could conscientiously have a drink with. Do you remember the old days? You only had to stick your nose inside the bar here, and it was good-bye to sobriety for the rest of the day. Now you never meet a soul. Do you remember Esko in his prime?"

"Yes," I said curtly, and raised my glass to the memory of bygone days. But not even genuine *brännvin* could compare with the French brandy.

"Good God, the muck one swallows nowadays!" said Julle, eyeing his glass with distaste. "One got better stuff during prohibition. Have you tried mixing *brännvin* with cloudberry liqueur? At least it's sweet."

We shuddered and raised our glasses. The smarting of the cigar smoke had left my lungs and I was filled with gloom.

"You're quite right," I said. "I can just as well go through those papers tomorrow—or the day after. They'll only lie about in some government office. And the British still won't pay more than fifteen pounds a standard. What hell it all is!"

"Let's have another," Julle said. "I must get just a little plastered; there's a theater fellow coming to dinner. Quite young; he's even got a dago mustache. How am I to find anything to say to him if I'm sober? He's just back from Paris; I met him on the boat from Stockholm. I'd been there buying shoes for my wife. She's mad about theater people. You'll come too, of course."

"Certainly not," I said. "I haven't been to the theater for a year. No time. Got to earn my salary. The bank keeps me chasing about like a terrier—inflation and all that."

"Of course you're coming," said Julle. "I'll telephone your wife."

"No, for God's sake don't do that!" I exclaimed in alarm. "She's told me often enough what she thinks of my friends; she has her father's principles. Look, haven't you any timber deals on just now? You owned a sawmill at one time; why not come with me to the bank and discuss things there? The old man's got some real brandy in the strong-room. I'll get my secretary to ring up my wife."

"Have you got a real live secretary?" marveled Julle. "Wonder your wife allows it. Pretty?"

"She can do Finnish and English shorthand," I replied stiffly, adding after a few moments' reflection, "she wears nylons."

"That settles it; we'll go at once," declared Julle, and he rapped on the table with his knuckles. "Waiter!"

I was filled with sudden recklessness. "Let's go, then," I said. "I'll pay."

If I'd only known! But what's the use of talking? No one can see into the future—at least no one like me.

2

The old man himself was at some Treasury meeting, but he had left the keys in the chief cashier's office, and I was doing nothing wrong in going down to the vaults and taking a half-bottle of brandy from his safe-deposit box. Julle Cypress was no negligible client and he would certainly be in need of funds next spring, when the sea was frozen, what with money sunk in the

timber forests and nothing coming in. My chief had pre-
dicted that timber prices would rise in the spring, so I
had every reason to offer Julle a brandy; though as it
turned out his sawmill was only a two-framed one. However, it was from clients in small businesses that the bank
made its profit.

"Mr. Cypress is going to Kemi tomorrow," I told my
secretary, looking her brazenly in the eye, "so we must get
this business cleared up today. Would you mind ringing
up my wife and saying I shan't be home for dinner?"

My secretary had very bright eyes, and was wearing a
white silk blouse fastened at the neck with a brown
speckled fish made of pottery. I was surprised not to have
noticed this before; but then as I said, my room is very
dark.

"Your occupation seems to have its lighter side," Julle
Cypress remarked with genuine enthusiasm, as he followed
the girl with his eyes. "How can she afford nylons, working in a bank?"

"How should I know?" I retorted. "She's new; she's
only been here a month. The old man engaged her for the
directors, and I'm allowed to borrow her for dictating
foreign correspondence."

"We'll ask her to dinner too," said Julle lavishly. I
glanced first at him and then at my chief's portrait on the
wall. It looked even more disapproving than usual, and
the goiter seemed to me to have grown since last I looked
at it. Julle followed the direction of my eyes and shuddered. "Perhaps you're right," he admitted.

At four o'clock there came a knock at the door, and
automatically I moved the bottle from the table to the
floor behind the desk before answering. But it was only
my secretary, to ask if I needed her again that day. I told
her I didn't, and promised to sign the bills of lading next

morning. "By the way, what did my wife say?" I asked somewhat uncomfortably.

"She was out. She left a message to say she wouldn't be in to dinner."

A stone rolled from my heart and I heaved a sigh of relief. The girl still lingered. Her neck was a warm brown against the white silk blouse, and the pottery fish had one eye shut and the other open.

"You look tired," said Julle Cypress. "I'm sure a glass of brandy would do you good."

"I don't know that Miss—er—cares for—" I objected stiffly.

"Don't be mean!" said Julle. "A glass of brandy won't break the bank. If it does, then the bank's better broken. Don't you see the young lady's quite pale?"

The young lady had in fact turned fiery red, but there was nothing more to be said. "Fetch yourself a glass," I suggested. "You'll find them on the top left-hand shelf in the office safe."

She fetched a glass, I poured her out some brandy and she sipped it without winking, sitting on the arm of a chair as if she meant to stay no more than a moment or so.

"*Skål!*" said Julle. "Valter, don't be so damned pompous."

I stole a glance at the portrait on the wall. The old man looked more pop-eyed than ever, and I put up a silent prayer that he might not suddenly walk in and find me carousing with my secretary. He had an unpleasant way of entering at any moment without knocking, and always when one least desired his presence.

"*Skål!*" I said. "Delightful to have a young lady with us. I have a daughter of your age, Miss—er—" For the life of me I couldn't remember her name.

"I'm sure you're not as old as all that," she said gently.

Her eyes were clear and bright as dewdrops. I was tired of pretense.

"Why this everlasting humbug!" I exclaimed in exasperation. "My wife, my tailor, my barber—they all do it. And for no reason at all. Now listen: I'm old; I'm putting on weight; I get breathless going downstairs. I've just passed the point where one's body starts to decay and life goes downhill."

"Never mind," said Julle consolingly. "We're still alive, you and I. We might easily be dead. Esko shot himself, do you remember? Kurre was killed in the winter war, Rafu trod on a mine at Syväri, and Martti has a cork leg. We've got nothing to grumble at."

I suppose I've grown slow with age, for I find it hard to get going on my story. Yet I feel that all this somehow belongs to it, so I'd better come to the point in my own way. At five o'clock the cleaner invaded the office, and we went to Julle's to meet the producer. The girl came too. I couldn't forbid Julle to invite her, but I was surprised that she wanted to come; perhaps a bank employee is glad of a free meal now and then. It's different for me: the chief gives me a percentage, for naturally his daughter must be supported in suitable style. And Julle talked of pork chops, which were still only to be had on the black market.

3

The dinner passed off without mishap. I was surprised to see how well Mrs. Cypress had preserved her youth and how tastefully she was dressed. Indeed I complimented her on being more beautiful every time I saw her; whereupon she apologized for her failure to remember that we had ever met before. Julle told me with composure that I must be thinking of his previous wife. I didn't even know he'd been divorced, and in attempting to retrieve the blunder I only made it worse, for it appeared that he'd been divorced twice. He gave us some atrocious Hungarian wine, but it was at least wine; and the producer told us of his experiences in Paris.

He was still a young man with a silky, reddish mustache. He wore a crumpled flannel suit with coffee-colored checks, and he was as cocksure as only a conceited youth can be on returning from his first trip abroad.

"What do you know of Paris?" I demanded. "Only those who lived there in the twenties know what it's really like. Never before or since has the world been so free. No, you don't know what it was like to live in Paris after the First World War."

But the words stuck in my throat as I noticed his tie. It was a tie from Paris, bright yellow with glaring red and green spots. In a flash the world was young and free again; it was a Sunday in summer and I was sitting on the roof of a railway carriage, choking in the smoke from the engine, on my way to the trotting races at Maisons-Laffitte. And beside me sat Jeanne. She clung to me as closely as a girl can cling only in Paris, in the summer, to a young man wearing a Parisian tie. I stared across the table into the limpid eyes of a girl. Nearly thirty years had passed since then, but once more I was gazing into Jeanne's eyes. Then it all crumbled; I felt that I was nothing but the ruin of my former self, and that life had trickled away between my fingers.

"True enough," said Julle. "It's no good your shooting a line about Paris. Valter here *knows*. He lived in France for a year to learn the language. Weren't you going to get

a timber agency there, Valter? Why the hell didn't you?
You'd have been a rich man by now."

"Could one really travel wherever one liked then?"
breathed the girl. "Oh, to go to Paris!"

" 'Course you could if you had the money," said Julle.
"Now you have to run from department to department
with your tongue hanging out before you can get permission to run over to Stockholm and buy shoes for your
wife."

I was still staring as if hypnotized at the man's tie.

"Wh-where did you get that tie?" I stammered, point-
ing at it. "In the Boul' Miche, wasn't it?"

He straightened it, stroked his mustache and looked at
me haughtily. "A little gaudy, perhaps," he said, "but
modern. I'm going to use it in a play; should be rather
effective, I think."

I emptied my glass, though the wine was really dire.
The tie was of a fierce yellow, and the dots on it were so
vivid that they killed the colors of Julle's pictures on the
walls. I was lost. I had to have that tie, cost what it might.
Jeanne, Jeanne—warm, generous Jeanne! I had forgotten
her as completely as only youth can forget. A whole world
had toppled since then, burying my memories beneath it.
Yet at this moment—this fleeting moment—nothing seemed
to me so vitally important as to recall that youthful experience in all its fullness and glory. I stared across the
table into the warm brown eyes of Jeanne, until the girl
opposite was thoroughly uncomfortable.

"What's wrong with you, Valter—surely you can't be
tight?" asked Julle in surprise. "We shall be having coffee
soon."

Not for nothing had I worked in a bank; I could hardly
have failed to pick up one or two things during all these
years under the leadership of the old man. I said no more

about the tie. Instead, we learned that the producer had written a play himself and was going to put it on. No doubt he would also have played the leading part in it if this had been possible; judging from his remarks it was an excellent play.

"How wonderful to be an actress!" sighed the girl. "Or a film star."

One doesn't have to be particularly intelligent to do Finnish and English shorthand. Nor was it intelligence I was looking for in Jeanne all those years ago. No indeed; so long as a girl is young and gay and has warm brown eyes, intelligence is of secondary importance. Moreover, a woman's intelligence resides in her body, and is of a more mischievous kind than any contained in a man's head.

Mrs. Cypress was crazy about the theater. During coffee she prattled volubly with the producer, while Julle expounded his plans to expand his sawmill from two frames to three and I stared at the tie from Paris. The girl said nothing; she looked from one man to another, and her gaze was still as pellucid as water. The brown pottery fish heaved gently on her breast, with one eye coyly closed. Mrs. Cypress surveyed the girl's legs with a certain hostility, and then glanced at her husband. I understood her feelings, if it was true that Julle had been twice divorced.

My thoughts were confused and my heart thumped as if it would burst. It was two in the morning. Soda water had been spilled on the table, and in it floated a cigarette in a state of dissolution. Two empty bottles stood by the leg of the table. The producer had sprung to his feet and was holding forth about his proposed regeneration of the Finnish stage. I had kissed Mrs. Cypress and Julle had kissed my secretary—or at least he had traces of lipstick at the corner of his mouth. We had all long ago arrived at

Christian names. My image of the girl had split in two: one I called Inge and the other Jeanne.

"Jeanne," I said sternly, closing one eye to make sure I was looking straight at her. "Remember we've got a heavy day tomorrow. We must saw up those bills of lading at once. Give me a pen and I'll sign them now."

She gave me no pen, however, and in some peculiar manner she landed in my lap. I shook her off quickly and rose, holding on by the table. "Brother Leo," I said to the producer. "Your name is Leo, isn't it? Give me your tie; you shall have mine instead. Yours brings back my lost youth. It's a trotting-race tie. We don't have trotting races here—you don't need it. Give it to me—I need it."

I put my arm round his shoulder and told him what an excellent fellow he was and what a brilliant play he had written. But he still refused to give me the tie, and at last I had to take it by force. Julle helped me, for the chap was stronger than I'd thought. A glass or two was smashed, but Mrs. Cypress assured us it didn't matter. At last I got the tie on and the girl knotted it for me. Mrs. Cypress tied mine round the neck of the producer, assuring him that it was a much better, smarter one than the other. She also told him that Julle didn't understand her or share her passionate love for the theater, so that she often felt lonely. Also that she longed to travel abroad.

"We've got a heavy day tomorrow, Jeanne," I said again. "We must get to the trotting races. Come on."

She looked at the men in turn with her limpid eyes, and despite Julle's vehement protests she came with me. To Mrs. Cypress's credit be it said that she made no very strong opposition to our going. Julle helped the girl on with her coat, squeezing her into a corner of the hall so that at last I had discreetly to separate them. Not being altogether sure whether I had one or two girls with me, I offered her both arms and let her choose for herself.

She told me in the taxi that she'd never dreamed I could be such fun. I kissed her and invited her to sleep with me, but she suggested tactfully that we should postpone this for the present. I thought this showed sense. She was a well-brought-up girl.

It seems clear, when I look back on it now, that I did and said a great many absurd things that evening; but I was far from drunk. I even remembered to wipe my mouth thoroughly on my handkerchief as I went upstairs; one learns at least some things in twenty years of marriage. My wife's dog came to meet me in the hall, but merely sneezed disapprovingly when it saw me. I paid small attention to this, however, being long used to its regarding me as an inferior member of the household. I never even tried to kick it; it would only have bitten me.

My wife pretended to be asleep, and I undressed as rapidly and noiselessly as I could. But when I took off the tie, another wave of exultant joy welled up in me. I had kissed Jeanne once more, and when I passed my tongue over my lips I could still taste her lipstick. I looked defiantly at my wife's back and crept over to my bed. Even after I had put out the light I beheld in my mind's eye the vision of myself on the way to the trotting races at Maisons-Laffitte, and with a happy sigh I fell asleep.

4

My awakening, however, was not so happy. Indeed it was dreary, as so often after a carefree evening. Until I opened my eyes I wasn't absolutely sure where

I was, and the fleeting relief of finding that at any rate I was in my own bed was soon dispelled by a heavy shower of recollections, which caused me to groan with anguish. There was a foul taste in my mouth, and to the right of my stomach beneath the diaphragm I felt a familiar grinding pain: my gall bladder was displeased with me and my habits, and was doing all it could to make its displeasure known.

But pain or no pain, the time was five minutes to nine. The habit of years roused me punctually and more reliably than an alarm clock, irrespective of how the night had been spent. I mustn't be late at the bank.

It's wonderful what a thorough shave can do for one's morale. As I patted the eau-de-cologne over my face I even ventured to hum a little; it was when I took my tie from its usual place that the shock came. The sudden shrill yellow with its mass of red and green dots dancing before my eyes nearly brought on a nervous collapse. At first I couldn't remember how this ghastly object had come into my possession, and for ten seconds or so I stood and quaked.

Then I remembered. Away rolled the clouds, and sunshine poured its burning rays over my defenseless head. It was the tie from Paris. With trembling hands I slipped it round my neck, stifling certain cowardly misgivings. Rubbing my hands and forcing a smile I walked into the dining room and said good morning. The children had already left for school, and my wife was sitting in there alone reading the paper. She neither answered nor looked up; nor did she ask where I'd been the night before. Her dog came up and sniffed suspiciously at the bottoms of my trousers, and I put out my hand cautiously to stroke it. I had the feeling it would have liked to bite me if it hadn't been afraid of the taste.

I drank a bottle of Vichy water and then devoted my-self to coffee and an egg. The newspaper rustled disagree-ably, and I could feel my wife's eyes upon me. She was staring at my neck with an expression of unutterable amazement on her narrow, well-preserved face. Like her father, she had pale blue, somewhat prominent eyes which now threatened to drop out altogether.

"What's that round your neck?" she inquired, in a thin, strained voice.

"A tie," I replied as casually as I could. "From Paris. Just arrived. Latest fashion. I got it from a business friend."

I was talking too much and betraying my sense of guilt. The fewer explanations the better; would I never learn? I felt I might have put up a better fight if I hadn't been hampered by embarrassing recollections. I fancied, though I was not certain, that I had kissed my secretary in the taxi by mistake. I couldn't imagine how I was ever to face her or anyone in the bank again. It was not the thing to kiss the employees, even off the premises: so much my wife had taught me in the very first years of our marriage, and I had faith in her. I was therefore in a weak position.

"Take it off at once," said my wife decisively, and with that she considered the discussion at an end.

I fingered the tie and seemed to feel new vitality flow-ing from it into me. I was indignant: I, an aging, peace-able man who never uttered a harsh word to anyone. What right had others to trample on my tastes and feelings? It was thanks to my diligence and punctuality, my knowl-edge of the timber trade and of languages, that I had at-tained my present position in the bank, and I was entitled to dress as I chose. My chief could wear a shoelace round his neck if he wanted to, without exciting remark. Not that he would ever have dreamed of doing so—though as it happened his ties were not unlike shoelaces. Now *I* had a superb Parisian tie, a real trotting-race tie, from which I was not going to be parted without a struggle.

"I shan't!" I retorted fiercely.

To my astonishment my wife made no rejoinder; she merely shrugged her shoulders slightly and shook her head. I wondered what was the matter with her, and again I felt the stirrings of conscience. Brushing them off I attacked my egg again; I was in a hurry.

When I was leaving my wife came out into the hall. She stood before me very slim and erect, and her narrow, finely cut nose quivered. "Wear the tie if you want to," she said mildly. "It's just that I don't like you to look a fool in front of other people."

It was radiance, joy—it was my own youth I was wearing round my neck, and I couldn't bring myself to put it from me, let my wife stare as she would with those great blue eyes. I had always been strangely in love with her eyes. "Good-bye," I said hastily, and fled down the stairs. Outside, the streets were bright with September sunshine. The Virginia creeper on the house fronts was beginning to turn red, but its splendor was as nothing to my tie. I was feeling a little anxious lest the producer should ring up and demand its return, for I couldn't imagine anyone voluntarily renouncing so glorious a thing. It was unthinkable. I made up my mind to tell him I'd lost it on my way home, and that I would pay him compensation.

I drew myself up and walked briskly to the bank, wearing my youth round my neck and reflecting that during all these past years I'd been carrying it inside me, like something forgotten and already unfamiliar. The day I first met Jeanne. . . . A rainbow-colored haze hung above the roofs of the city, and I had bought a bag of cherries from a fruit-seller's basket in the Rue Hachette, where there was a piebald cat, I remembered. Its eyes were yellow cracks, and at the corner of its black mouth there was a fetching white dot. I ate the cherries from the bag, leaning my elbows on the window sill in my room, and spitting the stones at passers-by. I had been turned out of the respectable *pension* where my uncle left me before returning to Finland via England, and had moved to a charming, dirty little hotel on the bank of the Seine, where complete freedom reigned. Suddenly I heard someone laugh, and when I turned my head I looked for the first time into Jeanne's warm brown eyes. She was leaning out of the next window to mine, in the same hotel, and laughing at me; there was barely six feet between us.

I roused myself from these bittersweet memories on hearing the doorman of the bank respectfully greeting me. He had just opened the heavy doors and admitted the first customers. "Nice day, sir," he said unsuspectingly, and raised his uniform cap. But the cap remained in the air and the arm holding it trembled violently as his glance fell on my neck. He looked about him in alarm as if meditating flight, and a glazed look came into his eyes. But he was a seasoned old fellow who'd served the bank longer than I had; with an effort he replaced his cap and opened the door for me in silence.

I was glad he'd said nothing, for the experience of years had taught me to respect his views. During my early days at the bank, before I had adapted myself to my new way of life, he had once or twice turned me firmly away and advised me to go home and rest. (The first time, I ignored his advice, but the consequences were so unpleasant that I prefer not to recall them.) I had an uncomfortable feeling that he knew more about me and the business of the bank than was strictly necessary. I therefore responded coldly to his greeting and entered with an air of abstrac-

tion, holding my hand protectively under my chin as if
I had a sore throat. Nothing happened, and with a sigh of
relief I slipped into my room.

There was a drop left in the bottle that I'd hidden in
the drawer of my desk. I poured it into a tumbler and with
my back to the door to avoid being taken by surprise I
swallowed it down; I needed fortifying before meeting my
secretary's eye. Then I rinsed the glass, sat down at my
desk and coughed with determination. Yet I didn't immediately start going through the mail as was my habit.
A light, delicate savor of cognac lingered in my mouth,
reminding me of Paris, of youth, and of France, which
Jeanne had taught me to love.

Jeanne, Jeanne! I handed her cherries as I hung out of
the window: we could just reach the tips of each other's
fingers. She had dirty nails and stained hands. Ah, that
dear, grubby little paw! She was eighteen and I was just
twenty. And I was in love with quite another woman:
someone of good family, fair, cold, and ten years older
than myself. She had well-tended pink nails, with which
she clawed, smiling, at my heart. One night I bought a
double armful of roses in the Halles and strewed them in
the street before her door. I fell asleep there, but was
roused by three soldiers in blue. They were sympathetic
and very drunk and they offered to take me with them to
a pleasant, inexpensive brothel.

On the way there one of them pushed his elbow through
the taxi window, and I left them there in the hot street,
wrangling about who was to pay, amid the sulphurous
curses of the taxi driver. I was young and unhappily in
love, and that first time I looked quite indifferently into
Jeanne's eyes. But I did give her cherries.

That, by the way, was not the first time I'd slept in the
street. Another night I lay in front of the same little gray

church where, on a heap of straw, Dante is said to have spent his nights. I wanted to do the same, and the street didn't seem unduly hard, for I'd been drinking Pernod, as a substitute for the forbidden absinthe. When I awoke once more to the noise of the day, the world was as fresh and dewy as when Dante awoke three centuries ago, and I determined never again to drink Pernod. No one forbade me to sleep where and how I liked, and I had nothing for anyone to steal; my uncle had got in ahead of the Paris apaches, whom at that time I regarded as pleasant enough types. The world was free and there was no fear.

But the *pension* soon wearied of its lodger, who often didn't come in till morning, and then only to shave before going to work, and who countered remonstrance with obscenities. I must add in my own defense that I didn't know how obscene the phrases were. I had picked them up from a Negro; they were not to be found in any dictionary. The Negro was a big, blue-black fellow who needed money to get his saxophone out of pawn. He never paid me back and I don't know that he even had a saxophone. But in those days I didn't take such things too seriously.

My secretary entered with the bills-of-lading folder under her arm. Her eyes were scared and brown and dewy bright. Sighing a little I prepared to explain. But she only stared uncomfortably at the tie, and I realized that she might be feeling even more awkward than myself. It was perhaps better to say nothing at all, and let time bury its dead. I was as cordial and polite as ever; I dictated a couple of letters and felt a guilty relief when she told me that the chief needed her at a conference. Not by one word did we allude to the previous evening. A most understanding girl. The light brown speckled pottery fish at the neck of her blouse kept one eye discreetly shut.

When she'd gone I slipped easily back into the old

groove, did my work, went through the letters and gave
negative answers when people rang up to know whether
there was any money in the bank. A vague melancholy
possessed me, and to the right of my stomach beneath the
diaphragm I felt once more that quietly grinding pain.
My gall bladder was still resentful.

Just before twelve Julle rang up hopefully to propose
a sequel to the party. But I knew Julle's sequels, and refused firmly, on the pretext of important conferences. I
asked him to convey my greetings and thanks to his wife.
This seemed called-for, as I had a hazy recollection of
having kissed her; and it had the effect of making Julle
hang up, for he disliked hearing his wife mentioned when
he was planning one of his "sequels." This may account
for his having got to his third wife already.

My refusal made me feel a better, nobler man, and to
carry my asceticism still further I decided to lunch off
potato soup, which the bank provided for its staff in the
common dining room. The chief considered it desirable
for the directors to partake now and then of this work-
house fare, the object of which was to shorten the time
allowed off for meals and at the same time demonstrate
the bank's solicitude for the welfare of its employees. On
the wages they were paid, the girls could afford no better
breakfast than a cup of ersatz coffee and a bit of dry bread,
and this had noticeably impaired their efficiency, as well
as causing them to faint on the premises from time to
time. Hence the old man's introduction of this impressive
social service.

Sitting thus engrossed in my work I had entirely forgotten my tie, and I felt flattered at the soft murmur of
delight that rose above the clatter of plates and spoons
when I came in. The head cashier—a woman—dropped a
spoon, and all round the table shy, enchanted eyes were

raised to look at me. I felt I had been remiss in not coming to their meals more often, and resolved to make up for it in the future. Not until I straightened my tie did I remember and understand and feel embarrassed. But defiance rose in me again. I took a plate, the waitress ladled potato soup into it and I sat resolutely down beside the chief cashier.

The talk and the clatter of spoons began again. My secretary was nowhere to be seen, but as I looked furtively round and observed all these aging, sallow, hollow faces I realized that she was the only young, fresh, well-turned-out woman in the place. I wondered if the day would ever come when even she would be as dried up, worn, and stale as the rest who day after day, year after year, sat at their desks—most of the time by artificial light—and in mute resignation bade farewell to their dreams. I wondered whether the old man shed some blight on the lives around him. The dining room was like the entrance hall of a mortuary chapel, where relatives and friends talked together in low voices as they waited for the funeral.

All this time I was painfully conscious of my tie, which was unsuited to that subdued atmosphere. The dingy potato soup reminded me suddenly of a little workmen's restaurant in the Rue de la Harpe, where Jeanne took me one Friday; for on Fridays the *patron* used to serve all his customers a glass of Málaga on the house, by way of dessert. Otherwise the food he provided differed little from this potato soup, and was perhaps even cheaper; but in those days Jeanne was beside me at a table spread with dirty paper, gaily sharpening her knife on her fork.

The *patron* had a bushy black mustache, and his Málaga tasted like burned sugar. Jeanne knew him, and he and his friends joked coarsely with us. They assumed we were lovers, and gave me practical advice as to the best way of dealing with girls in bed. At that time my French was still so poor that I had to listen very closely to catch all the allusions, and I think it was the gravity of my countenance that so tremendously amused them, and made them laugh till the food spattered from their mouths. Jeanne laughed too, putting her warm arms round me and kissing me unashamedly. The world was free in those days and everybody could do as he liked, without others feeling it their duty to blame him.

Jeanne muddled all my ideas and robbed me of my sense of sin. When I came to Paris I was full of the average Nordic youngster's inhibitions, and longed with all my heart to be rid of them. So I went to the other extreme. Until then I had never so to speak tangibly sinned with a woman, and when one evening a cold-eyed and no longer very young woman offered, for the modest sum of twenty francs, to perfect my knowledge in that field, I accepted her invitation without misgivings. It was a revolting experience. I felt nauseated afterwards and I determined never to repeat it. Even later, whenever I passed the little hotel where it happened I was aware of an inner, clutching chill, as if I were looking down into a coffin; and indeed it was there I had buried many youthful dreams. Jeanne cleansed me of the sour aftertaste of that transaction.

I started violently when the chief cashier touched my arm. She was a gray-haired, thin-lipped woman. Her piercing gaze was on my tie.

"Straight from Paris," I said feebly. "Something to liven up the day's routine."

She shook her head, shut her eyes and looked again. Her wan cheekbones turned faintly pink and she lifted her chin so that the wrinkles in her neck were smoothed out. "Ah, yes," she said. "If only one were young again!" With fingers worn from handling untold bundles of notes she timidly touched the tie, as if afraid it might explode. Then she rose quickly and left the room. I stood up too and went out, so as not to be the last, feeling as staggered as if I'd seen a cash register blush.

5

Towards the end of the day the old man came in. He didn't knock, of course, but my conscience was clear, for a pile of papers lay before me and I was busily making notes on a pad. He wandered up and down the room, fingering things as was his habit, rattling his keys, banging the paperweight on the desk, winding his watch and running a pencil along the edge of the table. At the most formal dinners he would sit balancing spoon or knife on his finger, but it never entered anyone's head to think this odd: he was chairman of the board of directors.

He talked of many things that were self-evident and needed no comment, repeating his instructions over and over again, as if I were the slowest pupil in a school for backward children. Suddenly he paused and the pencil fell from his hand.

"What's that under your chin?" he asked, badly shaken.

"Straight from Paris," I replied patiently. "Latest fashion. A spot of color in our drab North."

He still stared, as if unable to believe his eyes.

"Oh, well," he said at last. "I suppose you know what you're doing." But the sight had disturbed him. He walked to the window and turned again to look at the tie. "I don't know," he went on dubiously. "I've always been of the opinion that bank directors should dress discreetly, to inspire confidence. But in these days— Things are pretty dull, you know. We're getting old. It's nothing but routine and drudgery and everlasting responsibility— H'm, well, yes; perhaps a splash of color might cheer up the clients. I must think about it."

He had lost all his old assurance, and as he fiddled nervously with his keys I reflected that he was visibly aging and mellowing. I actually liked him: something I could never have believed possible. Might it be that behind that stony façade there lurked a timid, cowering man? The idiocy of this fugitive idea made me jump. I would have given much for a nip of brandy, for I felt I was losing my grip.

He withdrew his gaze from the tie and his prominent eyes resumed the icy expression that made one's flesh creep. "I really wanted to talk about your secretary," he said. "She's been here two months now. Are you satisfied with her?"

My conscience began sending out distress signals. I confined myself to nodding, and displayed no particular enthusiasm. This annoyed him.

"She's efficient," he said. "Punctual, quiet, and discreet. I think she'll do. We'd better give her a raise soon, or someone else will nab her. You might tell her, will you?"

He was quite right, but his suggestion came at an unfortunate moment for me. Good heavens, what would she think if today of all days I told her that her salary was to be raised? She might imagine—I sweated to think what she might imagine. The old man banged the desk so hard with the paperweight that he dented the wood. But there were deeper dents there already, from former visits.

"You can tell her I'm pleased with her and that I hope she'll be happy with us," he went on. "She's a good worker, and that's worth paying for. When I think of all

the rubbish that's drifted in and out of here—" He snorted
and scratched his head, then turned and went without
another word. It was his way. I straightened my tie and
stared at the portrait on the wall; it really looked quite
human.

My secretary appeared before the end of the day and
asked whether I had any instructions for her. As she was
going I said rather hoarsely, "One moment." She turned
and looked at me in alarm. Her eyes were large and bright
and clear. The previous night's lack of sleep had left no
trace on her smooth, soft young cheeks. She was evidently
afraid of me. Or perhaps she was merely afraid I was going
to be tactless and talk of things there's no sense in talking
about afterwards. I choked as I looked at her: she was so
young and so pretty.

"The chief wanted me to tell you that from the first of
the month your salary will be increased. He—we're pleased
with your work." I tried to smile and said playfully, "I
think he's afraid you might run off and get married."
Then in all sincerity I added, "And I can't think why you
haven't done that already. You don't want to bury yourself here for the rest of your life, do you?"

She smiled slightly too, and was tactful enough not to
remark that all the best men had been killed. "I've got to
live," she said, "and the nicest men are married already.
And I don't like very young ones."

She came nearer and half-sat on the arm of a chair, as
if willing to prolong this cozy discussion. "Young men are
so scatterbrained—so unstable," she said. "You can't rely
on them. During the war they got used to having things
all their own way; they're no support to you. If I marry
I shall choose a man who has steadied down—someone I
can depend on. But they're not to be found; they're already married. And so—" she raised her shoulders a little

as if to imply that she didn't mind working in the bank, so long as I was her boss. I was touched.

"That tie quite alters you," she said. "It makes you more human. It's frightful, of course, but it cheers me up whenever I look at it. Why are you so sad, I wonder? You shouldn't be. There's nothing to be sad about."

How touchingly young and virginal she was! She took my breath away. When I imagined what it would be like to unfasten that cheeky fish and—and so forth, I had to avert my eyes. I knew I could fall blindly in love with her, just because she was so young and warm; and that would be dangerous and unnecessary. I'd do better not to look at her.

"Your eyes are so sad," she persisted. "Like Charles Boyer's. I expect you've seen him in the films?"

I straightened the tie and felt a surge of warmth—but I pulled myself together.

"I'm no Charles Boyer," I said dryly. "Why, my dear girl, I'm bald."

She regarded me dreamily; a soft haze seemed to have fallen over her eyes and veiled their luster. "You'd hardly notice it," she said softly.

There was an awkward silence, and my pulses raced. She came quickly over to me, passed her hand gently over my hair, turned and almost ran from the room. I was shaking like a jelly.

Presently I went to the washroom and looked at myself in the glass. The mirror was kindly and discreet, not pitiless and revealing like the one in my bedroom. When I looked at myself in it the bald patch didn't show; nor was I as bloated and revolting as I had fancied that morning. The dullness of my crowned teeth couldn't be seen if I kept my mouth shut. Damn it, there must have been something about me once, or my wife would never have married me in the face of such strong family opposition. Since the old man couldn't stop her, he determined to make a banker of me—and he did, though it was heavy going. Now and then he'd been almost in despair.

I had kissed my secretary in the taxi, and now I was annoyed because my memory of it was so dim. For all I knew she might have been kissed far too often already. What did I know of her? Her white silk blouse looked so virginal. She was quite afraid of me. I would have given a lot to hold her in my arms now, in a sober state. Her eyes were so bright and brown as she stroked my hair. Good God, why had she done that? Surely she hadn't fallen for me just because I kissed her after a few drinks? It was only good manners.

Jeanne hadn't put up any resistance either; on the contrary, she thought it the most natural thing in the world when, after long hesitation, I kissed her. I gave her cherries as she stood at the neighboring window, and as this was awkward I invited her into my room. "Oh no!" she said, and smiled. I showed her how many cherries were still left in the bag, and she came without delay. I ran to open the door for her, and together we leaned out of the window, spitting cherry stones at the passers-by. Our shoulders and arms touched. She wore a dress with short sleeves and her arms were brown and warm and covered with fine, shining down. I dared not talk to her; my heart was beating too fiercely.

A gentleman with a white beard got a cherry stone on his hat, and looking up he threatened us with his umbrella. We drew back abruptly from the window, and found ourselves standing face to face. I was looking straight into those laughing brown eyes. My hands were clenched, and their palms were sweaty; then I kissed her and she responded warmly, with full, cherry-moist lips. It was as simple as that.

Someone knocked furiously on the washroom door. I woke up with a start and found I was still staring at myself in the mirror; my eyes were as round and foolish as those of a dead fish. Outside the door stood one of the boys from the exchange department. He was horrified to see me, and bowed twice. "I—I didn't know it was you, sir," he stammered. "I—I've got a pain in my stomach."

I hadn't an idea what he was saying; I was completely dazed and my scalp itched. I went home to dinner.

6

On the table at home, four bright red carnations in a silver vase glowed in the bright evening sunlight. I was still moving in a dream—a dream pleasant enough now, though I felt that at any moment it might turn into a nightmare. Touching the carnations hesitantly with my finger tips, I dreaded lest I should wake up screaming and gasping for breath. My wife was sitting up straight in an armchair reading a fat book. She raised her head and looked at me in something like alarm. Her cold blue eyes had a warm gleam in them.

"Thank you, my dear," I said. "But it's not my birthday."

"Oh, the carnations," she said absently. "They're not for you; they were given to me."

This didn't surprise me. I supposed that she had once more taken the chair at some committee, or arranged a mannequin parade in aid of some charity; the sort of function at which one may enjoy, for a dizzy price, a cup of real coffee and a cake sweetened with saccharine.

"They're lovely," I said. "I was thinking yesterday—" but I broke off in time, and for once she didn't seem interested in what I'd been thinking. The spicy fragrance of the flowers was in my nostrils as I touched them again. It was like touching the cool, clean skin of a girl.

"What are you reading?" I asked sociably. She rose, marked her place in the book carefully and said, "Dinner's ready." The gentle glow faded from her eyes and she looked at me with distaste.

We had boiled fish. My son explained volubly with his mouth full how to build model aircraft. It seemed there was a boy in his class who had a model plane with a real gasoline engine.

"Where does he get the gasoline from?" I asked, by way of showing intelligent interest. He fell silent and looked at me, then ate more slowly and stared down at the table-cloth. My daughter wanted to go to the cinema and began begging money for a large supply of American chewing gum; she said it was cheaper that way. There was a boy who got it direct from the sailors. My wife asked whether I minded her going to the theater that evening; she'd been offered a ticket.

"Oh, not tonight, do you mind?" I said wearily. "I just can't do it. I've had a heavy day."

"Nobody asked you," she said coldly.

After dinner I lay down and fell asleep, with the wonderful illusion of a young hand stroking my hair. When I woke up my wife was dressing to go out. Watching her sleepily I reflected how amazingly well preserved she was for her age. But she was no longer young.

She caught my eye in the mirror and said, "Don't stare like that."

Guiltily I withdrew my eyes. She put on an evening dress which had stretched through being on a hanger in the wardrobe all the summer. She lifted the hem and scrutinized herself in the mirror. There was a good deal of rouge on her cheeks. She passed her tongue over her thin lips and smiled slightly.

"Have I got too much make-up on?" she asked.

"I don't think so," I answered, and getting up I went and stood behind her. I looked at her image in the glass, and then bent and kissed her neck. It was thin and warm and a pulse beat beneath the skin.

"Leave me alone," she said, bored. Before she went she took a carnation from the vase and fastened it to her dress with a diamond pin.

In the hall I helped her on with her evening coat. Turning suddenly she looked straight into my eyes. Hers glinted like the edge of a razor.

"When did we last talk to each other?" she asked. It was like her to make this sort of remark in the hall, just as she was going out. And perhaps it wasn't exactly "talk" that she meant. I sighed deeply when the door had closed behind her. To the right of my stomach under the diaphragm the grinding pain began again. And it was the maid's evening out. I was alone in the twilight rooms, and all the familiar things in them seemed suddenly strange.

Without switching on the light I sat down and began slowly smoking one cigarette after another, oppressed by the "morning-after" sensation of being a stranger in a strange world; a world in which everything happens by blind chance and nothing is straightforward or natural. It wasn't such fun to be alive when one was breathless and bald and had a bellyache.

When I was young I took pride and delight in my own body. What joy it was to walk out of the little hotel in the freshness of morning and draw the air of the city deep into my lungs, feeling young and healthy and terribly unhappy! That was before Jeanne—or was her name Inge? Their figures blended in an irritating way. A wilderness of years separated me from that time, when with a fine languor and deep satisfaction I could sigh, "Ah, women, women!" Only in extreme youth does one sigh like that and imagine one knows all there is to know about the opposite sex. I sat in that comfortable armchair in the darkening room, wheezing away like a sick ox. What most annoyed me was that here I had a free evening and didn't even know her telephone number. She might have come for a walk with me, or we could have sat together at a table by the light of a little lamp in some quiet restaurant where there would be no one we knew, and where she could have told me simply and confidingly about herself, her studies, her life—perhaps even her dreams. We might have come nearer to one another. She had known instinctively that I wished her well, and that when I touched her it was with respect and tenderness. Perhaps, perhaps— For a moment I wondered what would happen if I rang up the chief cashier and asked her for my secretary's telephone number. I could say I'd forgotten something important which must be done at once. But the idea didn't appeal to me. The chief cashier had shown today that she was human; she might be capable of groundless suspicions.

I chafed, I sweated. What wouldn't I have given to be young, poor, and alone once more! Life was so straightforward and easy then. Like the day we ate the cherries and I kissed Jeanne's warm lips for the first time. She was glad I did. That evening I was to have tea with my boss's wife. I knew I should meet my cold, blonde ideal there, but the thought of it no longer excited me as it had in the morning.

"Jeanne," I said frankly. "What would you say if when I came home this evening I knocked on your door and said good night?"

She smiled at me and her brown eyes were gay. She had come to Paris from the country to take some sort of course; I never discovered whether it was a course in needlework, child nursing or what, but I felt that she enjoyed the life and the freedom of Paris as keenly as I did. When late that night I crept up the creaking stairs with my heart thumping, and knocked at her door, an alert voice answered. She didn't sound at all sleepy. She had left the key in the door and was already in bed when I entered. When I had kissed her she said in a matter-of-fact way, "Go to bed, darling. I'll come when you've undressed. There's more room there."

It was true. My room was exactly twice as big as her little cubbyhole which cost only ten francs a day: I had to pay eighteen for mine. Mine even had a marble fireplace, though it had never been used since the hotel had had central heating put in.

I undressed and washed. It was a hot night. Through the window I could see the red and white lamps of the Pont Saint Michel reflected in the dark, gleaming waters of the Seine, which by day was yellowish green. When I'd climbed into bed Jeanne came; she took the key from the door and replaced it on the inside. Then she came to my bed.

"It's hot," she said presently; she drew off her night-dress, wound her arms round my neck and kissed me happily. "It's better like this," she said; and generously, without reserve, she offered me her naked, warm body. It was youth's gift to youth, and since then I don't believe I've ever been given anything with so generous a heart. It was all so simple. Out there beyond the window the lamps were reflected in red and white ribbons on the water.

But that was long ago. A whole world had been dissolved and drowned since then, to say nothing of the degeneration in myself. The room was dark now and full of tobacco smoke. I opened the window to air it, and from the street below that nostalgic autumn scent of the young lime trees floated up to me through the cool evening. All that had vanished—all the madness and delirious young joy. Life demanded more solid and lasting values: home, family, responsible work, social position. But the autumn fragrance of the limes made me bitterly aware that everything was crumbling round me and that all the old values had lost their meaning. I felt weary of it all, and as I undressed my thoughts began to run along their accustomed channels—until suddenly I was holding the Parisian tie in my hand. Regarded with the eyes of an aging banker it was a fearful object. But the stranger beside me, my own young self, smiled to see it. I hardened my heart and went to bed.

Lying there waiting for sleep, I cursed the weakness and softness that had involved me in these needless complications. One short evening's conviviality had upset my life and left me at the mercy of my conscience. Whereas Julle Cypress, for instance, had been twice divorced, and for him a night's carouse was merely a welcome excuse for a "sequel" next day. If I'd asked him whether he had a guilty conscience he would have gaped at me; he wouldn't have known what I was talking about. Inge, Inge, I whispered, staring through the darkness at her limpid eyes. She had said herself that she didn't care for very young men. She had said something about my eyes. She was probably laughing at me.

I woke when my wife came in, and looked sleepily at

the clock. It was two. I wondered vaguely where she had been; but my dreams had been so pleasant that all I wanted to do was to return to them as quickly as possible.

7

After a hard moral struggle I vanquished my cowardly self at last and made up my mind to take my secretary out to lunch. This was most irregular, and I had therefore prepared a short speech in which I would make clear to her that we'd better not leave the bank together, but meet at the restaurant. But my precautions proved quite unnecessary. I had only time to begin, "I wonder what you'd say—" when the telephone rang and the old man informed me testily that he had to take my secretary out to lunch with the representative of a Swedish firm of machinery makers. He rang off before I could reply, and his picture stared at me from the wall with noticeably bloodshot eyes.

I could only sigh and tell her what he'd said. Was I mistaken, or did that young face really take on a look of disappointment? She sighed a little too, and fingered the pottery fish under her chin. Today she was wearing a white knitted sweater so bewitching that my eyes constantly strayed in one direction. The sweater indicated almost too alluringly how enchantingly young she was; merely to look at her took my breath away.

As she was gathering up her papers to go I said with constraint, "Pity the old man's in such a tiresome mood. I was going to ask you to lunch with me."

Her face lit up in a smile of surprise and pleasure. "Perhaps—perhaps some other time," she said confidingly.

Her eyes smiled as she bent towards me. She may have feared I might forget myself and take her in my arms, for she blushed and went quickly from the room. The old man looked down at me from the wall in indignation, but I fingered my tie defiantly and thought, "Another time."

Although the day dragged without her, I was aware that life had changed and become exciting. I enjoyed telling inquirers on the telephone that there was no money in the bank; I enjoyed signing papers destined to lie buried indefinitely in government departments; I enjoyed comparing the controlled home-market timber prices with export prices. I was in excellent form and was actually pleased to see the chief when he walked in just before four. "I promised them three and a half million for the machinery," he said. "They've something to do with electricity. What's plastic? I can't find it in any encyclopedia."

I told him what I knew about plastics. It wasn't much, but I assured him that it was the material of the future. He snorted skeptically, took a piece of paper from the desk, and began poking holes in it with his pencil. "The girl's copying out her notes," he said. "You can have a look at them. Plastic, plastic," he repeated to himself vaguely. "The girl did excellently. I let her lunch with us." He gave a sudden roar of laughter. "She had a glass of claret and asked if it was frightfully strong! Could you have imagined that there were still girls like that about?"

He sat down, put his thumb through his key ring and rattled the keys. "I'm getting old," he remarked. "My memory isn't what it was. I'm bothered by that plastic they kept talking about. One ought to take one's secretary along more often. She's a decent type of girl, and not at all in the way. How would it be if she came to Tampere with me tomorrow?"

"Tomorrow?" I exclaimed, disconcerted. He looked at

me crossly with his eyes popping out of his head. "Of course," he said. "I'm going to Tampere tomorrow—had you forgotten? We can give her a meal allowance if she wants it."

Still rattling his keys he went away, and I had no choice but to tell the girl. She hesitated and was plainly uneasy. "I'm a bit afraid of him," she said. "He makes one feel so small."

"He's delighted with your work," I told her reassuringly. "Don't you see this is a mark of favor?"

She wrinkled her nose slightly. "What about the letters?"

I assured her I could manage the letters by myself. "And I can always ask someone in the office to help me."

"No," she said. "I should hate to think of someone else sitting here with you and—" she broke off in confusion and lowered her eyes, while a slow blush spread down to her neck. The white sweater heaved so violently that again I choked. Mechanically I smoothed my hair and straightened my tie.

I can't say how it happened, but when I left the bank it was with her at my side. It would have been uncouth to leave her at the first street corner, and automatically I walked on beside her. Our ways lay almost together. She was very quiet. Sometimes I felt her glancing shyly sideways at me. When we reached Mannerheim Road she laid her hand lightly on my arm and said,

"Mr. Cypress rang me up last night and invited me out."

"How did he know your number?" I demanded.

"He asked me for it that first evening," she said demurely. "He said he thought he could get me some English to copy. I—sometimes I have to take extra work." She looked away with a little sigh. "I didn't want to seem rude, but I thought he was rather—" she shook her head and went on confidentially, "It seems to me that perhaps Mr. Cypress isn't altogether—dependable. . . ."

I assured her warmly that Julle Cypress was a heartless rake and not to be trusted. In fact I hardly regarded him as my friend any longer. I warned her as plainly as possible against the copying job, and was still upset when we reached her door. We paused here. She gave me her hand; I held it fast and she didn't attempt to withdraw it. She looked very young, standing there gazing into my eyes with her hand in mine.

"I wanted to ring you up last night, too," I confessed. "I was sorry not to have your number."

"Really?" she said. "I should have loved that; I was at home all the evening with my mother. I was thinking of all kinds of things—of you too."

"Oh, I can't let you go yet!" I burst out. "I—I wanted to—"

She was obviously wavering. "You could come in for a bit," she said, "if you're not in a hurry, and—and if you think it's all right."

In the lift she explained, "I live with my mother. It's a very poor little flat; you mustn't look at anything." We were standing close together in the lift and I felt her breath on my neck.

"Mother doesn't seem to be back yet," she said in surprise when she'd opened the door. "Do come in. I'm sure she'll be home soon."

The flat wasn't in the least poor, but I didn't look at anything—only at her. She seemed unsure of herself and sat smoking for a time without venturing to look at me. Then she laid down the cigarette, saying it tasted nasty. My throat tightened, so keenly conscious was I of her nearness. I fingered my tie, and at once a flame seemed to spring up in me. Leaning forward I put my arm round her; she averted her head but I forced her face round to mine and kissed her. Shyly she responded, with closed lips, like a schoolgirl.

"Oh," she said, "You shouldn't—" But her eyes were bright; she put out her hand and stroked my cheek gently.

"Oh, Inge," I groaned; but she rose and slipped with surprising adroitness from my arms. "No, no, you mustn't," she murmured, breathing fast, and she moved to the other side of the table. "You mustn't touch me. It feels so—so queer. You've got marvelous hands—they make me go all limp."

"Inge!" I said, "Oh, Inge! How beautiful, how glorious life is. I never imagined such a wonderful thing could happen to me again. Listen—" I hesitated a moment. "If you're not doing anything special we could dine together and—and—" She regarded me silently with those brilliant eyes.

I was troubled, and felt as if somewhere inside me a flayed patch were being rubbed with sandpaper. But I pulled myself together and went into the hall where I had noticed a telephone. My wife's voice answered, cool and remote.

"Listen, darling," I said. "I just can't make dinner to-night. Your father's going to Tampere tomorrow, and before then I've got to see various people, and—and—" I gasped for breath, "Plastic!" I said in desperation. "You know what that is, don't you? Well, it's to do with that. I shall eat out somewhere."

There was a singularly long silence at the other end of the line and I had time to feel nervous as I awaited my wife's reply. At last she said evenly, "That fits in very well. I thought of dining out too. Thanks for ringing." She hung up before I could stammer out my "Good-bye for now, then, darling."

I drew a deep breath and re-entered the room. When I looked at the girl I was thunderstruck: two bright tears were rolling down her cheeks. I saw them clearly, though she tried to hide them by turning away her head. "Inge, my dear, what on earth's the matter? Why are you crying?" I exclaimed. I knelt before her and put my arms round her, but again she turned away.

"I think it's so awful," she said. "I'd hate to make anyone unhappy. I loathe women who force themselves between husband and wife, and break up marriages."

"But it's not a bit like that," I protested. "My wife and I have nothing in common any longer—absolutely nothing." Far in the distance I seemed to hear a cock crowing, long and raucously, but it only goaded me to continue. "She has never understood me."

My hand was resting on her bosom but she didn't notice. Doubtfully she turned her face towards me and I kissed the tears from her cheeks. I grew ardent and embraced her more violently, until I felt I possessed her hesitant lips and that she responded to my kisses. She was now lying relaxed in my arms and I was firmly convinced that my wife had never understood me.

"You see," I explained, "we've been living our own lives for years now. We each have our own interests. In my heart of hearts I've always been alone—terribly alone."

Shyly she touched my cheek. "I felt you were lonely, Valter," she whispered. She took my hand gently from her breast and stood up. "I must go and change if we're dining out," she said. "Have a cigarette while you're waiting; I shan't be long."

And indeed she was out of the room less than half an hour. When she returned she was wearing a very lovely frock, whose simple perfection told of an expensive dressmaker. "Somewhere quiet where we can talk," she said dreamily. "Perhaps the Savoy? They have such good food there."

It was impossible to explain that I'd thought of going to some place where I shouldn't come across anyone I knew, or rather where people I knew shouldn't see me. So we dined at the Savoy, where I was conscious the whole time of piercing, inquisitive glances on the back of my neck. For this reason I drank more than was necessary. She was happily oblivious of all the admiring, scrutinizing eyes that were turned upon her, and of the caustic remarks inspired by me and my bald patch. In the taxi I kissed her again, and she responded gently and without reserve; but with firmness and skill she warded off my hands. I paid off the taxi and wanted to go in with her, but this she had to refuse. "Mother wouldn't like it," she said. "It's much too late." Her voice told me that she regretted this as much as I did. "Good night, my dearest," she said, hiding a slight yawn with her hand.

I walked homeward breathing the sharp, autumn smell of the lime trees. I was hot and there was a thudding at my temples. I felt her body in my arms and her soft caress on my cheek. She was young enough to have been my daughter, but in some queer way she made me feel as if the difference in our ages was of no importance. She understood me better than any woman had understood me for years.

8

Before the old man left for the station he came into my room. He had his hat on and was carrying a disgracefully shabby brief case. "Don't do anything silly while

I'm away," he admonished me amiably. "In fact you'd better not do anything at all. That's the best way of dealing with difficulties these days." With his free hand he began absentmindedly shifting things on the desk, and I felt him looking at me askance in some embarrassment.

"Your secretary," I began nervously. "Don't let her travel third class. She might feel hurt."

"Of course not. Don't be a fool," he retorted, and began knocking gently on the table with the paperweight. "Do you know, Valter," he said almost abruptly, "I had a dream last night, and it's still bothering me."

If the roof had fallen in I couldn't have felt more shaken, and I looked at him in consternation, wondering whether I ought to warn the other directors about the state of his mind. He noticed my amazement and made a dent in the desk with the paperweight. "I haven't dreamed for years," he snorted, "and it bothers me. I was swimming in warm water—yes, yes, swimming—a long way out. And some sort of sea monster, or fish, came along and bit off my nose." Mechanically he touched his thin, bluish nose. "It made me very depressed—unpleasantly depressed."

"Some psychoanalysts—" I began, but he waved away my words and snorted, "Rubbish! It must be something I ate last night. But all the morning I've been thinking about my poor wife. If it wasn't so idiotic I'd say that fish had my wife's face." He stroked his nose again with a troubled air, and returned to reality. "Get hold of some facts about plastics; we shall need them. I've been going into the matter, and it's the material of the future." He repeated the same thing three times in different ways, addressing me as usual as if I were feeble-minded. Then with a look of disgust he dropped the paperweight and began fidgeting with the calendar. "I hope your family's well," he said. "Your wife might remember her old father now and then, I think; I feel lonely sometimes." With that he stroked his nose again, patted my shoulder, and left for Tampere.

At dinner I conveyed his greeting to my wife. "I'm sure he's ill," I remarked. "He dreams and he's gone all tender-hearted. What do you think—should I warn the board?"

My daughter was out riding and my son had been kept in for testing a rocket-driven model aircraft in the school yard. As usual we were dining alone together. We had roast mutton, which was easily heated up for the children later. I ate greedily and marveled at the slow passage of time. In thought I was following the rhythmic clank of the train to Tampere, and lingering in the corridors of the Tammer Hotel. I was blindly, madly in love; it was an intoxicating feeling, and life itself was transfigured.

"Will you have some more?" my wife asked. When I shook my head she said abstractedly, staring past me, "Has it ever struck you, Valter, that our best years are slipping away? One's body is losing its youth and life has begun to go downhill. It's as if one wanted something without know-ing what it was; as if something were missing from life—something one wants to reach out for and grab, before it's too late."

She looked at me with the prominent blue eyes that I'd once been so strangely in love with. "You're right," I said meekly, though I had hardly taken in what she'd been saying. She sighed. "Have you ever thought about a di-vorce?" she asked, in a matter-of-fact tone.

"No," I lied automatically; then, more honestly, I added, "What's the use, anyway? It can't be done."

"Why not?" she inquired with a cold stare, and I averted my eyes. I was too polite to say that in no circumstances would she give me cause. Yet as I thought what might have been, there came a ringing in my ears and a surging warmth in my throat.

Like her father she sat playing with her fork. "Perhaps
I feel I'm losing something, too. Perhaps I too want to
snatch at life while I can."

"You *too*," I said guardedly. "Then do you mean that
I—"

"Oh, *you*," she cut in. "You've got your Parisian tie."
Her voice was as sharp as a glass splinter, and it annoyed
me.

"But you'd never give me a divorce," I said stiffly.

"No. On the contrary," she replied, staring past me into
the distance. Her beautiful eyes had a veiled look in them
as in the old days. "I'd like you to think seriously about
giving me one. In a friendly way, of course. Now don't get
worked up. Let's discuss this calmly, like adults. The children are old enough to understand that I have a right to
my own life, too."

"What are you raving about!" I cried, springing up in
dismay. She was talking as smoothly and evenly as a ma-
chine; that's what made it so horrible. My head was in a
whirl. The carnations, the theater, her frequent late home-
comings. Had I been blind, then, to trust her so implicitly?
I turned cold, and felt as if hailstones were rolling down
my spine.

"Who's the man?" I demanded.

"Who's the woman?" she mimicked, adding with something like pity, "May I remind you that sooner or later
your handkerchiefs get into the wash? The girl's surprised
to find so much lipstick on them."

I felt myself slowly turning red, and it enraged me.
"What about you?" I blustered. "What time did you get in
the other night?"

"Well, what of it? What have you got to yell about?
We've been strangers to one another for a long time. We
each have our own interests. If I've found someone who

really understands me, why shouldn't I seize my opportunity while I may?"

"I'm not yelling," I said heatedly. "Are you out of your mind? I could never have imagined such a thing about you —*you*." I drew a deep breath and swallowed repeatedly.

She rested her elbows on the table and with her chin in her hands she regarded me with amusement. "Does it go so deep? I couldn't know I was touching a tender spot, now, could I?"

I recovered myself. "Who's the man?" I demanded once more. She looked bored. "Oh, never mind that," she said. "We'll talk about it tomorrow. I must go now. You can be thinking it over."

She tried to pass me, but I seized her wrists. "You're not going anywhere," I told her.

"That's what you think," she retorted. She was staring at me and breathing hard. And somehow—I don't know how it happened—she was in my arms and I was kissing her, inquiringly. At first she resisted me, then relaxed and shut her eyes. Softly, dreamily she answered my kiss, and all the time I could feel her thinking about the other man. It was no pleasant sensation. Suddenly I released her.

"Do you believe me now?" she asked. I believed her without further assurances, and she walked proudly from the room. I remained blankly staring at the door, which closed after her.

I rushed from room to room, hand on head; what was the matter with me? Why wasn't I glad she was willing to set me free? Inge's lustrous eyes smiled at me; nothing now prevented me from taking youth into my arms. It was as if a magic door had flown open. All I had hardly dared dream of was now suddenly, effortlessly within my grasp. I could begin a new life, without fighting for it and with a clear conscience, and yet—why did I hesitate? Thinking of what lay before me I felt a dreadful weakness.

Was it so formidable a task? Did I lack the strength? And Jeanne? To hell with Jeanne! How shattered I had been when I found out that, as gaily and naturally as she had loved me, she was deceiving me with an Albanian student she had met. Later I discovered that during the brief course she was taking she had found time to form a new branch of the League of Nations, by means of her warm, generous body. When I reproached her with it she laughed in my face and told me that her little brother collected stamps. Besides, she said, it was fun to get letters from so many different countries.

I sank exhausted into a chair and with trembling fingers lit a cigar. But it wasn't soothing, it tasted foul. I mixed a brandy and soda, and that tasted foul too, and my gall bladder reminded me of its existence with needle-sharp stabs. I wanted to think about Inge; I wanted to relive the sweet intoxication of the evening before, but my wife's face intruded into my thoughts in a vexatious manner. She had had rouge on her cheeks; there had been a mild, liquid brilliance in her eyes and a softness in her straight, slim form. It was revolting, unbearable, to imagine her in another man's arms. The thought of her thin, lovely lips parted for a kiss made me sweat. I couldn't understand why it should upset me so much, yet the mere notion of her attraction for some loathsome, unknown man made her intensely desirable to me.

I couldn't sit still, and in wandering restlessly round the room I noticed a photograph album lying on a table. I opened it vaguely and began looking at summer snapshots taken during our first years together. She wore a fringe in those days, and really looked extremely attractive in a bathing suit. A tender, troubled feeling stirred in me as I beheld these pictures of a time that would never return. Our first summer shack. The children when they were small. The boy. How terrified I'd been when he was born! I quickly shut the album again. Then I wondered how it got onto that table, and in a wave of tenderness I understood: my wife had been looking at these photographs, seeking strength perhaps to withstand the passion that was drawing her away from me; I fancied her twisting her long, lovely fingers in anguish. I found I was bathed in sweat. But perhaps nothing irrevocable had happened yet.

I went to bed early. When I undressed I found the tie from Paris in my hand again. I stared at it spellbound, as if at a snake. Youth, the stranger, stood smiling ironically at my side, and, my torment past, I felt only defiance. For like a dream, a rapture, youth was in my arms. I lay in bed in the dark unable to sleep, feeling the hard, smooth limbs of youth beside me. How could such intoxication last? It *was* intoxication and it would pass. But the drink was worth the price, I told myself stubbornly.

How far, how very far behind me lay my rampageous youth! I remembered the old photographs in the album. I remembered all that my wife had saved me from. I used to drink too much, and had money troubles; she had saved me and made a decent man of me. Decent in what way? Decent enough to sit in a bank year in year out, gazed at with condemnation by her father's portrait on the wall, until I grew slow and breathless and bald. If we divorced amicably I might keep my position in the bank: there was nothing petty about my wife.

No: better cut loose altogether. The bank had helped me to form other connections; I might get a good timber agency and travel abroad, to France or South America. Every half hour I switched on the light and looked at the time, my fury mounting. Very well, then; if for the sake of a momentary whim she was ready to lay waste the life we had shared, then let her do it. It was finished for me too. Not that we hadn't been happy together; there had been a time when I was proud of her and admired her more than any other woman I knew.

At about two o'clock I heard the outer door open. My wife's dog barked softly and rushed to meet her. In the hall a coat hanger clattered to the floor; the dog returned crestfallen to its basket and stayed there with one eye glittering like a black diamond and one ear pricked, to await developments. For once I felt a real affinity with the beast. My wife appeared and stood leaning against the doorpost.

"Are you still awake?" she said in surprise. She was smiling amiably and as she undressed I saw that she'd been drinking. The undressing proceeded slowly, and once she paused with a stocking in her hand and gazed smilingly into space. Her lipstick was smudged all round her mouth, and I shuddered to see her—I suppose with disgust.

"Don't stare at me like that," she said, still with that bland smile. Yes, she could smile at me, still bearing the marks of cheap caresses on cheeks and neck, and elsewhere for all I knew. This clinched it: there was nothing for it now but a divorce. Yet she was lovely. . . . My throat dried up at the sight of her, and I could feel my pulse in my finger tips.

She gave me a quick glance and her smile faded. Her eyes were hard as she stood for a while in thought. Then she began gathering up her bedclothes. "I see I'd better sleep in another room," she said with meaning.

I lost my temper. "Don't flatter yourself I'd touch you—not if I—" I stammered and was at a loss what to say. "I detest you!" I cried from a full heart. "You're behaving like an animal."

She made no answer, but sank into bed, tucked the bed-

clothes round herself and sighed sleepily and contentedly.
"Put out the light," she said in a drowsy voice. I gritted
my teeth and did so, and presently I heard a thud as the
dog jumped onto her bed. She kicked out, but feebly;
the dog with a grunt of satisfaction curled up at her feet.
I'd seen this happen so many times that even in the darkness I could follow the creature's every movement.

Tears of disappointment, resentment, and weakness
stung my eyes. "So we're to be divorced," I remarked bitterly. She said nothing, but presently I heard the sound of
smothered sobbing. She was crying, then! All this was
costing her something, after all. Relenting completely I
groped for her shoulder in the darkness, but she pushed
away my hand and went on sobbing.

"Darling," I said. "Darling, are you crying?"

I stroked her narrow shoulder, until she suddenly raised
her head out of the bedclothes, turned on her back and
snapped, "Don't be idiotic. I'm laughing." In my disbelief
I felt her face, and it was true. Her eyes were dry and she
was shaking all over with suppressed laughter. I was cut to
the heart. "You're drunk," I said, and turned my back on
her.

"Permit me to get a little drunk too, now and then," she
said affectedly. "It's a glorious feeling. I'm so bursting with
laughter that I can't stop."

I clenched my teeth and pressed my head down into
the pillow. I suppose I fell asleep then. I never woke until
morning, to find my wife pouring out Vichy water.

"It's nine o'clock," she said. "Do you know, I believe
I've got a hang-over. I think I'll stay in bed for a bit."

I couldn't look at her. Her dog glanced up at me in
triumph and pressed its chin harder against her legs. I
dressed. The tie from Paris lay on the dressing table, dimming with its brilliance the natural colors of the room. It

glowed like some exotic, poisonous reptile. I should have liked to tear it to shreds, but without looking round I knotted it savagely round my neck. I had a bitter taste in my mouth and I was pale from lack of sleep. The look in my eyes—yes, it was misty and staring. Like Charles Boyer's. But this was small consolation.

9

The weather was overcast and I had to have the light on in my room all day. The old man rang up from Tampere to say that he was staying on there until tomorrow. He was testier than ever. His face stared past me from the wall with an expression of utter boredom and distaste. The drab weekday brought with it deadly, crushing monotony; unrelieved dullness rolled over me like a giant tank; the rapture was over and to my astonishment I found myself thinking of my secretary with a marked lack of enthusiasm.

I wondered what I was to say to her. "Inge," I would say, "we can't go on like this; you know that as well as I do. I have my home, my children, and my wife, to whom I owe loyalty at least, even though we may have drifted apart. Inge my dear, you'll soon forget me. You're young—you have your whole life before you. But you must never think that I was just amusing myself with you, and nothing more."

I was troubled, and unconsciously I fidgeted with the things on my desk. Inge was so sensitive. I remembered the bright tears on her cheeks. I remembered the taste of them on my lips, and the memory was unwelcome. Suppose she began crying and someone came into the room—the old

man himself, perhaps! I should have to say something wise
and beautiful—something that would make it easier for her
to bear: "Inge, you know I love only you, but for that very
reason we must end this before it's too late. You know I
shall never forget you." Something of that sort: frank,
noble. It might comfort her. As for me, I would live out
my life in loneliness and self-chastisement; only now and
then would I gaze into the distance with a sad smile. I
should never forget her.

At the same time I felt a nagging certainty that she
would vanish as swiftly and completely from my mind as
Jeanne had, a quarter of a century ago. It was the con-
founded tie, the ill-fated encounter with Julle Cypress,
that had caused it all.

At the end of the day I once more surveyed myself in
the washroom mirror. My face had acquired an expression
of stern, manly resignation; my eyes reflected a secret and
profound suffering and I was noticeably pale. With weary
though resolute steps I made my way home. My wife was
waiting for me, and reading the paper.

I took off the Parisian tie and handed it to her. "Here
you are," I said simply. Then in a sudden burst of temper,
"Take it—tear it to bits and throw it away. I never want to
see it again."

But my wife's long and lovely fingers folded it carefully.
"I think I'll keep it," she said in a mild tone, "in case you
ever want to look at it and revive old memories." But there
was no malice in her words, for she rose and put her arms
round my neck.

But I was not to be mollified so easily. "Let me go," I
said, and thrust away her arms. Wounded pride, disillusionment, and a vague melancholy weighed on my heart
as I avoided her eye and stared stubbornly out of the win-

dow. In the street the lime trees rose wet and dark green towards the cloudy autumn sky.

"Perhaps we needn't separate after all," said my wife, gently fingering the tie. "I've been thinking—" she didn't finish her sentence, but I knew what she meant to say.

"Put that beastly thing away!" I cried. "Where the hell's dinner? Can we never have meals on time in this house? Ugh, that blasted dog!"

Her dog had risen on its hind legs and was gently licking my hand. It didn't feel at all bad.

From then on, I believe, all was well. Much later, in the dark, I asked again, "Who was that man?" She laughed, and after a silence said, "I've asked you no questions."

"It's all over," I said curtly. "And it was nothing anyway. Just a slight mistake."

"Mine's all over too," she said quietly. "And it was nothing anyway. Just a slight mistake."

"A few kisses, a rush of something to the head, some foolish thoughts," I said. "What does it amount to?"

"A few kisses, hardly any rush to the head; what does it amount to?" she echoed.

I was assailed by a strange suspicion. I raised myself on my elbow, bent over and kissed her narrow, lovely mouth. "What color are his eyes?" I asked.

She hesitated for a moment. "Steel gray," she answered, with some constraint. But the moment's hesitation had given her away. I kissed her again and my spirits soared: she had just been teasing me and had never so much as thought of another man. And the carnations—she had bought them herself, of course.

Or had she . . . I was not absolutely sure. I was never absolutely sure about her; but this amounted to no more than a faintly unpleasant feeling.

Next morning my secretary came into my room and

when I saw her I felt horribly guilty. She was very pale and she had dark rings under her eyes. She looked as if she'd been crying, and she avoided my eye.

"Valter," she said. "I've had time to think. We can't go on like this." She gazed into the distance and her lips quivered. She was wearing a blue silk blouse with yellow buttons.

"Perhaps you're right, Inge," I said, with a sigh of relief. "You're a sensible girl. We must think of what's best for you."

"There's something—something fine about you, Valter," she confessed softly, and she sought in vain for the right word. "Let's always be friends, shall we?" She held out her firm young hand spontaneously, and I pressed it warmly.

"Perhaps we'd better drop the Christian names during office hours," I suggested. "The staff might think it funny."

She looked at me with her limpid eyes. "Oh, Valter," she said with a low sigh. I moved swiftly to the other side of the desk. "You know I shall never forget you," I gabbled, and grasping the paperweight I began tapping it lightly on the desk top.

In the afternoon the old man walked in, unexpectedly as usual. He was in a remarkably good humor and his fine great nose was aglow. I explained what had been done in his absence, and he listened abstractedly as he shifted the things on the desk. His eyes were startlingly prominent, and not once did they meet mine. I read out extracts from some notes I'd got from a plastics expert, and he rattled his keys busily and dug into his pockets.

"It's the material of the future," he observed, taking an object from his right-hand waistcoat pocket and tapping the desk with it. He became more and more vehement, and to give emphasis to his words he knocked so hard that a piece of the object broke off. Startled, he opened his hand. In his palm lay a brown speckled pottery fish, one of whose eyes was modestly closed. A bit of its fin lay on the desk.

To cut a long story short: my former secretary is now my mother-in-law and wears mink. My wife and she are good friends, for my wife is a wise woman. But at times I feel embarrassed by those limpid eyes. The old man has begun to suffer from breathlessness, and his bulging eyes have sometimes a wavering look in them.

Goldilocks

1

Perhaps it's all a result of my having been born in sin. That sounds odd, and I'd better explain. I was the third child, and when I was born my father had been away from home for eighteen months. I was six months old when he returned, and he was far from pleased to see me. Mother was afraid he would kill me, for he was not remarkable for self-control—at least not when he'd been drinking. At that time he was still in the prime of life; black as the devil, as people said. He had shiny black hair and a black mustache. He cursed and swore, but he couldn't do anything to me then: I was too small. He and my mother got through that year together somehow, and later two more children were born, so that we were five in all. All survived, so sturdy were we, so stubborn our will to live; although even then there was war and famine in the world, although we were all crowded into one room and a kitchen in a wooden shack over the yard, and although my brothers sometimes screamed with hunger. Father drank. If it had not been for this we should have done well enough; he earned good wages when he was working; better than most other artisans.

The war took him abroad for two whole years. He wanted to earn more. He wanted change. He was restless. He was perhaps all the things that I am. For from my mother I inherit nothing; I take after my father, despite the fact that he was not my real father, and that already I differed in looks from the rest of the family. Father and the boys were dark and so was my mother; I alone was fair. "Goldilocks," I was later called, when I became what I became.

While he was away in Estonia and Poland, Father learned to drink and to enjoy a brawl, or so Mother said afterwards. I don't know if it was true. It may have been the shock of the home-coming that started him off, when he returned without the dreamed-of savings to find a stranger's six-months-old baby in the cradle at home: a silent child with downy fair hair. It must have been a queer sensation for him, for presumably he loved my mother; they had children after this. It was my quietness that annoyed him most, I believe. If I'd cried, if I'd yelled like other babies he might have been able to put up with me. But I was too quiet—unnaturally quiet—and this was something alien to him. He was the roaring, swearing type, and gave free expression to his feelings. My stillness got on his nerves, for perhaps there's nothing more disconcerting than an utterly silent, solemn, wide-eyed baby in arms.

From the time he came home my father drank, whether because of his foreign habits, because of Mother, or because of me I don't know. But drink he did, though he never became sodden enough to ruin his own life, or incur more than a fight now and again, and a fine or two. He never drank himself out of a job, for he was skilled in his trade and could handle men well when he chose, and so his drinking bouts were always pardoned. It was not until he was older that he became reserved and gloomy.

But it doesn't matter what he was like when he came home, for of course I remember nothing of him then. I was too small. I only know what Mother has told me. Who my real father was I never discovered; she kept it from me. I have no idea what sort of man he was—what whim, what aberration gave me life. I shall never know now; I can only imagine—dream, perhaps—though there was a time when I longed to know, so that I might spit in his face and claw his eyes out. This was childishness, of course. I don't feel like this any longer, though I sometimes fancy that he's still alive somewhere. It's not impossible: I'm not very old. Perhaps he lives here in the same town, not dreaming of my existence; for Mother never gave me the smallest reason to suppose that she met him again. Probably she never did. Children have sharp eyes—terribly sharp—and I should have felt it, known of it by invisible signs, if she had.

My real father, then, is a shadow. There is nothing to tell me what he looked like except my own face, the color of my hair, and perhaps my eyes. He must have been a good-looking fellow.

For I was pretty even as a child, and I knew it. Too soon and all too well I knew it, and it was therefore a mystery to me how my father could dislike me. God knows I exercised all my childish wiles to win his affection. When I was small I admired him above everything in the world, and never dreamed of course that he was not my real father. He was the finest person I knew. On Saturdays he spent a great deal of time changing his clothes and combing his hair. His hair was so black as to be blue. He would have had a drink or two by then, and as he stood smiling in front of the mirror he sang songs he had learned on his travels. He had a full, deep, manly singing voice—an irresistible voice—and the melancholy and passion of the foreign songs stirred me profoundly, though I didn't understand the words. God! It made me weak at the knees to see him, so strong was he, so dark and handsome! I would have given anything in the world for him to bend down to me just once and rub his freshly shaven, blue cheek against mine, as he sometimes did with the boys. And with Mother.

Then he would go out and not come back until late at night. He was another man then, at once frightening and fascinating, like a thunderstorm. We children would be already in bed and asleep, of course, but we were wakened by slamming doors. Mother put on the light and there would be Father, holding onto the doorpost with both hands, wild-eyed, wet-lipped, with a torn collar. Sometimes he brought other men in with him, to continue their carousing in our kitchen. This most often ended in a fight, which was why so few of our possessions were whole. The chairs limped, the table wobbled, and had to be propped up with blocks. Once Father was knifed, though not at home.

Of course I was afraid of him at times like these; but if I could I would creep out of bed and peer through the crack of the door into the kitchen. Some power within me impelled me to it, with curiosity and icy fear, knowing that if I were caught I should be dealt a blow that would deafen me and make my cheeks sting. When Mother was younger she would often get up and have a drink with the men. It was the only thing she could do, having no longer the power to control her husband. She lived in continual dread lest something terrible should happen to him. And so she took a nip sometimes on Saturday nights, though the other women in the block condemned her for it. But their condemnation was mixed with envy because of the dash, charm, and good looks of my father. And there was still a sparkle in Mother too, for all her five children. When we were older she took a job as office cleaner to bring in more money, for when Sunday was over there was little enough left for food. The rent Father paid regularly, however, and now and then if Mother nagged enough she was given money for clothes.

Not that Mother was a scold by nature. Why do I talk so much about Father when I have so much more reason to talk of her? She was certainly the more admirable of the two, though this never occurred to me while she was alive. Only when she was dead did it dawn on me that Mother would have been the proper object of my admiration. As a child I never thought much of her, nor indeed after her death, though reason told me that I had cause. Some unexplained contrariness in myself repelled me from her, although she would have liked to make much of me when my father and brothers were out of the way. Perhaps she felt she had wronged me by bringing me into the world, and wanted to atone for this by lavishing a larger share of affection upon me than upon her other children. But I cared nothing for her, and ungraciously warded off her attempts to fondle me.

Sometimes, when Father had had a good Saturday wage, he gave the boys money. To me he never gave anything, though I put myself forward ingratiatingly—never a farthing. When he'd gone and the boys had dashed out into the yard or the street, Mother always let me have at least as much as Father had given my brothers: a whole mark, or even two. She was careful to see that I was never given less than they were, even if she had to take it out of the housekeeping, and failed to realize that this secrecy merely embittered me and heightened my sense of injustice.

It wasn't the money I wanted, though it did mean cakes and lemonade and sweets, or a red hair ribbon. What I longed for was for *Father* to give me something. One coin from him would have been infinitely prized, whereas those I had from Mother I took with mulish sullenness.

At times I tried to comfort myself by imagining that Father thought I didn't need money because I was a girl. Perhaps he thought that only boys found use for it. But this explanation didn't console me. I felt, I was convinced in my heart, that Father looked upon me with ungentle eyes; he made it all too plain. If he happened to catch my beseeching gaze when he was giving something to the boys, a cold, hard look came into his eyes and he would turn away with a toss of his wild, dark head.

On Sunday afternoons it was his habit to lie half-dressed on the bed reading the paper. At such times he would take my smallest brother up beside him. The older boys knelt on the floor at the head of the bed while Father read and explained the comic strips to them. I would have given anything to lie beside him in my little brother's place—to lie close against him with my head on his shoulder and his arm round me. I used to imagine how I would stealthily let my face brush against his hard cheek, and how with a hard yet tender hand he would have squeezed my head and pinched me, as he did with the boys when they crowded too close.

There he lay, big, hung-over yet smiling, his breath still sour with the spirits he had drunk, an opened beer bottle on the floor by his bed; and I loved and worshipped him as only a little girl can love her father. I knelt at the foot of the bed out of sight, and under cover of the newspaper I sometimes laid my hand very lightly on his legs. Yet he would notice it and kick out.

"For Christ's sake what's the girl gaping at!" he would exclaim. "Get to hell out of here!"

I can't remember that he ever spoke to me without swearing.

Thus I grew up as a stranger in my own home; every day Father made me feel it in one way or another, until even my brothers withdrew from me and wouldn't let me share in their games. Mother would have liked to make it up to me, but it was not *her* tenderness I wanted. On the contrary, when I saw that my sullenness and obstinacy saddened her, I increased them in revenge for Father's indifference to me. It was childish, pitiful, hopeless. Just as Father shunned me, so did I try to shun my mother—with agony in my breast, with an aching throat and eyelids smarting with tears. But I never shed those tears.

Life is mad. I can't bear to recall for how many years I waged this futile war, but one Saturday when Father had gone out and the boys were tormenting a cat in the yard, Mother offered me money and I struck her hand, sending coins rolling all over the floor; then with sobs and screams I fled. I wept for a while in the woodshed; then went out into the street and never came home until the boys had had their supper and gone to bed. From that day I sought fun and friends in the street and hated my home; but it was only the dreary hatred of a despised child, and it hurt me more than anyone else. Yes, after that day I sought my fun in the street, and learned all the ugliness and evil that it has to teach: the foul words, the malice, the pilfering, and the unrest. By this time I was attending the primary school and the bigger boys tried to paw me about; but their hugs left me cold for I was still a child. I was unawakened, a child longing for tenderness. And this was not tenderness.

But on Saturday nights I would crouch on the bare floor, shivering with cold and biting my fists, to watch Father come home and Mother take a nip from the bottle he brought. Her eyes shone then and her cheeks were flushed, and she was beautiful. They wrangled together; she took off her clothes and made him undress too and come to bed. But when the light was out I lay as if on glowing embers, listening to every sound, hating Mother and her sighs and laughter in the darkness. I was afraid of my father and I hated my mother with so violent and suffocating a hatred that when at last I fell asleep, my sleep was more like a swoon.

2

Mother carried her secret—my secret—to the grave, and I shall never know who my real father was. When she was dead I would often torture myself with self-reproach for not having made her tell me the truth. But these regrets were futile, for she would never have spoken, old, frail, and blind though she became. Mother was strangely proud and silent. She never complained, or called for help, though in later years Father often beat her when he was drunk. She held her head up and kept her own counsel so long as she was able to work; it was not until her sight failed that she gave in.

But I can still remember her smile: it was the unconsciously alluring smile of a woman aware of her own power, and proud of it. A smile that caught my father's eye and compelled him to smile back. And although in his absence she was untrue to him, I am sure she sinned with an air, in the full realization of what she was about, and in the conviction that it was worth the price. Yet I suspect she never thought of me; I was an accident, a mistake, a cruel trick. It seems to me quite possible that she met that man only once and never wanted to see him again. But there must have been something very special about him to induce her to be false to Father and to herself.

Or was it merely that Father had been away too long

and that Mother was a young woman, caught in a moment of weakness? I believe, though, that she smiled the same smile then: abstracted, unconscious. But why worry about something I shall never know? At the reformatory I used to daydream sometimes; and in bed after the whispering had died down, I would lie awake with my eyes closed, speculating about my unknown father and imagining all sorts of things about him.

At the time, my mother had been a cleaner in a hotel; so much I knew. My father might be some blond Russian officer, perhaps a prince, who boarded his warship next morning never to return. Or he was perhaps an eminent landowner visiting Helsinki on business. This was a fancy that charmed me mightily, and I pictured a lean, distinguished-looking, gray-haired man riding along the edge of a plowed field on a splendid horse towards a big white house, followed by a loping setter, against a vivid autumn sky. Such were my fancies then, and I had no desire whatever to scratch his eyes out, or even to spit in his face.

These were of course absurd and childish notions. My father can have been nothing like this. He was most likely a perfectly ordinary citizen of Helsinki of the type I know all too well, with pouches under the eyes, a face puffy with alcohol and rich food, with one hand in his wallet pocket and the other busy unbuttoning some girl's blouse. God knows, I may even have slept with him at one time or another in those worst years.

No, I won't think of him like this either. To me he's a mere shadow, a possibility, and it's better that I should know nothing. My eyes, my own face, are my only clue to him, and there's a grain of consolation in knowing that he was good-looking, and probably of finer clay than the legal father, whom I loved. Mother never spoke of him, which means I never really knew her either; anyone with any pride lives and dies unknown to even his nearest and dearest. But at what a cost is this pride preserved!

By the time I was ten I knew I was pretty, better-looking than my brothers—better-looking than anyone of my age in our street. I used to eye myself in the glass like a monkey and tie ribbons in my hair, detesting my shabby clothes, darned stockings and broken shoes. I wanted to be beautiful because then Father might get to like me—he might even relent so far as to stroke my cheek now and then. My playground might now be the pavements, my lips might now be inured to coarseness, I might now have become infected by the fever of the streets—yet still I burned with an unquenchable desire to win his affection.

I had dark eyebrows that needed no blackening with charred matchsticks, as was the practice of others of my age. I had brilliant dark eyes, and my hair—when I had learned to wash and brush it properly—was of a dazzling fairness. Even the older boys loafing at street corners used to whistle after me as I passed, and offer me a puff at their cigarettes. I was glib and noisy—I who had been so silent as a baby—I yelled and racketed about like the other girls, as if from some inward compulsion to be even livelier, noisier, more violent than the rest. I was a little savage: I teased, fought, kicked, and bit—and yet it was not really I who did these things. I didn't like the street; it was something quite different I yearned for: kindness at my father's hands. Yet it seemed to me that if I shrieked louder, ran faster, bit more wildly, something inside me would close up and I should feel better.

At thirteen I became a woman. I'd been waiting for this with impatience, and also with shame. The man-woman relationship was not foreign to my mind. Boys had pawed me and the older girls had told me, sniggering, all I needed to know—or rather all I ought not to have learned in that

manner. Mother had said nothing to prepare me. No
doubt she lacked the right words, as many women do. But
I needed no help from her. I wasn't frightened when it
happened; on the contrary I triumphed. I was something
more now. I steadied and became quieter, with a sense of
having been initiated into a new realm of warmth and
delight.

We were so overcrowded at home that it was impossible
for me to keep the matter to myself. My brothers made
faces and teased me, but I was unmoved—indeed I ignored
them. I was a woman now. I began to choose my company; wild games no longer amused me. I entered on a
mute, dreamy phase and began indulging in vague fantasies about the future awaiting me by virtue of my
pretty face. My limbs were straight, my body developed
as the months passed and my waist grew slender. I began
to sense something of my power. The boys who once used
to pinch me now looked sheepish when they met my eye,
and didn't know what to do with their hands. The grocer's
son took me to the cinema and gave me raisins and sweets
from the shop. There was something immensely attractive
in the idea that I could get something for nothing.

One Saturday when Father had come home and, without changing his clothes, sat down to his meal, I went up
to him. I had made myself as attractive as I could; I had
combed my curly hair and tied it with a red ribbon, and
was wearing a blouse and skirt like a grown girl. Father
had had a drink or two before he came home, and had
put the bottle in the lobby cupboard. He was in a good
humor. Quaking with suspense I pressed myself against
him, put my arms round his neck and let my cheek touch
his.

"Father," I said with a shy smile, "I've got a new blouse
on."

He looked at me and his mirth left him. His eyes grew hard, he shoved me roughly away and stared at me for a long time. Then he looked at my mother and cursed, and with a thrust at the table that set the plates rattling he rose, though he was only halfway through his meal, picked up his hat, and went out. On his way he took the bottle from the cupboard. Mother gazed stonily after him, then turned to me and began absently fingering my hair ribbon and straightening my blouse at the back. So shaken and unhappy was I that I never even edged away from her as I usually did.

In itself there was nothing extraordinary in Father's going out on a Saturday night without bothering to tidy himself or change. The depression was then at its worst; it had made him reserved and bitter, and he never smiled now until after the first few drinks. Although he escaped unemployment, he was earning less than formerly, and little by little our home was deteriorating. When I was fourteen I left school and went out to work.

By then I was being invited out to dances and longed desperately to have money of my own, so as to buy better clothes, thinner stockings, prettier shoes. I didn't mind having to find a job; it was rather thrilling—just as it was thrilling to let the boys hug me and kiss me after dances, and fumble at my blouse. I was quite cool and indifferent myself, and when, thinking they'd gone far enough, I slipped adroitly from their grasp, leaving them panting and swearing, I reveled in my sense of power and superiority.

A job also enabled me to get away from home, into new streets among new people. I became an errand girl at a carpet dealer's in the center of the town. Mother found me the situation, and I was to have four hundred marks a month. The owner of the shop was a foreigner and he scrutinized me closely with a veiled, close-bitten expression on his shiny face. He seemed to me a very grand old gentleman, for he wore flashing rings and a gorgeous tie. I worked hard for him for a fortnight, and enjoyed it, for my work took me to many different shops and offices where everyone, especially the men, were kind to me.

The carpet dealer too liked looking at me, and I would smile and coquet with him as well as I knew how. Both my mother and I had lied about my age, for I could easily pass for sixteen and there were few jobs going at that time, even for errand girls. It was now the summer; the merchant had sent his family into the country, and one day when he was at a meeting he rang up the shop and asked me to bring a number of papers and invoices round to his flat.

I was thrilled. I tidied myself as well as I could, deploring my worn shoes and darned silk stockings; but the summer green of the trees was so fresh and gay that I was soon humming to myself and almost dancing along the street. My employer lived in a fine block in a residential suburb, and he opened the door to me himself when I rang. He was in shirt sleeves, his face glistened and smiled, and he smelled of hair lotion, spirits, and cigars.

He asked me to come in and said I need be in no hurry to go back to the shop. The flat was the grandest and most expensive I had ever seen; there were deep armchairs, Oriental carpets, tall pier glasses, and gilded console tables. I felt shy and walked on tiptoe, thankful that his family was in the country and that he was alone here. I should have had no idea how to behave if his wife had come in.

He invited me to sit down and offered me chocolates from a newly opened box. "Take as many as you like," he said kindly. "You're a pretty girl, Maire. How old are you?"

"Seventeen," I lied, and smiled at him as sweetly and alluringly as I could.

"Seventeen," he repeated, and a gleam came into the coffee-brown eyes. Laying his hand on my knee he pressed it gently and looked suddenly sleepy. "Take off your coat," he said. "You haven't got to rush off anywhere." He drew off my knitted cap and in doing so let his hands touch my hair. "I'll show you some nice pictures," he said.

I was flattered and a little dazed by his polite attention, by the chocolates, and the luxurious surroundings. He brought a big German book and laid it on my lap; then sitting on the arm of my chair with one hand on my shoulder, he turned the pages. But at the sight of them I went hot and cold all over, for those pictures were all photographs of naked men and women making love. I was so horrified that I dared not look at him, and pushed the book away. But he held my shoulders, seemingly amused by my dismay, and went on turning the pages in an attempt to force me to look. I was numb with horror and afraid of angering him. But when he pressed me down under himself in the chair I screamed. There was nothing else I could do, and the screams were a relief, so I continued at the top of my voice.

He lay upon me with all his weight and pressed one hand over my mouth, but I bit his hand and managed to tear myself free. Blinded by tears I dashed away, found the door somehow and raced down the stairs still yelling at the top of my voice and paying no attention when he shouted after me.

I was too badly frightened to return to the shop, and simply wandered about the streets not even daring to go home. But home I must go at last, and since my coat and hat were still at my employer's flat I had to come out with the whole story. For once my father took my part and having asked me for the address he set off. When he came back he had my coat and hat and four hundred marks—a whole month's wages—though I hadn't held the job for more than a fortnight.

Terrified though I had been I was soon ashamed of my fears, and I lay awake many summer nights thinking about the naked photographs and about the plump, beringed hand that pushed me back in the armchair. It made me hot and flustered and I shut my eyes tight—yet I couldn't help thinking of what had happened.

Later on, when some boy or other saw me home one evening and wanted to kiss me under the archway, I pressed against him, responded violently to his kisses and allowed him to fumble a little nervously. Then something seemed to stab me in the pit of my stomach; I tore myself loose and rushed away.

3

In my next job I had no better luck. Father found me work in a shoe shop and one evening the storeman told me to stay on overtime when the others had gone; then locked the door and tried to assault me. But this time I was not so frightened; I clawed and kicked and shrieked until he had to let me go. Father once more picked up his hat and went to beat the fellow up, but I had to leave. When Father came home afterwards with the corner of his eye cut and blood on his forehead he looked at me somberly and said, "You'll be a whore like your mother. It's not the men's fault: you egg them on. But I'd rather thrash you to death than see that happen."

He gave me a look that convinced me he'd be as good

as his word if I did anything to bring shame upon him.
For a time I was without work; then I became an assistant
at a florist's. The wages were only fifty marks a month and
the woman who owned the shop was harsh and exacting,
but Mother wanted me to stay on there so that at least I
shouldn't be idle. The idea was that I should be taught
how to make wreaths and so learn a trade, but the woman
taught me little enough, nor did I care to learn; I preferred to dream away my time with visions of cars and
films and money and boys and beautiful rooms. The other
assistant in the shop was a girl older than myself named
Viola; she taught me to use powder and lipstick and told
me ways in which a pretty girl could earn money, given a
little luck. It was gloomy in the shop, and mostly I was
employed on errands outside. This meant trudging about
the streets all day ringing doorbells, for a miserable wage.
But now and then I was given a tip so that I could buy
silk stockings, and Viola let me have a pair of her old
shoes, though they were rather too big for me. I dared not
give notice, but I wasted a lot of time in the town and the
woman called me lazy and scatterbrained, and prophesied
that I should take to evil ways. But perhaps I wouldn't
have been so lazy if she'd paid me a fair wage.

Father had begun to observe me more closely than before, and one Saturday night he caught me in the archway
kissing the grocer's son. I was terrified, but Father said
nothing at the time, for he was with another man. They
went up the steps into our place, banging the doors. It
was midnight, but so light—being summer—that he must
have recognized me.

Not for a long time did I venture to creep in after him,
but he only laughed when I entered the kitchen, and said
to his companion, "Well, she made it at last." They were
both very drunk and Mother was not in the kitchen.

"Show us how you do your kissing, then—you seem to have learned how," he went on. He was always full of notions, and I didn't know whether he was being malicious or not, or whether he was just so drunk that he'd forgotten he hated me. "Ugh," I said, as the other fellow in his grimy working clothes leaned forward. But I was so dazed by father's jocular attention that I let the stranger hold me and kiss me, twisting my head away to look at Father.

"What's that supposed to be?" he cried, with a raucous, tipsy laugh. "That's no good. Come here and I'll show you."

He drew me to him. My strength left me as he bent me backwards, pressed his mouth to mine and kissed me. None of the boys I knew could kiss like that. He kissed me as a man kisses a woman, and I went moist and limp in his arms. Such was the one kiss he ever gave me, but there was no tenderness in it—only hatred. He released me so abruptly that I had to steady myself against the wall, while he looked at me malignantly, his face swollen with excitement and alcohol. Then he hissed, "I guessed you were that sort! But remember, Maire, I'd rather kill you with my own hands than see you come to that."

I was still too much of a child to understand, but when he packed me off to bed in a rage I still seemed to feel his sinewy arms round me and knew that no one else had ever kissed me in that way. I still felt his firm lips against mine. Something sweet and terrible seemed to have happened; perhaps after all Father was fond of me? For my sake he had braved the great merchant and fought the storeman. I thought of all the characteristics in him that I admired: his strength, his violent temperament, his boldness, and his moods, and to this day I believe that if he had shown me any kindness or affection at that time, I should have turned out very differently from the way I did.

But after that evening he was more hostile than ever. Next day he tore up my pretty blouse and my hair ribbon, saying, "I'm going to keep an eye on you, Maire." From now on he watched me, forbade me to stir out in the evenings, to go to the cinema with a boy, or to dance. Sometimes after work he went out into the street just to keep me in sight; and if, all unsuspecting, I happened to meet him when I was laughing and talking with the grocer's son, he dragged at my arm, led me home, struck me, and threatened to thrash any boy he met in my company. It was not long therefore before the boys sheered off.

But if I sat demurely at home reading library books, he took no notice of me except to glare, or to snap at me if I happened to get in his way. His behavior goaded me into doing the very things he forbade me to do; for then at least he was compelled to notice me, think about me, and watch me. And I wanted him to think about me. I don't remember now all I felt, but I do know I would cheerfully have endured a beating if by this means I could have won a moment of his attention. It seemed almost as if he did like me after all, since he went to such trouble to watch me.

Nevertheless I made efforts to be good and stay in at night. I tried to sew and read, and whenever I'd been given a tip for delivering flowers I would bring the money home and lay it before him. But he only swept it aside with a curse. And so as soon as his back was turned I ran out into the streets again, and since I dared not hang around our own neighborhood I took to visiting Viola, and going to dances with her. But afterwards I always said good-bye to my escort before we reached the corner of our street, and aching from his kisses I went panting and trembling home by myself, fearing—and secretly hoping—

that Father would be sitting up waiting for me. Yes, I feared and hoped at the same time.

Sometimes when I came home like this Father beat me until I was bruised all over, and I cried. I never uttered a sound while he was doing it; but afterwards I lay trembling in bed, my face wet with tears, feeling the pain of the blows and still hearing the dance music; and thus the pain turned to a sort of dreadful pleasure, as I lay thinking of Father, sick from the kisses and the blows.

These things happened in quick succession during the short summer; I played truant more often every week and sometimes stayed away for nights on end. Mother could restrain me no longer, for I ignored her remonstrances. One Sunday the grocer's son took me into the country. His family had had a party the night before, and he had got hold of some wine which he brought with him in a lemonade bottle. It was brown, sweet wine; we both drank it, while the sun beat down on the burning rocks and the breeze blew from the sea. I turned dizzy from the wine and let him kiss me and touch me with his clumsy hands, and he whispered in my ear, "There's not another girl in the whole world like you, Maire."

But I cared nothing for him; I simply approved of his being well-dressed and always having money to spend; I approved of his attending high school and studying to graduate—which by the way he never did. His touch meant nothing to me; I lay still on the hot rock with my eyes closed while he stroked my arms and legs. I was thinking then that life might be wonderful after all, and that splendid things might be in store for me because I was pretty —prettier than other people—even though I did live in a wooden hovel in a back yard with a father who drank and a mother who was a charwoman. I had read books from the library and always tried to talk like the characters in those books whenever I met a boy who didn't know me and was unaware that I had grown up in a back yard. Such was I at fourteen; no better and certainly no worse. I might have enjoyed working if I could have earned a decent wage; I might have gone to evening classes and studied Swedish and tried to enter a commercial school, if only Father had encouraged me and been fond of me. If he'd been fond of me I could have done anything, for I was still young and pliable, and always ready to admire him, for all his drunkenness and moodiness.

But I was pretty, which gave me self-assurance and inclined me to flirt, as I was now doing with the grocer's son. There must have been something in me that egged them on, as Father said, though it was unconscious on my part. I've since fancied that if I'd cut off my hair and worn shoes and stockings with holes in them and had dirty hands, it would have been all the same: men would have been attracted to me, whether I'd wanted it or not.

Having once experienced the feeling of exaltation that wine gave me I wanted to try it again. Wine freed me; it made me feel the world was mine and that nothing could stand in my way. I began taking nips from the bottles that the boys brought to the dances, though this was not wine but diluted alcohol. Horrible though it tasted I drank out of defiance, because Father did; but I never had more than just enough to make the boys talk about me and to shock the gossips.

I hardly know how it all happened or why, but I believe Father suspected even then that he was mortally ill. The boys had grown up and the two eldest were at work; Mother had aged and her gray cheeks no longer flushed when he frolicked with her. And perhaps he'd had enough of our home in the back yard, of the shabby furniture and ragged bedding, and felt that his life was running down.

Brooding over this—contemplating me through his darkness—he felt that I was to blame for it all, and hated me. At any rate, for a week he was gloomy and hardly spoke, and on Saturday he never even had his meal with us, but went straight out to drink, so that I was able to wash and change and comb my hair and make up my mouth in peace, to go dancing.

Viola had shown me the place. It was an old stable building near the shore, not far from where we lived. It had been hung with gay paper lanterns and people danced there on summer evenings. Not that it was a particularly pleasant place, for a lot of drinking and brawling went on there, and some time later it was closed down by the police. But it seemed to me great fun, and although the other girls were older and more experienced than myself, this only made it more exciting to dance there and pretend to be older than I was. None of the men there did me any harm, or wanted to; they just laughed and fooled around and jokingly offered me a pull at their bottles.

But that evening some scandal-mongering woman, shocked to the core, went to Mother and said, "You'd better keep a sharper eye on your daughter. She's reeling about in those stables, dancing and hanging round the boys—and it's not doing them any good either."

Father had come home early and was sitting gloomily befuddled with his hands on his knees, listening. He stood up then, saying, "By God, what I've said I'll do! I'm going to bash the life out of her." It was useless for Mother to hang on his arm; he swore and pushed her over, and having fetched a hatchet from the woodshed he slipped it under his coat and set off down the street, steadying himself against the walls.

Mother knew that if he caught me he'd kill me. Overcome with dread she took a short cut through the yards and reached the stables before him. She dragged me away in the middle of a dance, though I struggled and indeed swore, for I was perhaps a little drunk, as the old gossip had said, though I didn't realize it at the time.

Mother wept—a rare thing with her—and babbled the whole way, "Maire love, you must hide or Father'll kill you." Defiantly I retorted, "Let him get on with it then, and you'll both be rid of me. You all hate me anyhow."

Mother said, "Hurry now, run, child; Father's on his way and he took the hatchet with him."

Mention of the hatchet scared me, and instead of slipping away from her as I could easily have done I went on with her to the wall of the dark churchyard, where we were well hidden. It was August. We stumbled over heaps of rubbish by the wall and sat down with our backs against it in the warm grass. Mother wept, and so did I a little.

"I've done nothing wrong," I told her. "I've done nothing wrong at all."

"You've been drinking," said Mother sorrowfully. "I can smell it in your breath, though I didn't believe what the old creature said. Don't try to deny it!"

"What about Father, then; doesn't he drink?" I retorted. But my defiance melted when I saw how grieved Mother was, and I added defensively, "I only did it for fun, because the boys were teasing me. There was no harm in just a sip. I did so want a little fun. At home you do nothing but shove me out of the way." I was sorrowful now too and began to cry, for I was only a child. I laid my head in Mother's lap and wept and said, "Mother, I'm not bad. Why does Father hate me so? He's never said a kind word to me so long as I can remember, and now he wants to kill me. Is he mad or am I?"

But Mother only moaned, "We'll hide you tonight, my dear; you mustn't come home till he's sober."

I caught both her hands in mine and thrust her back against the wall.

"For God s sake, Mother, won't you tell me why Father's so angry with me? Nobody in the world has such a terrible father as I have; I can't do anything right for him, however hard I try. And I have tried—you know I have!"

I doubt if Mother would ever have told me if we hadn't found ourselves alone together in the dark like this. Before us the sky was aglow with the lights of the town, and perhaps in looking at this glow Mother was overcome by a sense of futility. For these were the lights of a city in the grip of the depression—a city full of poverty, prostitution, and smuggled liquor—and she saw perhaps no future for herself but increasing age, destitution, and lingering death. Therefore she said,

"It's my fault, child. I ought to have told you before, so you might have understood and been more careful. He's not your father. You were born when he'd been away eighteen months; I didn't even know whether he was coming back. You were born of my sin and it's not you he hates, but me in you, because he couldn't help loving me still and having more children by me. That's how it is, Maire love. I've wronged him and you. Can you forgive me?"

But I was mute. I was still too young even to have imagined such a thing, although all my life I'd known that there was something ugly between Father and me. All my giddiness drained from me, leaving me cold. I felt emptiness and space—I felt a sort of death as I stared at that glow in the sky. There was no need to grope among my thoughts and sort out what Mother had told me; in an instant everything was clear. I understood it as if I'd experienced it myself, and only wondered why I hadn't seen it all before. I was mute, therefore, and Mother held my cold hands in her work-hardened ones, sobbing softly as she went on to speak of what I've already told about my birth. But of my real father she said nothing, nor did I ask; I had enough to cope with in what I'd already heard. The revelation lay like a gaping wound within me—such a wound as is barely felt so long as one lies still, though at the slightest movement it gives excruciating pain. So I sat quite still and silent against the churchyard wall, while Mother held my hands and sobbed.

4

We sat there in the warm grass for perhaps two hours. It was late and the glimmer above the town slowly faded as the lights below went out. At last Mother said, "What's to be done with you now, Maire my dear? I daren't take you home."

I pressed my hands together and said, "Don't worry, Mother; I shan't ever come home again. You needn't be anxious about me." Alarmed, she began protesting and I said, coolly and sensibly, "What would be the good of my coming home? He'd beat me to death sooner or later, when he was angry. And that wouldn't do, with two boys in the house younger than me, because he'd be sent to prison. He's a bit crazy from drinking so much and brooding over this all these years; and he's been having a hard time of it too, now we're poor. I'll go to Viola's tonight and perhaps she'll let me stay with her. I'll manage somehow if you'll let me have my clothes. But I never want to see Father again."

I talked quite dispassionately, and perhaps I thought in this way too; yet somewhere in my hidden self there was a terrible, searing sensation that I couldn't explain or even understand. It spoke, so that the words I was uttering became a mere empty shell—a semblance—compared with this secret voice. All I knew was that I never wanted to see Father again, since he was not my true father.

At the same time I felt stunned by the cold, empty sensation of being free—freer than other people—and by the realization that it rested with me to steer my life either to hell or to heaven, without asking anyone's advice or leave. For in telling me what she had, Mother lost her power over me; I determined to obey her no longer, no matter what she said. Were I to return home and live there as before, some irreparable disaster would be bound to follow. Father might kill me, or something even worse might happen; for in and around me everything would fall to pieces. Thus I felt and thought; and Mother made no further objections, but assented to my going to Viola's for the night and promised to send on my clothes.

Yet no sooner had we agreed on this than I was ready to weep at the knowledge that suddenly, at the age of fourteen, I was free. My throat tightened and burned, but I wouldn't let Mother see me cry, since I was now to be in charge of my own life. For the first time for many years I felt affection for her; I remembered that *she* had never hated me or been anything but kind, though I had shunned her kindness. Had she not reason to hate me? Had I not been constantly before her eyes, a perpetual reminder of the sin for which Father in his heart would never forgive her? But Mother never hated me; she was too strong for that, and therefore admirable. No doubt she judged me by herself and allowed me to go out into the world because she was confident that I should make my own way as successfully as she had at my age. But I was not like her; there was that in my nature which was as formidable in its way as Father, though I didn't know it then.

Some time after midnight we left the churchyard wall. First I went hand in hand with her part of the way home; I dared not go all the way lest Father might still be waiting for me with the hatchet. But Mother had not the heart to leave me, and in her turn accompanied me all the way to Viola's lodging, with my hand in hers. Viola lived in a house with a paved yard; the iron gate into this was shut, but I could open it by slipping my hand between the bars and working the bolt along; and so I got in. Only then did Mother turn and set off for home.

Viola's room had a separate entrance. At this time she had no roommate, and I thought she might let me stay with her until I'd earned enough to pay my share of the rent. She was scared by the knock on the door so late at night and at first was reluctant to answer it, for she had a man with her. But I went on knocking for so long, having nowhere else to go, that at last she was compelled to open the door. She hadn't much on and she'd been drinking.

"What a fright you gave me, Maire!" she said. "My landlady will throw me out if she hears us."

I was ashamed at having disturbed her when she had her fiancé there for the night—for I assumed that was who it must be. But Viola said to him, "You needn't worry about Maire. I must let her in—her father's thrown her out of the house."

I told them how Father had come after me with a hatchet, and being fuddled they both pitied me and made a fuss of me. They offered me a drink too, but I didn't want one and was unwilling to disturb them any further; so Viola made up a bed for me on the floor, and when they'd put the light out they took no further notice of me. I was so tired that I paid no attention to them either, and despite my curiosity fell asleep at once. I never woke until the man was leaving next morning, and then Viola wanted to go to sleep again, since it was Sunday. When we woke the second time I went to the dairy for milk and then brewed coffee for Viola, and she showed me the hundred-mark note the man had given her, saying, "I feel a bit mean taking money from them, but what the hell can I do when I'm behind with the rent?"

I asked, "Where did you find him?" and she answered, "In the street." And we said no more about it, but had a cozy time together, drinking quantities of coffee and spreading big sandwiches for ourselves; I felt freer than ever before, though somewhere inside was a wound I was afraid to touch. Yet at times I was even happy during my stay with Viola, for I was too young to worry about the future, and I loved the town as it was in August with its hot streets and its dark green trees in the parks; and I reveled in having so much time to myself.

I dared not go back to the florist's, for Father might have come looking for me there, but Viola said, "I know how we can make some money." Every day when the shop closed she would bring back a quantity of flowers—those which were fading and would have been thrown away. We made them up into bunches, put them in a basket and sold them from door to door. This was illegal, of course, but being young and gay we never thought of that. It was exciting to ring the bell and see who would open the door. Women usually slammed it in our faces, and sometimes snapped at us as well, but if men answered the bell they often bought our flowers. They were mostly those whose families had gone into the country, and who were either bored or having a good time: it made no difference which.

Once we were invited in and given crayfish and wine, and often we were asked to step inside with our flowers. Viola wouldn't always do this, and used her own discretion as to when we might venture in and when not.

In this way I earned enough to pay Viola my share of the rent. Clothes I never troubled about, as I was content to be a flower seller and nothing more. Besides, it was best not to be too well dressed for this job. So I went bare-legged in a short, ragged skirt and spent all my money on food, for so much walking made me very hungry. During the day I roamed the streets or played at keeping house in our room. It was magnificent to have a whole room to ourselves, and I swept and dusted it vigorously, aired the bedding on the little balcony and beat our bits of carpet in the yard. I was happy and carefree with Viola; I seldom thought about my family and felt indeed as if I had escaped from something dark and evil.

During that period I fell in love for the first time. I must tell how it happened, for it was quite serious, and if circumstances had been different I might have loved very deeply. One evening when we rang a doorbell it was answered by a man in overalls. I offered him my flowers, smiling as prettily as I could, and Viola smiled too, though she kept more in the background. He was a dark, cheerful-looking man with curly hair and shining white teeth, and he said laughing, "But this is great luck; I was just wanting some flowers, and I'll buy some if we can agree about the price. Perhaps you ladies would care to come in while we talk business?"

I glanced at Viola, who nodded, so I stepped inside with my basket on my arm, Viola following. Talking all the time the man showed us into a big, light room full of books and tobacco smoke, where there was a table strewn with drawings. He told us he was an architect and was at the moment designing a house. He jokingly handed us cigarettes and regretted he had nothing else in the flat to offer us; we said we didn't want anything, but he promised to be better supplied when next we called. Then he pretended to choose his flowers very carefully, to find fault with them and to beat down the price. But it was only in fun; he smiled and kept looking at me, so we stood firm and he paid what we asked, digging the money carelessly from his waistcoat pocket. He was as polite to us as if we'd been grand ladies, and when we left he opened the door for us.

Some days later when it was raining and our feet were wet and we hadn't sold a thing, Viola said, "Shall we go and see the architect?" I was overjoyed, though at the same time rather nervous of bothering him again so soon. But we went straight to the house where he lived, though it lay in quite a different part of the town. We were both drenched when we arrived, and my broken shoes were squelching.

He looked surprised to see us, then remembering he said, "Ah, you've guessed that my flowers are dead. I appreciate your thoughtfulness. Come in, won't you, and let me offer you something better this time."

Bowing deeply he showed us in and spread our coats out to dry. "Let's celebrate the rain together," he said, and having switched on the lights and poured wine into small glasses he put on a gramophone record. The wine warmed us gloriously; I felt as if summer had come again and I was lying on warm rocks by the seashore. Viola laughed and talked but I could say little; I felt solemn and reverent in the face of so much kindness. Every time I ventured to look up at him I met his warm, twinkling eye. We stayed for at least an hour and he talked to us as if we'd been grown-up ladies from his own world. Viola shot him bold glances, and I was jealous of every word he spoke to her. Yet I felt that in talking to her it was myself he was addressing, and this was an intoxicating sensation. I was unsure of myself, however, and really felt shyer of him now than I did the first time, in spite of the wine. He prudently gave us no more than two small glasses each.

After that evening I thought about him for days on end —about his kind face and twinkling eyes and the grasp of his hard hand when we said good-bye. I looked forward to the day when I might go and see him again, and decided to tell him that he needn't buy flowers from us every time if he didn't want to. But when I talked of him to Viola she said, "You can go alone next time, Maire. It's you he wants to see, not me."

I glowed at these words. I protested and vowed that I would never go there by myself, but in reality it was what I longed above everything to do. I had already been puzzling over how it was to be managed, for I was jealous and wanted to be alone with him if he should ask me in. That evening Viola and I toiled up and down many staircases, until at last she gave me a nudge and said, "Perhaps the architect will buy the rest. Go along and see; I've got some other things to do."

I went, and my heart thumped in my breast as I climbed the stairs to his door, both from my dread of bothering him and my intense shyness. I'm relating all this at length because it seemed to me very beautiful, and I have nothing else of beauty to relate. He opened the door himself and said, "Ah, Miss Goldilocks is alone this time. Where's your friend?" I looked at him, almost too shy to smile, and stammered that Viola had gone elsewhere. I wanted to add that he needn't buy any flowers if he didn't want to, because only the worst were left; but he took the basket from my hand and led me in, saying, "How few you have left! I'll take them all, and then you won't have to climb any more dark staircases today."

He never even asked the price of the flowers, but drew a crumpled note from his pocket and held it out to me. I felt horribly embarrassed, because I hadn't wanted any money from him at all. I said, "That's far too much," but he wouldn't take it back; and I arranged the flowers in his vase as well as I knew how. For he had gone at once to fetch a vase and fill it in the bathroom; and while I was arranging the flowers for him he stood beside me, touching my hair and smiling and saying softly, "Goldilocks." When his hand touched my cheek I started as if it had burned me, and thinking I was afraid he moved a little away from me. "I expect you'd like to go now," he said; but I shook my head. "I don't want to go yet," I said, "unless I'm in the way."

He stood looking at me with his head on one side and whistling softly to himself. Then the smile faded from his face; he looked grave and stared right through me into some far distance. "What will become of you, little one?" he said as I looked up at him and adored him. For I did adore him, though he must have been twice my age; I can find no better word for it. Then he laid his arm lightly round me and kissed me gently and kindly on the lips. An almost physical pain cut through me, so desperately did I wish that he would seize me in his arms and kiss me as one kisses the person one really loves. But he led me over to a chair and fetched me a glass of wine.

"Child, child!" he said, but I felt the searing pain of love and longing, and answered stubbornly, "I'm not a child any longer." Then he bent down again and kissed me, and stroked me very gently, meaning me no harm. I parted my lips when he kissed me, but he wouldn't kiss like that.

"How old are you, Goldilocks?" he asked. I wouldn't—couldn't lie to him, and whispered, "Nearly fifteen." He gave a little start and looked round as if afraid that someone might have seen us. "I see," he said, smiling again. I thought you were older. You've developed early. Well, what's to become of you? Don't you know you're a very dangerous girl?"

"How am I dangerous?" I inquired in astonishment. He demanded sharply, "Does your friend know that you're here with me?" I was frightened and stammered that if he thought it best I could tell Viola that he wasn't in when I rang the bell. He smiled then and said, "I don't want to believe anything bad of you, Goldilocks, but I've heard there are two girls in the town—one's under sixteen, and they go about together; the young one offers things for sale at the door while the other hides on the stairs, waiting."

I had no idea what he meant, and he explained, "For instance, if I touched you now and you screamed for help, the other girl might come and threaten to report me to the police, and blackmail me; because one can be put in prison for molesting children."

I stared at him in horrified dismay, and my cheeks burned. I said, "I'd rather die than do such a thing to you. No one has ever been so good to me as you."

"Tell me about yourself, Goldilocks. How do you come to be with a girl like that?"

I told him what my home had been like and how Father had chased me with a hatchet because I'd had a drink with the boys and let them hug me, and that therefore I hadn't dared go home again. I also explained that he wasn't my real father, though this was something I never thought I could tell a living soul. He listened attentively and then

said, "Soon it'll be winter and you won't be able to sell
flowers any more. What will you do then?"

I answered cheerfully, "Oh, I'll manage somehow."
Then a mad, childish hope sprang up in me, and with a
strained smile I suggested, "Let me be your maid during
the winter. I could do the housework—and I can cook too."
He jumped, but I went on, "I don't want any wages; just
a corner to sleep in and my food. I'd be quite all right if
I was here."

He stroked my hair absently, as one might stroke a
puppy, and said regretfully, "No, my dear, that wouldn't
do. I'm married and I've got two children—they're all in
the country now. My wife's delicate, you see, and in the
autumn the climate of Helsinki doesn't suit her. Didn't
you know I was married, Goldilocks?"

At this something snapped inside me—but perhaps he
was just teasing me, rather cruelly. In an attempt to
breathe life into my dying hope I said dubiously, "You
don't wear a ring." But he explained, "I never wear it
when I'm drawing. And as you know, I usually sit and
draw in the evenings, so as to earn money and to make the
time pass more quickly when my wife's away."

Feeling him slipping away from me I threw my arms
round his neck and hugged him, and kissed his cheeks and
chin and mouth as hard as I could, to stop him sending
me away. Disconcerted, he forced my arms loose, saying
reproachfully, "My dear! My dear girl!" Nervously he lit
a cigarette, tried to smile and said, "It's time you went
home to bed, Goldilocks."

"I haven't got a home," I said, staring at him with
scalding tears in my eyes, and in a whisper I went on. "I
should like to sleep here." I couldn't explain what I meant
at all, and burst out crying in my unutterable distress,
sobbing, "I want to lie with your arm round me like my

little brother did and you'd show me pictures." For I wanted this too, and I blurted it out like that because I couldn't express my deepest need in any other way.

He laughed a little and said, "We'll do that some time. But now you must go. I'm only human, you know." He led me out into the hall, helped me on with my coat, shoved me out and shut the door behind me.

I went there once more after that. We lay full length on his sofa; his arm was round me and he showed me pictures in English periodicals and translated for me, kissing me lightly now and then. I lay quite still with my head on his shoulder, loving him the whole time more than I can say; I don't think I've ever known such comfort and consolation with any man as I did with him, lying on his shoulder. But when the time came for me to go he said, "It would be better if you didn't come again, my dear. My family will be back any day now, and my wife mightn't understand. It might be awkward for you and for me too. But come again next summer and tell me how you're getting on."

He wanted to give me some money, but I refused it because I was so unhappy. And next summer I couldn't go and see him because by that time I was at the reformatory, where I stayed for nearly four years. After that I didn't want to meet him again, even if he remembered me, for I had no wish to see him as I saw all other men. It might have been better though, if he hadn't been so timid and cautious, but had taken me and loved me just a little as I wanted him to, even if it had ended badly for both of us. I don't think I should have regretted it; it would have been better than what actually happened. He too would have had more to remember. But he was afraid and he didn't understand me, at the time when I was so free and so happy because of him.

5

Things turned out as he foretold. Autumn came, and cold weather, and no one bought flowers any more, and it was no fun running up and down the stairs of endless blocks of flats with a streaming cold and soaking shoes. Viola grew irritable and made it clear that she preferred a roommate who brought in money. I knew she couldn't keep me. I did my very best to get work, but the only vacancies were for errand girls, and carried a wage one couldn't exist on unless one lived at home. If I'd had friends and money for clothes I might have been taken on at some restaurant, and so at least been given my meals, but I had no such friends. There's no point in blaming anyone; bad times would have caught up with me sooner or later. But I do wish I'd never met that woman. I did meet her, however, and she told me that as a girl lodger of hers had just moved she had a room free. I might live there for the present, she told me, in return for cleaning the room, and then we'd see what could be done to put me in the way of earning something. I disliked and distrusted her from the first, but I had no choice, for I couldn't go on being a burden to Viola. Viola seemed to have misgivings about letting me move in there, for the woman had an evil reputation; but she held her tongue, reflecting perhaps that I should be in for it any way, sooner or later.

It was a horribly dirty, smelly basement flat, with a door into it from the archway. There was a kitchen, where the hag lived with her husband, and an inner room usually occupied by girls, though now it was empty. The man was a doorman at a restaurant and made good money, but they were both extremely miserly. They thought of nothing but money and lived on the food scraps that the man brought home from the restaurant. The old woman had money in the bank and whined everlastingly about having to think of the future and laying by for a rainy day. I didn't know then that they made most of their money by keeping girls for the benefit of drunken customers from the restaurant; for this reason there was always liquor in the house. The girl who lived there before me had gone into the hospital, having been infected by one of the clients.

Soon after I moved in, the woman began grumbling and saying she must be paid something for the room. A day or two later the husband came home with an elderly gentleman from the restaurant; they had brought food and wine and brandy with them, and the stranger looked at me hard, so I knew the doorman had told him about me. The hag hissed at me continually, telling me to be polite and attentive to their guest, for then he would give me money. I tried to look cheerful, and I was grateful for the good food, for I was very hungry. I drank wine too, since it was offered me. But I felt cold, very unhappy, and alone.

There's no need to say any more about this. Their only object was to make me drunk. They fooled me into undressing and going to bed when I was tired, and when I had fallen asleep the customer came and got into bed with me and raped me. When I shrieked he was scared and let go, but the doorman came in, took me by the throat and threatened to knock my teeth in and report me to the police for indecency if I screamed. So I screamed no more.

I think the visitor must have given the hag and her husband a lot of money, and he offered me some too, but I didn't take it; I just cried. So he left it on the table and the woman snatched it as soon as he'd gone. I had no idea who he was, but his face I never forgot, and later I met him again, as will appear. He was not so very much to blame, perhaps; he didn't hurt me more than he had to, to get what he wanted, and no doubt he felt that business was business. He was wealthy, and both the doorman and his wife had persuaded him that I was acting of my own free will, and that I put up a show of resistance to get more money.

Not until the morning, when I was torn and ill, and ugly from crying, did I realize that their threat of calling in the police must be a bluff. But when I tried to go out the man hit me and the woman locked me up, telling me that if I informed against them I should be put in a reformatory, whereas they would be none the worse; they would bring evidence that I was depraved and vicious.

I prefer not to think of that time. For exactly two weeks they kept me locked up in that basement room, and every night the doorman brought men home—two and even three at once—who sat drinking in the kitchen and took it in turns to visit me. I never once submitted willingly; they had to hit me every time, so that at last I was ill and worn out and bruised and sore all over.

I caught the names of some of these men and memorized them, so as to take revenge one day, and from a drunken fellow who amused himself all night by torturing me I stole a visiting card when he fell asleep. For I was so defiled and shattered that I thought I should never be happy again, and I longed for revenge. But as the days passed and I found I couldn't escape, I began to be afraid they'd keep me locked up until I died.

I don't know how it would all have ended if the doorman hadn't brought a man back one night who listened to me and believed me. He was horrified when he heard how young I was, and I made him promise faithfully to report the matter to the police, so that I might escape from this hell. And this he did, though he brought nothing but trouble on himself and got his name in the papers, so that he was disgraced on my account, though he had done me no harm.

For it all came out and a great fuss was made about it in the press, since the scandal involved no one influential enough to necessitate hushing it up. And because of the publicity the police were anxious to display alertness and activity, for at that time they were being accused of turning a blind eye to the rot that was spreading through the city. Helsinki was sheer hell for young people in those days, for many who had become unemployed through no fault of their own had turned bootlegger, and there were women who kept houses where workless girls could sell themselves, when they had nothing else left to sell— though they asked nothing better than a job and a living wage. I hardly knew anything of all this at the time, but I learned about it afterwards in the hospital and at the reformatory. But it was no good blaming the police for this state of affairs, for not even they could have shut down all the speakeasies and brothels, however hard they had tried. Hunger was stronger than the police. But when my case came out they acted with great energy, and I didn't enjoy it.

No, I didn't enjoy it at all. I don't know how I should have borne the shame of it if I hadn't lain ill for weeks. The experience was like a bad dream in which I took no part. They had to put me in the hospital at once, for the thrashings and ill-treatment had brought on pneumonia. In the hospital they found I had contracted venereal disease, and later that I was pregnant. I might have longed to die if I hadn't been too maimed and numb in spirit even for that.

Three men were jailed and the doorman and his wife sent to the penitentiary, though they swore that they were innocent and laid all the blame on me. My mother and father were also interrogated, and Father testified that I had shown vicious tendencies from childhood. I had run away from home out of sheer wickedness, he said; and I never attempted to contradict him, for he and Mother had already suffered disgrace enough. "Why didn't I kill you? Why didn't I kill you?" he muttered to me as we stood opposite one another at the questioning. These were the last words he ever spoke to me; I never saw him again, for he died a couple of years later. Even at the time of the trial there must have been something wrong with his liver, for his face was yellowish-brown. He suffered a great deal of pain before he died, but without complaint; he just cursed. The principal of the reformatory would have let me attend the funeral, but I didn't want to, though the other girls would have given anything to get out into the town, for whatever reason.

My child was premature and stillborn, fortunately, for in my heart I had sworn to kill it, whatever they might do to me afterwards. I had will power enough to desire its death—for what would become of it, when I had been able to do no better than this for myself? At first the doctors talked of abortion, but in the end, as I recovered so quickly from my illness, they did nothing. Perhaps there was some reason. This is all true.

But for me the worst part of it all was certainly this: that there was no one who fully and truly believed me; they all thought I'd got into this willfully, through my natural depravity. Or such was my impression as I lay there, sick, and obsessed by a sense of guilt, as a child feels guilty of all the ills that befall it. For I was still quite childish. It was in the reformatory that I lost all my child-ishness; the girls there rubbed it off—with coarse emery.

But the man, the first, whose face and hands I shall re-member forever—he escaped. I had no idea who he was and so I said nothing about him, nor did the doorman; I fancy he was bribed to hold his tongue. But I too had my reasons for keeping quiet about him—not that it would have done me any good to talk, for I didn't know his name. The three who were sentenced were the worst kind of scum, but the other, the first, was by way of being a gentleman.

6

I don't want to speak ill of the reformatory, for they did their best there, and were even kind to those who were willing to behave and work and learn. There were good girls and bad girls, and if I'd made friends with the good ones I might have been different. But the good girls were oafish and plain and boring, while the bad girls were keen-witted and attractive; and they knew too much ever to be dull. My impression was that the ones described as "good" were those willing to live as hard and drab a life as possible, while the "bad ones" wanted to live light-heartedly and without regrets.

I, of course, was notorious before I arrived, for my name had been in all the papers, and young though I was I was regarded as the worst of the worst. Many envied me for the money they fancied I must have made and gaily squan-dered, and I didn't disillusion them, for it was less painful for me to imagine that I had been in control of my own actions than to know that I'd been a passive victim. So I exaggerated here and there and enjoyed talking about all the ugly things I knew, and the girls enjoyed listening, for there was nothing they were so keen to hear about as men and their ways. I lied and made myself out to be as vile as possible, but only because I was unhappy and because everyone needs something to boast about, if it's only wickedness and impudence.

From the appearance of these girls and the tales they had to tell, I concluded that being good was foolishness, and that only plain girls found it easy. And in this place even the good ones were pilferers and gluttons and telltales. When I thought of the trifles for which they had been sent here I could only marvel at their stupidity, and the bad girls and I were soon of one mind in thinking that the only crime was to get caught.

I learned a great deal. I learned for instance that men are gold mines for a pretty girl and that the older they are the more infatuated they become. I learned that the higher the price a girl puts on herself, the more desirable does she appear, and that no man can resist temptation if the tempter is only wily enough. I learned that nothing is more idiotic than taking a wallet off a drunk, for that's just what one most often gets pinched for. Only beginners and nitwits do it; the bright ones know plenty of ways of fleecing a man without landing themselves in trouble. For theft is a worse crime than fornication, and the police are not there to protect young girls from lecherous men, but to protect the men's wallets from girls. Yes, I learned a lot at that institution; among other things that by far the cleverest plan was to marry, for as a married woman one could do as one liked without the police being able to interfere, so long as one was careful not to be brought up too often for drunkenness.

I cooled and hardened during those years, and as I looked back at all that had happened it seemed to me that society owed me a big debt and that I had no reason in the world to pity anyone. I grew taciturn too; I kept my thoughts to myself, and didn't chatter as I had done at first. The girls came to think me dismal. I tried to take care of my hands, though, and keep them smooth and clean despite all the peeling of potatoes and grubbing in the garden that had to be done. My most precious possession was a piece of mirror which, like all the others, I kept hidden under my mattress. I tried to look after my hair too, for an attractive appearance seemed the only weapon against the world. But I didn't mean to drift with the stream, like the rest of them. They were merely awaiting release so as to drink again and get themselves clothes and walk the streets and catch men.

But I wasn't thinking of things like that; I felt they'd been talking a lot of nonsense, and that with a little honest effort it would be possible to build up something in life instead of landing straight in the gutter. In the streets one was lost: there one's only certain future was either alcohol, syphilis and TB, or toil and drudgery at the reformatory, where prostitutes were sent after a sufficient number of warnings. I therefore resolved to do my best, and perhaps find a man who would be good to me and marry me, were he but a simple workman, and give me a home of my own. By the time I reached my eighteenth birthday and left the institution I'd become cold and silent, and I determined never to set eyes on any of the other girls again, but to build up my life alone, asking neither advice nor help of anyone.

First I went home, which I could do without fear now that Father was dead. I entered the same old yard; the steps were even more lopsided and worn than before and the woodshed had a hole in the roof. My heart melted as I went upstairs, knocked at the door and groped for the key in the dark lobby.

"Why, Maire!" said Mother. "You've got out then, love!" She was kind and good; she made coffee and went out to buy buns. My eldest brother had married and moved elsewhere, but the second lived at home and supported the family. The youngest was still at school.

When my second brother came home from the factory and saw me he exclaimed, "Maire! Is it really Maire?" Then his face darkened, and as he was washing in the kitchen I heard him say to Mother, "Does that tart think she's going to move in here?" At this my mood chilled; I went up to him and said, "Don't worry. The Home found me a job, so I shan't be a burden to you." To Mother I said, " 'Bye, Mother, and thanks for the coffee." And I went.

But I wasn't to start work until the first of the month, and having nowhere else to sleep I put up at a hostel which charged twenty-five marks a day. Here I sat staring out of the window at dirty roofs and gray rain, and had porridge and *wienerbrot* and coffee in the canteen. I was eighteen and pretty, though badly dressed, and in the canteen there was music on the radio and men who stared at me. There was music that spoke of everything that was bright and enchanting and joyous in life; I tried to imagine that I was sitting in a big hotel at some foreign seaside resort, and that I was one with that world of gay, laughing people. But the porridge stuck in my throat, for all I had was eighty marks and the clothes I stood up in.

So when evening came and the street lamps were lit I went to a big restaurant and began walking up and down in front of it, until a man came out, took me by the arm and said, "Where shall we go?" He was well dressed and a little drunk. I thought of my brother's remark, and answered, "I don't know." He said, "I can't very well take you home with me," and I suggested, "Perhaps the woman at the hostel will let you in if you give her something. But I want three hundred marks." He was in a good humor and said laughing, "Are you crazy? Don't you realize the town's crawling with girls who are glad to get a hundred?" I withdrew my arm and said, "Then why bother me?" But my reluctance provoked him; he came with me to the hostel and gave the woman money to let us in together.

When he entered my room he lit a cigarette and sat down, but I undressed as quickly as possible, showed myself to him and asked ironically whether I would do. But when he tried to touch me I said, "Money first." He was disconcerted, but did as I asked. And perhaps he wasn't such a bad fellow, for when he got out of bed he said, "If you had at least laughed!" But I couldn't laugh; I went over to the basin and vomited, though he was not at all a repulsive or cruel man. Instead of being angry he said in quite another voice, "Was it so horrible? I'm sorry." But I didn't want his pity, and all I said was, "If you've had enough, get to hell out of here and let me sleep." Even then he wasn't put out, for no doubt he saw my despair. He merely brushed my hand with his, took his hat and coat and went. He was no fool.

Thus I was able to buy myself decent stockings and shoes and a white collar for my dress. On the first of the month I went to my job, thinking I should be content with a corner to myself, food and a couple of evenings off a week.

But the kind of situation the reformatory finds is nothing to boast of, for it's always in a family that wants a maid for half-price and expects her to toil like a slave and be grateful into the bargain. But I was so timid and depressed that I took little notice of my employer's nagging and scolding, and struggled on as best I could, looked after the children when the mother was out, and didn't even insist on my evenings off. For I resolved to learn Swedish; even at the institution I had begun to study it, thinking that perhaps one day I might serve in a shop or a restaurant. So I would sit and work at it sometimes on my free evenings, but one night when the wife had gone to the cinema the husband came into the kitchen for some soda water, and seeing me sitting there with the grammar in front of me he offered to help me. I was glad, until I found what he was after.

When I struggled he got angry and said, "Don't you act the prude with me, you little bitch. I know where you come from." But I kicked, and butted him in the face with my forehead until he was forced to let me go, and afterwards he didn't dare persist for fear his wife should come home.

It would have been no good complaining to her, for she would have put all the blame on me and thrown me out, as is the way of wives; for what else can they do to preserve their peace of mind in such cases? But after that I could never escape her husband, for I had tantalized him. One night after I'd undressed he came into the kitchen, sat down on the edge of my bed and said, "Don't be stupid now; I can do you a bit of good. I could get you a job in the club kitchen if you like, and then you'd have more time off." This got him nowhere with me, so then he tried threats: "I'll get the better of you yet!"

He was beyond even wanting to resist temptation, and I don't wonder, for his wife was older than he was and a great nagger. And so one evening he came home early—having said he would be late—walked into the kitchen and asked with a sly smile, "Have you seen my cigarette case?

I left it on the writing table when I went out this morning."

I hadn't found it, but he said, "We shall see. One has to
be careful with people like you in the house." He pulled
out from under my bed a cardboard box that I kept my
things in, having no suitcase, and started to open it.
"Leave my things alone!" I cried, but he took no notice;
he opened the box and pulled out his cigarette case from
somewhere among my clothes. It was of silver and quite
heavy. He weighed it in his hand and looked at me tri-
umphantly. "This is a matter for the police," he said. "I
shall have to ring up and report it."

I stiffened. "You put it there yourself," I said. "You did
it when I was out at the dairy."

"Well, what of it?" he returned scornfully. "Which of
us do you think they'll believe—you or me?" Then taking
me by the arms he said, "Good God, you're driving me
mad, girl! I shan't let you go until you've done what I
want."

I looked him in the eye and saw that he would certainly ring up the police, just to pay me out for my stub-
bornness. But I was cool enough to speculate as to just
what power it was that drove an otherwise pleasant, decent man to this madness; and I wondered too whether
that power lay in him or in me. I realized that in the war
he was waging against me there was neither mercy nor
compassion, neither law nor justice; it was a war in which
pity must be silent.

I snatched up a carving knife and said, "If you touch me
I'll drive this into you!" And I added, "If you report that
cigarette case business you know what'll happen to me.
But *if* you do I swear I'll kill you—and if I can't do it at
once I'll do it the day I get out of prison—I swear it!"

He saw I meant it, and with something like admiration

he said, "Yes, I believe you would, you crazy girl." He picked up the cigarette case and turned to go. But as I stood there with the knife still in my hand I felt numb and limp, despite my victory. I don't know what came over me, but I was suddenly indifferent, knowing that it was useless to fight a power that was stronger than ourselves. The knife fell from my hand; I went after him, took him by the arm and said, "Don't go."

Never had I known so fierce a delight as when he threw himself over me and possessed me. It was then that I first realized that my body could experience things that many women never know. Perhaps it was this which without my willing it had made me what I was. So I must mention it here, though one doesn't usually talk of such things.

But next day I gave notice, and if the two weeks I still had to stay there were hell for him, they were hell for me too. It was as if an abyss had yawned at my feet; I stared into it, turned giddy and backed away from the brink with the strength of despair. During those days darkness opened in me for the first time and I learned more of myself and of other people in one minute than in all the years at the institution.

7

I tried once more, though secretly I knew it would be useless. I wanted to prove to myself that at least I'd tried. But in my next situation there were two young students in the family, and less than a fortnight had passed when the lady of the house told me she couldn't keep me on because of the boys. She didn't blame me; she assured me of her conviction that I was an honest girl and had done my best; nor had she any fault to find with my work. But she just couldn't keep me.

I didn't try a third time. I was convinced.

I looked about me: there lay the town—the broad streets, the great shop windows with their beautiful wares, the lights at night, and the neon signs glowing red and green. Money was being poured out everywhere, engines hummed, music played. Where was the point in holding back? No decent man would have cared about me if he'd known who I was and where I came from; I was not the kind of girl to whom people offered marriage, so why not go the whole hog at once? Father's words rang in my ears, "Why didn't I kill you?"

Bad company was always to be had; good company was harder to come by. I hung around dance halls until I'd got together some decent clothes, and did pretty well. I found a lodging with an excellent girl who had a telephone and a nominal job, for one of her regular clients was a goldsmith who could testify when necessary that she was a saleswoman of his. I was even given a silver fox fur by a drunken furrier who invited us into his warehouse and treated us to liquor.

I then made friends among the taxi drivers, so that I didn't have to walk the streets, but could wait for customers at home. The only drawback to my roommate was that she drank too much. That was why she took me in: so that I could keep an eye on her, for I drank only when compelled to, and merely pretended to be tight with those who preferred me so. Often she would ring me up in the small hours and ask me to fetch her, because she was too drunk to get home on her own.

Apart from this she was a gay, carefree soul, generous and good-tempered. Men liked her very much and were free with their money in her company, for she was full of fun and never disguised her enjoyment of her relations with them. "Why shouldn't we both get a kick out of it?" she would say. "I'm going to have a good time while I can." And all might have been well with her, for I think the goldsmith would have married her if she'd wanted him to; there are such men. But she preferred drinking, and a year or two later she was stabbed in some speakeasy and died. She was by no means a bad girl, despite the life she led.

I was quite different. I never gave men an atom more than I had to. I enjoyed making them feel that I was only doing it for the money, for this degraded them more perhaps than it did me. They never possessed any essential part of me. "What's the matter with you, anyway?" one of them once asked me. "It doesn't matter what one does— one would think no one had ever touched you." For it's possible to seem untouched, even when one sleeps with men for money every night. I was cold, reserved, and silent. When I began to learn my business I did all I could to emphasize the innocence of my appearance. I dressed plainly, used as little lipstick as possible, spoke carefully and avoided coarse words. I believe that at first glance no one could have distinguished me from any girl from a good home. Many of these indeed behaved far worse in restaurants and dance halls than I did. My hair was innocently fair and my dark eyes had always had a shut-away expression in them, as if nothing—not even the worst degradation—could touch my innermost self. It was easy enough to keep this manner up, for I soon tired of men. The great majority were fundamentally alike; when one had known a few one had known a hundred. There was nothing new or surprising about any of them. Their secret wishes and desires were simple and gross, though each one of them fancied himself in some way remarkable and different from the rest.

I was expensive, and choosy about my clients; but I knew this couldn't go on for long. My companion drank too much and I was afraid of being cautioned by the police, so I married a taxi driver. He knew what I was, having often rung me up at night and brought me customers, calling on me next day if he were free to collect his commission. Other drivers wanted money, but he wanted me, and at last he said, "You know, Maire, you'd be better off—safer—if we got spliced."

He may even have been in love with me, at least in the beginning. But it wasn't long before he began bringing men home. First he sold them liquor, then me. Finally he took to driving only at night, cruising slowly round the town in search of suitable customers. I soon got tired of him and I felt that my life had become a dirty, stale, stagnant pool. And so I took to drinking too, sometimes. But I knew that my life couldn't go on like this—this was merely incidental. Something was bound to happen to me soon. But my marriage lasted for three years, and those years so wrought upon me and wore me down that I fancied I was as hard as a diamond, without a thought of anything but money.

I tried to save, but it was hopeless, for my husband drank, and would often lie in bed for days on end instead of plying for hire, and then I had to buy food and alcohol for him. He grew careless about the rent too, so that in time it fell to me to pay it. I had expected to exploit him, but it soon proved to be the other way round. Then we quarreled, and I irritated him as much as I could. He was lazy and dirty and disgusting, and in desperation I sometimes picked up men in the parks or cafés and brought them home; I took no money from them, but gave them money and a drink or two if they wanted it.

I can't really explain why I did this, except that I felt terrifyingly alone and afraid of my life. I wanted someone to like me for my own sake and not just for my body; I wanted to talk to people as an equal and feel free to do as I wished. But it never went further than my body, for that was the best I had to offer; there was nothing else that my casual acquaintances would have valued. The other girls thought me queer in the head and the bawds thought me raving mad, and no doubt I was a little unhinged; but it was terrible to feel the years slipping away, young though I still was—to know that I had nothing better to look forward to, and to carry within me a perpetual darkness. Sometimes I flew into a rage and shrieked at my husband, and once I threatened him with a knife; after that he began avoiding me, and kept to himself; for he had quarreled with his fellow drivers too. They hated him for blackening their reputation with his goings on. He talked of divorce, thinking no doubt that he could easily pick a more cheerful and amenable wife from among his girls.

But it's time I told how I met Torsten. It must have been some hidden instinct that impelled me to wander about the streets when I was alone. Every time I went up and spoke to a man I was really waiting for a spark to be lit in my darkness, though I no longer seriously believed that such a thing was possible. But it is, though I don't know how or why. I needed no more than a spark to explode my darkness. At first he was just a fellow in working clothes standing at the corner of the street at dusk, under a lamppost. He looked at first sight like anyone else; there was nothing special about him. I just glanced at him sideways as I made my way home, but after a few steps I felt impelled to turn back.

Perhaps other women too know what it is for a spark to strike into their hearts. A glance, a glimpse of a face— even the curve of a shoulder—is enough. One can never forget it; it comes back to one again and again for years. Most women pass on, not daring to look back. Custom, decorum, fear, modesty forbid them; the spark dies and is lost, perhaps never to be rekindled.

But no convention or modesty could restrain me. I was as hard as glass and free to do as I would. I turned and went back and my heart began to thump. I looked more closely at him in the light of the streetlamp, and there was really nothing to admire. I've seen plenty of hand- somer, more striking men. He was even shorter than my- self, fair, with a rugged face. Two deep furrows ran from his nose to the corners of his mouth. He was standing there with his hands in the pockets of his overalls, a chewed cigarette holder in his mouth. He had clear blue eyes.

"Excuse me, but are you waiting for someone?" I asked. He looked surprised and examined me from head to foot, and as he took the cigarette holder from his mouth to answer me I saw that he wore a wedding ring. He looked at me without a smile, and I didn't smile either.

"I've been working overtime," he said. "I promised to wait for one of my mates here at seven; we were going to take a bath at the *sauna* and then have a bite somewhere, but it's past seven already."

When he answered I was lost, but for my life I couldn't have smiled; I felt as a fox must feel when it walks into the trap and the jaws close on its foot. I can't explain it. I only knew that this man was mine and that not for any- thing in the world would I lose him. His voice alone drained the strength from me.

"Come and have supper with me," I said. "I live close by."

He stared. "I oughtn't to—" he said doubtfully.

"Come," I said, and he came. It was as simple as that.

I laid the table and put food on it for him, but I wasn't conscious of what I did, nor of the unswept room; I simply looked at him and wondered how a complete stranger could feel so close. Nor could I pin down what it was about him that was so familiar, for I had never seen him before and had exchanged very few words with him now. I could hardly speak and my hands shook as I laid the table, in fear lest he should go and I never see him again. I offered him a drink, too, hoping it might induce him to stay longer, but he refused it. He ate with a good appetite, without fuss or ceremony, and when he had finished he sat silently at the table for a long time with his eyes on mine. He was neither surprised nor shy.

Then he rose and came over to me, laid his hands on my shoulders and said, "Thank you for the supper." And that was all he said, for I rose to meet him and the spark in me burst out in roaring conflagration. I remember little of what happened then. I only know that a darkness opened in me when he came to me and I cried out wildly, again and again, as he held me. No one else had ever held me like that.

He smiled afterwards and said, "You screamed."

"I thought I was dying," I said, and stroked his cheeks, his neck and shoulders and his hard knees.

"Mad," he said, and he lit a cigarette and began biting on the wooden holder as his habit was. But he didn't seem to want to go, although I was afraid he might. As I combed my hair I felt as if the earth had rolled over me, and I thought that perhaps after all it had been worth while to live and to become what I had become, just for the sake of this one hour. I knew I wanted him, whatever the cost. I never considered his side of it—of whether I were bringing him happiness or grief. It never occurred to me that I might harm him—burn him up, as iron is burned by the welder's flame.

I thought of none of these things. I knelt in front of him and stroked his knees and wanted to know all about him: who and what he was, what sort of life he led. Everything about him was so precious that I didn't want to lose a single word from his lips. I felt no shame, nor any fear that he might soon tire of me if I so readily and unreservedly showed him what power he had over me. I thought of nothing, only of him.

His name was Torsten. He was over thirty; a metal worker in a good job. He had been married for a couple of years, but there were no children. "I don't think one has the right to bring children into a world like this," he said. He talked politics too, as men will. "The world must be changed," he said. "Everything that's going on in it today is speeding up the rate of evolution." What did I care about the world and evolution? I looked only at him. His eyes were bright blue and hard, and sometimes as he was talking they flashed like sparks.

"What about you?" he asked.

"I'll tell you all that some other time," I said hastily. "Some other time," I repeated, and I touched him again as I could never have touched anyone until now, when all the dams and barriers in me were down. There was no sort of caress I would have been shy of giving him, so open, so whole, was my feeling for him.

"Perhaps there won't be another time," he said; then his mouth hardened and he grasped me again. Again I was drowned in the flood; the world rolled over me in thunder so that I was plunged into darkness; and I sobbed in his arms. I knew then that everything was real and not just a dream, and I knew that I should never let him go while it was in my power to hold him.

After one or two further meetings I told him that I could get a divorce from my husband at any time. This was true, for I knew far too much about him for him to be able to keep me, even if he'd wanted to. Torsten started when I said this, for he had hardly considered such a thing; perhaps he had vaguely imagined that he would drift with the current for a time and then climb ashore again as if nothing had happened. Men forget more easily than women, and every man is ruthless to the woman who desires him.

But I sowed the thought in his mind right at the beginning. Even if it had scared him and he'd wanted to draw back, he couldn't have done so now, for my body had already poisoned his; I knew that every night he thought only of me and that he no longer had any joy of his wife. Because of her we couldn't often meet.

I asked him about her and he told me everything—things indeed that no man ought ever to tell about his wife, though they all do it—and I went on asking, for it gave me a cruel pleasure, as if I'd been turning a knife in my own heart. It seemed to me a heavy curse that Torsten should be tied: the kind of thing that would happen to me.

I think he was really intelligent. He had read a good deal and was skilled in his trade, but his was not a sensitive nature and he had no imagination. He was reserved and silent and every word had to be dragged out of him. But I, who had believed myself to be as hard as glass, woke to the realization that there were emotions dammed up in me so violent as to frighten me. He was probably quite an ordinary man, as I said before. But he was meant for me.

Things went on like this for a time; we met secretly and no one found out—not even his wife—for he often worked overtime and could use that as an excuse for lateness. But the hours we spent together were far too brief, and the stolen happiness fretted at my heart—while every hour, every second, the fear gnawed at me that I might lose him: that the day would come when he wouldn't want to see me again. Yet I was happier at this time, I think, than ever before or since.

8

Just about this time I caught sight of *him,* the first, the one who had made me drunk in the doorman's cellar and whom I never mentioned at the trial. I saw him coming out of a restaurant, well-fed, well-dressed, and neat. His hair was becomingly gray at the temples and his eyes were shifty. I followed him along the street until he went into a big office block, and there, having waited for a time, I asked the liftboy the man's name and the name of his firm. And so at last after all these years I ran him down.

I didn't call on him at once; for some days I studied newspaper advertisements and looked at various shops. When my plan was made I called at his office and sent in my name, saying I wanted to see him on a private matter. My name meant nothing to him, for I used that of my husband, the taxi driver. The girl came back with the reply that the director had not the pleasure of my acquaintance, and that he could not spare the time to receive visitors. "Mr. —— will recognize me when he sees me," I answered, and waited once more. He kept me a long time, but at last I was admitted; he stood up behind his desk as I entered and looked at me inquiringly.

"Don't you recognize me, Mr. ——?" I asked with a friendly smile.

"I'm sorry, I'm afraid not," he answered; then he stared at me and his well-shaven face turned gray. He fumbled with his tie and his eyes wandered. But I wasn't going to help him; I just smiled at him until he asked, "What is it you want?"

"Exactly," I said. "I am Maire, though I'm no longer fourteen. But I never said a word about you at the trial, nor at any time since. So you owe me something."

"I see; blackmail," he said, and sat down again at his desk. His color returned, he pulled himself together and ventured to meet my eye. I went up and sat on the edge of the desk in front of him, and I said, still smiling,

"I'm not going to blackmail you, and I wish you no harm in the world. But you knew at the time that I was an innocent child, and you ruined my life. I now have the chance of starting a new life, if you'll help me. I have no one else I can turn to, and so I've come to you."

"How the devil was I to know you were an innocent child?" he demanded.

"You knew all right," I said, and laughed in his face. "That was the fun of it. Wasn't it?"

"How much?" he said, the man of business once more.

"I want to buy a flower shop and make an honest living by it," I said. "It's the only line I know anything about, and I think I can run it all right once I get into the swing of it. I'll tell you exactly what I want, and you needn't try to beat me down; you need only say whether or not you'll give me the money."

"How much?" he repeated.

"Nothing exorbitant," I said. "There's a little florist's business for sale, for only thirty thousand marks. Then I shall need ten thousand as capital. I don't think this is a big price to pay for a human life."

He was on the point of saying something—of haggling, perhaps—but he saw that I meant what I said. For a time he pondered, then smiled, took out a checkbook, asked me again what my name was and made out a check.

"I'd prefer it in cash," I remarked.

"This'll do as well," he said. He had regained his good humor. He rang the bell and sent the messenger girl to the bank with the check. While I waited he went to the typewriter and drafted an agreement in which I acknowledged receipt of the money, undertook to make no further demands and promised to say nothing to anyone of what had passed between us. I knew as well as he did that such a document was worthless, but he was a businessman and it was a satisfaction to him not to pay out money without getting some sort of paper in exchange.

When the girl arrived with the money he gave it to me and I signed the document. We said no more to each other, but when I went he held out his soft, well-tended hand, and I didn't refuse it.

I went at once and bought the flower shop. A back room went with it, where I could live at first, though it was not a healthy place, being cold and damp. There was an assistant who was competent to run the shop single-handed, so I kept her on with the promise of a better wage than she had been paid by my predecessor.

When I came home again I rang up a moving company and ordered a van to fetch my things. I had nothing of my own except a bed and bedding, a dressing table, and a couple of chairs; but it was enough to start with. While I was packing my clothes the doorbell rang, and on going out I found a man standing there, swaying unsteadily.

"For God's sake let me have some brandy," he said. His

face was swollen with drink and his hands shook. He wore
no overcoat, though it was late autumn. He may have
bought liquor from my husband before, or been given
this address by the neighboring café.

"Have you got the money?" I asked, unwilling to let
him in.

"No, but I've got a good pistol," he said. "Take it, and
I'll redeem it tomorrow."

He drew a worn, self-loading pistol from his pocket and
showed it to me. His eyes were bloodshot and I fancied
that by next morning he would scarcely remember where
he had been.

"That's no good to me," I told him. "And I'm moving
tomorrow, so you won't find me here."

"Take it," he insisted, thrusting it into my hand. "You
can keep it if you'll only give me the stuff."

I let him in. "Is there ammunition for it?" I asked.

"Five rounds," he answered, and with shaking hands he
took out the magazine and let the cartridges roll into his
hand. "Put them back," I said. "I don't like it. What am I
to do with a pistol?"

But I took it, giving him in exchange a bottle of brandy
and a hundred marks in cash, so that he wouldn't be
tempted to come back and redeem his pledge. I don't think
I had any object in accepting the weapon. When the furniture van arrived I put money for the brandy on the table
and wrote a note to my husband to say I was leaving him.
I didn't tell him where I was going, for he might have
come bothering me if he'd known I had money now and
owned a shop. But a day or two later I rang him up and
we went together to the lawyer's to arrange a divorce. I
was so keen to get this that I undertook to pay all the
costs, and made no claims for myself—not that it would
have been any good if I had. My husband took it all very

calmly; he was glad to be rid of me, and it wasn't long before he had another girl living with him.

Next time I met Torsten I took him to the flower shop, showed him the back room where I lived and said, "Now I'm free from my husband and I own this shop. I'm going to do well with it, and begin a new life."

I had told him all about myself, thinking it was better he should know everything now, rather than pick up odds and ends through gossip, as he would have been bound to do sooner or later. Nor did I want to hide anything from him; on the contrary, it was a relief to talk about it—even the worst of it. The only thing I kept to myself was how I raised the money for the shop, since I had promised not to divulge that to anyone. Instead I told him that unknown to my husband I'd been gradually saving up for my freedom.

I had bought wine and real brandy to show how well off I was; I made him drink and tempted him in every way so that he stayed the night with me. It was the first time I had ever slept with my head on his shoulder, and after all he had drunk he slept heavily and never knew that I kissed his mouth and face and his bare breast all night. That night I was happy indeed.

But in the morning he said, "Good God, how am I going to explain this to my wife? I've never slept away from home before!"

He was sitting on the edge of the bed, puffy-eyed, running his hands through his tousled hair. I knelt in front of him, and threw my arms about his knees, saying, "Torsten, tell her all about it! She must divorce you, and then we'll set up house together somewhere and have a real home. We could always be together then."

He said, "Damn all women! This is a nice mess you've got me into."

Clinging to his knees I whispered, "There's no life for me without you, Torsten."

But his wife would not agree to a divorce; she made a terrible scene and told Torsten that I was a wicked woman and that he would only be unhappy with me. She wouldn't divorce him; she clung to him savagely and made him swear never to see me again. We had to meet in secret as before. We plotted and planned, and Torsten proposed collecting his belongings and simply moving in with me; but it would have been hopeless to have his wife continually at our heels, ruining our life together. We thought of moving to another town, and even at one point to Canada; but Torsten had a good job and I had my florist's business, and it would have been hard to begin all over again in a foreign country.

I believe his wife knew quite well that we were still meeting, for a woman is always aware of that sort of thing once her suspicions have been aroused. But she preferred things as they were and said nothing, no doubt believing that Torsten would get over it if she had the patience to wait. And she was right in this—horribly right—for Torsten was not like me; there was no looming darkness in him. He was a man like other men. I knew the time was soon coming when he would tire of me. He would tire of the dodges, lies, and secrecy; he would be glad to go back to his wife and see me no more. It would happen quite soon, I thought, and therefore I wanted to bind him to me with unbreakable bonds.

A man's passion, even the most ardent, dies down in time, however serious it may seem to him. However fiery and violent his emotion there comes a moment when all he sees before him is dust and ashes, and he can't even remember or understand how it all came about. For a man everything is transient, and in order to hold him a woman must bind him to her, bind him with home and habit, so that he remains in the net even though its meshes are mere illusion.

Torsten's wife may not have known this, or may not have taken quite this view of the matter, but feminine instinct and cunning compelled her to act as she did. She must also have dreaded the shame of being deserted by her husband—dreaded the malicious comments of parents and friends. She was inconsistent in her treatment of Torsten, though, for at times she would plague him with her nagging; she also tried to make him jealous. She went dancing and stayed out late, implying that she too had her admirers. This had no effect on him; he merely grew colder to her. Outwardly, however, she went on as if nothing had happened, and not for her life would she have let her neighbors and acquaintances know that Torsten had another woman.

Torsten told me all this. How I hated that woman! She was small, dark, and plump, and on one red cheek she had a wart with stiff hairs in it. I saw her in the park one Sunday when she was out with Torsten. I wanted to know what she looked like. She didn't want to meet me. She was afraid to, knowing that she would get the worst of it in any row with a woman of my sort. But I saw her, and she had round, foolish eyes; she was hanging on Torsten's arm and looking beseechingly up at him. I hated her more than ever then. Torsten and she had known each other since childhood, though he went about with other girls before he married her. He had a strange magnetism for women. He was nothing much to look at, and he didn't have to speak, but in his eyes and his hard mouth there was something that attracted women, so that at times when we were out together I was stabbed by unbearable jealousy at the sight of other women turning and looking at him.

This was a further reason for wanting to bind him to me, and I realized with a feeling of helplessness that even if he got his divorce and I became legally married to him, I might not be able to keep him; for a man who has once been divorced, and finds out how easy it is, will do it again, and the girl who lured him to break with his wife in the first place can't complain, for she has only herself to blame.

These things were on my mind continually; every day I grew more desperate and my desire for Torsten greater. But I had to curb myself and not make myself too cheap, but rather worth the winning, despite the suffering this caused me when everything in me was crying aloud for him. I treated him more coolly, made various objections when he wanted to meet me, and tried to withhold myself from him, telling him to go to his wife if that was what he wanted. But in the end I could never resist melting into him, and each time my darkness was more searing and agonizing, until I wanted him with me every hour, to take him, fill him, smother him with myself and my caresses.

My shop was doing quite well and I could live on it, though I gave it little attention; I could think of nothing but Torsten, and my thoughts went round and round in the same old circle: the problem of how to hold him for good. I let the assistant run the business and deal with the orders, and just kept an eye on the shop and the till and helped with the selling at the rush periods when a number of customers came into the shop at once. I dressed plainly and spoke politely, and I became known among the ladies of the neighborhood. I realized that if I chose I could make friends with decent people. But I had no wish to live a respectable middle-class life with its coffee parties and gossip; I had no thought but for Torsten. Men of the better type often came into the shop for flowers and a chat, for I was still pretty; indeed the passion within me made me beautiful, and matured me. Yes, during those months I was seared as by glowing coals.

There was a certain councilor in particular who took a fancy to me. He would peer in at the window and if he saw me inside would slip in for a talk. He lived in the house next door. I don't know what sort of a councilor he was; he was known just as "the councilor." He was enormously rich and used to come in wearing an expensive fur coat, which he would pantingly unbutton. His eyes were misty and his nose and cheeks had a bluish tinge, and I fancy it was long since he had met the day sober; but he was always quiet and courteous in his speech and behaved like a gentleman. He must have been over sixty.

One Sunday morning he came into the shop, bluer than ever and very wretched, and asked if I had any brandy. His heart was troubling him, he said, and his guests of the night before had drunk up all he had. I took him into the back room and we talked together until noon, when the restaurants were allowed to sell spirits.

"You're drinking yourself to death," I warned him, for he was a nice old chap in his way, who knew a lot and wasn't too proud to sit and chat with me.

"I've done and seen too much," he said, "and I'm tired of life. Besides, there'll be war soon, and I don't think I can bear to live through that again."

He wanted me to go to his place so that he could offer me something in return, and one day I went. He lived in an old-fashioned flat whose walls were hung with weapons, old paintings, and portraits. He had a large collection of medals too; they were his one remaining interest. He would poke about in antique shops in search of them, when he was sober enough. He showed me this collection and gave me some fine Madeira, and when we'd been chatting for a little time he took my hand and said,

"Dear lady, won't you come and be my housekeeper? I shall soon have drunk myself into my grave, and I'll remember you in my will."

He was a widower and had lately dismissed his housekeeper because she locked away his drink and disturbed him when he brought girls home to see his medals and be petted. He held my hand now as he looked at me, and his eyes showed that there was something of the old Adam still alive in him, though he was elderly and had long since drunk himself impotent. I smiled and thought, "Just you wait, old man; I'll get you where I want you." I think he fancied that there was something unusual and peculiar about his appetites, and never dreamed I could know about such things.

I looked at him; I looked about at his handsome old home, thinking that there ought to have been an aristocratic, gray-haired old lady at his side, and children and grandchildren about him, so that he might have aged with dignity. But alcohol had soaked off his dignity, his courtly manner, and all the inhibitions that go with breeding and education, and laid bare the underlying lusts. He was a ruin, and as he said, in a few years he would drink himself into his grave.

"Oh, no!" I said; but I let him hold my hand and I looked him boldly in the eye. "I can't be anybody's housekeeper. I've got a good man of my own and I'm soon going to marry again."

He didn't pursue the matter, for he could conceal his cravings and perhaps was ashamed of them. He was old and had learned the art of waiting. Also he had had wide and varied experience and perhaps in me he sensed something to suit his needs.

But I teased Torsten about him, and told him how wealthy the old man was. He had millions, I said, and I might become his housekeeper and then marry him, and so inherit his whole fortune. At this Torsten would flare up. "But what am I to do?" I retorted. "At least I'd have money that way, and get all I want from life: I could buy gorgeous furs, travel abroad and perhaps make a good marriage. You'll never get away from your wife until you die. But of course you're fonder of her than you are of me."

"You know perfectly well that you're the only woman in the world for me, Maire," Torsten said, and his face darkened. He rested his head on his hands, his hair still ruffled from my stroking, and brooded.

"If she died—" I said, and added nothing more, for Torsten knew what I meant. He was no fool. We met each other's eyes and trembled.

"You're a devil," he said. I lay over him and kissed his cheeks and neck. "I've got a pistol that the police will never be able to trace," I went on. "She often goes out dancing with that fireman you've told me about. They stand for hours under the archway when he takes her home; the neighbors have seen them. No one would suspect you—and if they did they'd have no proof."

"But how could it be done?" asked Torsten doubtfully, and I knew I'd won, even though he was still only playing with the idea without really believing it practicable. But I poisoned him with my body and persuaded him that he'd lose me if he didn't get his freedom. Little by little the idea sank more deeply into him, and I dazzled him until he was in a perpetual haze.

Then he did it. We had decided not to conceal the fact that we were lovers; it was bound to come out anyway. My shop assistant had often seen us together. On that day I kept her at the shop until Torsten came from work; we had a few drinks and she was with us until quite late. When she'd gone I gave Torsten the pistol, and he made his way to a lonely road through a park on the outskirts of the town, and there lay in wait for his wife, who was at a party at the fireman's house. When she passed he shot her in the head, killing her instantly. The whole thing took him no more than an hour, and on the way home he threw the pistol into the sea. It was all very simple, with no complicated planning, and no one noticed Torsten on the dark road that night. If there had been anyone with his wife he wouldn't have fired. But she was alone.

We drank together all that night, and not until the girl arrived in the morning did Torsten leave, very late, for work. He was soon fetched from the factory for interrogation, but he was calm, denied everything and said he had been with me all night. His wife had begun keeping company with other men, as the neighbors could witness, he said, and they had been thinking of getting a divorce. I was also questioned, and bore out his statement. My assistant testified that he had been with me that night. Torsten had never either owned or borrowed any weapon. The fireman and one or two others whom Torsten's wife had been about with were questioned too; they were scared, but no one could throw any light on the matter. The crime remained unsolved, and no charge was ever brought. Torsten may have been suspected but there was no evidence against him. He had behaved calmly and naturally, and made no secret of his association with me.

And so I got him. So I bound him to me with stronger bonds than law or vows could tie. He could never break free from me, for murder never dies. It lay waiting for him in the police files.

9

That night as we drank together, Torsten simply told me, "I shot her in the head." But one evening some time later when the inquiry was over he said, sitting with his head in his hands, "She recognized me before I could fire." As I made no comment he went on, "I saw her eyes as I fired."

I put out my hand to him, but there was something missing between us. I didn't feel the same violent passion, the same cruel, drugging ecstasy. Something in him had cooled, and when he took me I knew he was thinking of that other woman.

I found a good flat and we moved in together as soon as my divorce was through. He didn't want to bring anything from his old home, and so he sold it all. We often went out together. We danced a lot too. He was now drinking rather more than formerly and seemed absent-minded; he lost interest in his work and did it carelessly.

One evening after we had moved into our little two-room flat on the fourth floor he asked me for a drink and I mixed him one. We could afford good stuff now, for the flower shop was doing well. He emptied his glass and asked, "What sort of poison was it you gave me?"

It was not the drink he meant. He was thinking of all that had happened to him because of me. Passion was past and his head was clear again, and for a man nothing is more ghastly than this form of hang-over, if he has done something that can never be undone.

"You don't love me any more," I said, and he swore and called me a bitch. We bickered on until he lost his temper and seized me—took me to himself as if he meant to kill me—and once more the earth rolled thunderously over me. It all seemed just as before. Yet something was missing.

"Supposing I gave myself up," he said one night. It was near morning and we were lying side by side, each aware that the other was awake. His wife held him faster in death than she had in life.

"You'd simply get me put in jail too," I answered. "What good would it do to give yourself up? It won't bring her to life again."

"No, what good would it do?" he repeated, and turned over restlessly. "What good's anything now?"

"You can't bring her to life again," I cried with mounting fury, and I thumped him on the shoulders with both fists. "Can't you understand? She's dead and won't ever come back! Can't you see you're free of her for good? It's just the two of us now, you and me and nothing else."

But Torsten said, "I saw her eyes." And so he went on every day: "She looked at me and knew me before I could fire."

But he was mine and now I mounted guard over him. I would meet him at the factory when he came from work and never for a moment left him alone. He was mine and I tormented him with my jealousy. I got furious with him if some woman looked at him too long, and I questioned him about what had happened at the factory, whom he had met and what he had talked about. I never let him attend any meetings, and if he sat at home trying to read, and forgot me, I made his life a burden to him.

For unlike him I had not sobered up; I was as besotted with him as before, and lived only for the moments when I could make him take me in his arms and possess me. But something was missing, and that was why I continually plagued and teased him until he hit me, in revenge for all that had happened to him through me. He hit me until I bled from nose and mouth—until I cried and sobbed with pain and begged him to stop. And all the time the dark fire within me flickered and flamed; and when in remorse he took me in his arms to comfort me, I knew again that terrifying bliss. So I teased him, played on his weaknesses and sore points, and found the ugliest words to wound him with, to make him rage again.

But it exhausted him and he grew terribly thin; the blue shadows under his eyes spread to his cheekbones, and he couldn't sleep. Sometimes he would make himself dead drunk so as to sleep, and I loved him perhaps best of all in this drunken stupor, for then I could do as I liked with him—embrace him, kiss him all over his body—and the unconscious body could make no resistance and lay helpless in my arms. I rocked his head in my arms and kissed his mouth and cheeks and gloated because he was mine alone.

But when he woke up he would say, "If only war would come and put an end to it all!" And once he said, "I can't go on any longer."

But I shut my eyes to all misgivings; I blinded myself into living from moment to moment. The hours he spent at the factory seemed like days, for I was only waiting until I could touch him again. One day in drawing the curtains I pulled down the curtain rod and couldn't get it up again. It was a job for Torsten, and I was glad to have found one, for he liked having things to putter about with at home; they helped him to forget. When he came home I said, "The curtain rod's come down."

"I'll fix it presently," he answered. "I want something to eat first."

He started on his supper, but soon forgot it and sat staring in front of him. "Open the window," he said. "It's as hot as hell in here." When I'd opened it he went to the cupboard, took out a bottle and began drinking, still staring in front of him with his elbows on the table.

"Don't you like my cooking?" I taunted him. "I suppose your wife's was better. Or do you think I've put poison in the food?" But he never even looked at me. His dark blue eyes stared fixedly ahead.

But the mere sight of him and his ignoring of me inflamed me. I went over and leaned against him and put my hands on his shoulders. He thrust me away, saying savagely, "Don't touch me, you devil!"

I could feel the pain of his blows in advance, like a dreadful quaking in my body. Leaning against him to provoke him I said mockingly, "There you go, thinking about her again! You're always thinking about her."

He turned to me and surveyed me from head to foot as if beholding me for the first time. "That's it, Maire," he said, and he sounded not at all angry, only terribly tired. "I'm thinking about her. I'm always thinking about her."

Having said this he stepped onto his chair and thence onto the table. I thought he was going to mend the curtain rod, but he leaned out of the window and let himself fall to the street four floors below. It was so quick that for a second or two I didn't grasp what had happened.

When I did I raced down the stairs, though without a clear thought in my head. I tore out into the street and threw myself over his bleeding, lifeless body, and I screamed like an animal. I embraced him and kissed the last spark of life from his lips, and the earth rolled forward over me until I drowned in my darkness, and all was dark.

10

For a week or two I was almost out of my mind: every second was anguish and every night in my dreams I held his limp, shattered body in my arms. People were sympathetic and kind, for they thought he had stumbled and fallen as he was putting up the curtain rod. The bottle and glass were still on the table, and so they supposed he had been drunk and lost his balance. I didn't want to explain anything, and I let them believe what they wanted to.

But after a fortnight or so I could think coolly and dispassionately again. If I'd thought myself hard before I was doubly so now, and nothing in the world meant anything to me any more. I must go on living, I thought, and it's better to be rich than to toil on from day to day. So I began amusing the councilor again, and I encouraged him to do what I wanted. This was easy enough, for he wanted it too, and when he found how well I suited him he was delighted, and no doubt thought that he could never have found anyone better. He marveled at my experience, and I concealed nothing of my former life when I saw how it inflamed him. It was he who suggested that we should get married. I insisted on a joint will and a legal provision by which the survivor, whichever it might be, should inherit the whole estate.

"This is business," I said. "I'll see to it that you drink yourself to death in peace and that your relatives don't come and put you in a nursing home. And I'll give you what other advantages I have to offer. Don't imagine that I love you, but I can stand you as well as other men, and I'll deal fairly by you."

He was old and shrewd, and for safety's sake he got two separate doctors to certify that he was in his right mind, before—unknown to his relations—we contracted a civil marriage and settled our affairs at the lawyer's. This was a prank after his own heart, and it appealed to me too, until I discovered that it was less easy than I'd thought to be married to a mad old man.

I saw to it that he always had plenty of good drink in the house, so that he need never meet the day sober so long as he lived with me. I cooked for him, to save him going out for his meals and having to keep himself neat and tidy as he had done hitherto. He degenerated visibly, but it was by his own wish. And I attended to him and his notions as well as I could. At first it was easy, but his appetite grew with what it fed on, and he had been on a starvation diet for some time, from shame and from the belief that no one could give him what he wanted. His decayed old body glowed like a furnace under my hands, and my only consolation was that the better I gratified his queer cravings, the sooner he would die.

But he was cunning; he drank less now instead of more, until at last I began to be afraid that he had tricked me and would live for years yet. I was filled with a great disgust and I began to put him off and refuse him, but by now I had inflamed him to madness, and he was wilier than I. So I began drinking with him; for some weeks we competed in this until the flat was like a pigsty and I never even bothered to dress, except when I went out to buy the bare necessities of food and alcohol.

Then he took it into his head to have a party; he hauled in loafers from the streets and gave them brandy. Other and worse fancies visited his mad old brain. "I want to enjoy life!" he giggled, and his gold teeth flashed. "Business is business, and I want to enjoy life while it lasts."

But when afterwards he lay in bed recovering, blackish-blue about the nose and cheeks and breathing heavily, he said very softly, "If this is enjoyment I'd rather be dead." Staring at me with sad, straying eyes he went on, "Why couldn't I die at the proper time? It's terrible to rot away alive. It's terrible when worms nibble at one's soul."

Something like compunction stirred in me and I came to my senses again. I kept him in bed and had the place cleaned and the rubbish, broken glasses, and empty bottles thrown out. I cooked good meals and gave him only light wines to drink; for I couldn't take him off alcohol altogether when he'd been soaking it up for ten years. He said, "You're very good to me, Maire, better than I deserve, for I didn't marry you out of kindness. It was the worms in me that made me do it." His trembling yellow fingers played with the medals that I brought to his bed so as to give him something besides worms to occupy his thoughts. In time I got him on his legs again, and summoning up the remains of his dwindling will power he dressed himself carefully, was shaved every day and went out with me. We went to good restaurants and to the theater. I looked upon him as a sick child and stopped thinking horrible things about him; I didn't even feel repugnance now, but tried my best to give him safe toys to play with instead of dangerous, ugly ones.

He enjoyed dressing me up, and made me buy three fine fur coats, for he was free with his money now that he expected to die so soon. So I did well out of him, though he was difficult to live with. Now for the first time I could appreciate the power of money, and I was staggered. For the sake of his money people showed him respect, and bowed to him, whatever they may have said behind his back. When we dined out he ordered lobster and oysters that had come from abroad, and at midwinter he bought roses and carnations flown from southern countries. Money brought him politeness and good service and there was nothing he couldn't buy, except life and death.

But what did I care for beautiful clothes and fine things, when somewhere within me was a blind spot that smarted when it was touched? Every night my inner self cried out for Torsten and I thought of how I had been unable to bear him a child, because of the damage done to my body before I met him. A child might have saved him for me, and created equilibrium in our lives; and even if he had died, the child might yet have saved me. Such were the thoughts that obsessed me in my handsome, luxurious hell.

I had been to see Mother now and again, and once I brought her back with me to show her how well things had turned out. I fetched her in a car and led her upstairs, for she was almost blind even then. The councilor did his best to be friendly and polite, as always in his better moments. Mother was shy and respectful and touched admiringly all the lovely things round her. But my brothers would have nothing to do with me, although the money I gave Mother eased life for them too. They hated and envied me and my life, but I had nothing they need have coveted.

For a time things went well. But then the old man began to get restless again, and badgered me. There was an edge to his tongue now and he found fault with all I did. Nothing satisfied him. He couldn't sleep, and when the light spring mornings came he would creep through the rooms, pulling out drawers and examining and rubbing up his medals. But the medals amused him no longer; he began to drink worse than before and forced himself on me with his horrible swollen body. In the evenings he roamed the streets annoying girls, and he dragged home all kinds of riffraff and drank with them and filled them up with spirits. He couldn't help it; those worms of his were stronger than his divided will, and no amount of remorse and woe on the morning after was any good; the same thing would happen all over again. He was a sick child, spoiled by life and money, but a malignant, frightening child for whose own sake, I felt, it would be well if death came soon.

No one can brood forever over sorrows and disappointments. It was spring again, the mornings were bright when I woke, and sometimes I caught myself smiling. I swept and dusted, humming as I did so, for I was not old in years, though I felt as if I had lived through many cruel lives. I found plenty to do; on those fine spring mornings I threw open every window in the flat, and there before me lay the streets with blue shadows across them, and sunlight gleaming on the roofs. Even the councilor was a little more like a human being. He passed his hand over his throat and his puffy chin and said, "What a vile old wretch I am, Maire! I've drunk sewer water all my life and now it's burning my throat."

Once when he had gone to the bank on business there was a ring at the door, and when I opened it a little girl was standing there with liverwort and marsh marigolds for sale. Her legs were bare and she had fair hair and a stained skirt. I remembered my former self and the time when I sold flowers from door to door, and when I saw the shy, tense look in her eyes a lump came into my throat. I asked her in and gave her coffee and good cakes, stroked her soft hair, and paid her more for a bunch of liverwort than she could have expected for the whole basketful. But this I shouldn't have done. I ought never to have let her in. I ought rather to have sworn at her and frightened her and slammed the door in her face.

She was a little girl, just as inquisitive, just as eager as I had been. She was shy of me, and admiring, and she answered trustfully all the questions I asked her about her home. Her eyes were bright and keen, and I loved her so that it hurt. I loved my own childhood in her and everything that was in me before I became what I became.

When she went I put a bag of pastries in her basket. Her cheeks were pink and she was so thrilled that she couldn't keep to a walk, but skipped and hopped along the pavement. She was ten. I should have known of course that I was setting a trap for myself in this, but I suspected nothing then, with the fresh spring air pouring in at the windows and the shadows lying blue across the streets and the roofs flashing in the sun.

I have little left to tell. A few days later when I came home from shopping and was putting the key in the door I heard a child crying inside. At once I knew what had happened—knew that I ought never to have let the child in and so tempt her to come again when perhaps I might not be at home. Everything went black before my eyes as I dashed in and snatched the child from the old man's hands. She was frightened, and was crying quietly and desperately. Her basket of flowers had been overturned and a few limp bunches of marsh marigolds were strewn in flecks of yellow-gold about the floor.

I took the girl into my room, dried her tears, and washed her with a damp towel. I had arrived before any harm was done her, but she was so frightened that for a long time she couldn't stop crying. I took her on my knees and rocked her as if she'd been my own little girl. When she had calmed down I fetched her flowers and talked to her seriously, warning her never, never to obey any man who asked her in when she was selling flowers. I gave her money to buy shoes with and told her to forget what had happened. And I don't think she was much the worse for it; it was quickly over and I managed to reassure her. But it might have been a very different story if I hadn't come home when I did, and that thought so upset me that I was inwardly seething when at last I sent the little girl on her way.

The councilor looked at me sideways, abashed and conscience-stricken, like a dog that knows it deserves a beating. Saliva was dribbling down his chin and he rubbed his yellow fingers together. "I didn't do anything to her," he said aggressively, as if wanting to start an argument and conceal his guilty conscience.

But I didn't want to quarrel with him. I fetched a bottle of brandy and two glasses and said, "We'll drink to that! May nothing like this ever happen again." He was a sick, unhappy man; life's sewer water scorched his throat and I relented at his pitiable condition. He could have been locked up in some institution, but that would only have made him unhappier, for more than anything he dreaded compulsion and locked doors. Yet if he went on like this, sooner or later something really ugly would happen, for when his worms got the better of his will he was not responsible for his actions. And I couldn't watch every step he took; he was cunning enough to elude me. I pondered over this as we drank together. The brandy was warming and relaxing, and it made everything easier; for I hadn't tasted any for a long time.

"Drink up!" I said. "Let's both drink the filth. To sewer addicts fresh water is tasteless."

So we drank together all day, and I neither reproached nor scolded him for what he had done, but was as good to him as I could be, so that at last towards evening he dozed off, tired and content. I waited until I saw that he was sleeping deeply and that even shaking didn't rouse him. Then I took his pillow and laid it over his face, and I lay on the pillow with all my weight. His feeble, rotten body

could make no resistance; he died under me with a few
faint rattles and a slight movement of his head.

I thought that no one would ever know of this, and
that not even the doctor would notice anything, since he
had been drinking heavily for so long that his heart was
no more than a flickering flame. I sat thinking about this
beside his bed; I thought of Torsten and of my whole life.
I should have a great deal of money now and be able to do
what I liked; yet when I thought of this I felt only revul-
sion and an unutterable despondency.

In the morning, when he was cold, I rang up his doctor
and told him that I'd found the councilor dead in bed.
The doctor soon arrived, made his examination and asked
what he had eaten and drunk the day before. "My deepest
sympathy," he said kindly, and sat down to make out the
death certificate. "I'm putting down heart failure," he
said. "It's pretty obvious, and I don't think there need be
a post-mortem, as he was my patient." He wrote, then
looking up at me he said, "Perhaps I'd better prescribe a
sedative for you at the same time. You don't look at all
well." He stood up and took my pulse.

As he touched my wrist I was overcome by such appalling weariness and self-loathing that the strength drained
from me and I reeled where I stood. My whole life seemed
to rise into my throat like the sewer water, and I thought
how much better it would have been for me and for everyone if Father had killed me with that hatchet all those
years ago.

"Don't bother," I said, withdrawing my wrist from his
warm hand. "You haven't examined him properly. It was
I who took his life, because it was best for him."

I sat down, for my knees had given way, and I said,
"Would you please telephone to the police? I want to be

done with it all and get some peace. I can't stand any more."

He saw that I was speaking the truth. When he had examined the body again he rang up the police. I was arrested and convicted of murder, and the court could find no extenuating circumstances. Soon afterwards war rolled thundering across the world, to blot out the past.

Before the Twilight of
the Gods

1

"The plane for Lisbon leaves in five minutes!" A loudspeaker, hoarse from much effort, bawled into the shabby restaurant. "Passengers will kindly take their seats."

A swarthy little man crammed a soft hat over his blue-black hair, gathered together wife, grandmother and babies, rugs, bags and brief cases, and walked purposefully out. A lame waiter, a cleaner, and the hang-overish lieutenant at the next table looked after him as if gazing into another world, with an envy so incredulous, so hopeless as to be devoid of bitterness. The panes of glass in the wrenched door had been replaced by cardboard, and near the ceiling the wall plaster had flaked away. I'd been here since early morning, but the thunder of the packed underground train still roared in my ears. I shook my head and lit my fifteenth cigarette, which tasted more like dried moss than ever. The porter at the press club, after peering warily round the hall, had given me the cigarettes in exchange for butter coupons. I'd been waiting here no more than a couple of hours, but already I felt abandoned and alone in an empty world.

"You smoke too much; you'll get shaky hands," said the lieutenant at the next table reprovingly, as with trembling fingers he straightened his collar. His green tunic was faded and bore only two medal-ribbons; he was just a subaltern on leave, a person of no importance, with an

275

intelligent, pleasantly ugly face. He licked his dry lips and was glad not to be dead yet.

"Leave up?" I asked, wondering how such a junior officer had achieved so satisfying a carouse. No doubt the girls had been saving their Easter allocation of spirits for him all these months.

"Two weeks in Hamburg," he said with a laugh. "My home town, you know. Now I'm on my way to Lapland. Where are you bound for?"

"I don't know," I replied truthfully.

"Military secret, I suppose," he remarked. "Same old bloody nonsense."

"Cigarette?"

He took one with trembling fingers. His face was the color of dough from his hang-over. Thawing a little he asked, "Foreigner?"

"Journalist," I told him, and it was true. I still had my press passport; it had been restored to me with a thousand apologies on my release, which was as sudden and unexpected as my arrest. They'd even reserved a room for me at the Adlon, because some men from a French forced labor battalion had been moved into my old room meanwhile. All my baggage was intact, and I had lost only two weeks of my life.

"My home's in Hamburg, you see," he told me, as if wanting to send a last greeting to the world, whether or not it arrived.

"Yes, I know," I answered. At that time Hamburg was already regarded as a devastated city. The waiter came cheerfully through the door behind the bar, limped up to us with his head on one side and said with a flush of enthusiasm on his gray cheeks,

"Some vermouth has just come in, sir; two-fifty a glass."

It was now eight in the morning, and naturally we each

ordered one. A man had to take what he could get. People queued every day at the Adlon bar when the day's allocation came in, and in a quarter of an hour it was sold out. After that one could get nothing but a bottle of white wine at an exorbitant price—that is, if one was on good terms with the headwaiter.

The waiter looked at me with the mild and mournful eye of an old dog without a bone. "Have one yourself," I said, for my fellow-feeling was not yet dead; on the contrary, it grew hourly more pronounced. Therefore I ordered another glass as soon as I finished the first. It was an excellent French vermouth.

"My love to Lapland," I said, raising my glass. "I was there once in peacetime, fishing." I tried in vain to remember the name of some river or place up there, but my memory was like a loosely woven bag full of ashes.

"Salmon!" said the officer, somewhat stirred. "We stun them with hand grenades as a rule. It's good sport."

Good sport. He said that with genuine enthusiasm. I drained my glass and reflected for the thousandth time that my world was blown to pieces and would never return.

"I brought some reindeer antlers for my mother, to fix on a cupboard or on the wall," he told me, in the nostalgic tone that all Germans adopt when talking of their mothers. "There was no cupboard left. No walls either, for that matter. The old lady herself was barely there. But there were girls—" and he smacked his lips reminiscently.

Through the crooked doorway came a very beautiful woman, wearing an expensive fur coat and carrying a pigskin bag. Her oval face was heavily made up, despite the earliness of the hour. Smiling she looked round, came up to me and spoke my name inquiringly. I rose.

"I was told you were waiting here," she said lightly.

"That was quite unnecessary. I could have fetched you in my car if I'd known. We're starting at once."

She evidently assumed that I knew her, for she didn't tell me her name. The lieutenant at the next table signaled his astonishment with eyes and hands and dropped jaw.

"Have a vermouth," I suggested. "It's very good—too good to leave for other people."

"Lovely," she said. "We've been drinking champagne all night, at Magda's." She took it for granted that I knew who Magda was, and this confiding attitude flattered me. The waiter came up, bowing ecstatically, and the woman smiled at him like a young girl.

"Schmidt!" the lieutenant introduced himself loudly, springing up so abruptly that the table was nearly overturned, and clicking his heels with a military bow. "If you'll allow me. Every boy in Lapland has a photograph of you. We admire you tremendously. We see all the new films at the front. 'Take-Off at Dawn'—ah, you were wonderful in that. We're all in love with you."

She dropped her fur coat over his shoulders and patted his cheek. "Would you hold this for me?" she asked him. The waiter brought the whole bottle of vermouth on a tray and quivered with excitement as he filled the glasses. "This is a great honor," he said.

Now I too recognized her. I ought to have known her before, of course, but film stars look quite different in real life: smaller, somehow, and less significant. One had to study her closely to perceive how alive her face was under all the war paint.

We drank the vermouth. Lieutenant Schmidt gazed at the actress with such rapture that he choked.

"The charter plane for the delegates leaves in two minutes!" roared the loudspeaker angrily. "Kindly take your seats at once."

In a collapsing world, under the corpse-pale fog of Berlin, the sunshine of the vermouth warmed my heart. She was really a charming woman—and she smelled good after the lysol of my cell. Her eyes were blue and they sparkled with gaiety and zest. With her gold fountain pen she signed the printed menu, on which most of the dishes had been crossed out with smudgy ink. "My heart flies to Lapland," she wrote in staggering letters; and only then did I realize that she was not entirely sober. Schmidt pressed the menu to his breast and a tear or two rolled down his doughy cheeks. "I shall never forget you," he vowed. I thought of Lapland and of two crossed bits of birchwood on a mound. It was a mad world.

The loudspeaker bellowed again; it seemed flustered.

"It's for us," I said with a start, as our names were called.

"They can wait," said the actress tranquilly. "They won't leave without us. This is extremely good vermouth. You have one too." This last was addressed to the waiter who with a grubby napkin over his arm stood resting his lame leg near by, and staring at her enraptured.

A huge, angry gentleman strode in and straight up to us, followed by a white-faced, narrow-headed man wearing the smart uniform of the Ministry of Propaganda. He was carrying a sealed packet. The giant seized the actress by the arm, dragged her to her feet and shook her.

"The plane's waiting," he snapped. "You're drunk again. You'd better be careful."

"I was at Magda's," she said haughtily, though with a hint of constraint, and she tried to free herself. "We drank champagne all night. Be careful yourself."

"Your parcel," said the official politely, trying in vain to give her the sealed packet. At last he turned to me.

"Would you be good enough to take charge of this?" he asked. "He'll take it from you when you arrive—he or someone else who knows about it."

"Of course," I said obligingly. "I shall be glad to." The parcel was so heavy that I nearly dropped it. It was a cube measuring about eight inches each way, and sealed with black wax. "It's darned heavy," I remarked.

The representative from the Ministry of Propaganda softened slightly. "I hope you have a good journey," he said, extending a chilly hand. "Your papers are in order. We can't change money for you here, but if you apply to the authorities at the other end you can get what you need for your expenses. I think you should find material for an interesting article; and you'll be the only journalist there."

I took this to be a sort of amends for my wrongful imprisonment. Lieutenant Schmidt helped the actress on with her fur, whereupon she threw her arms round his neck and kissed his wan cheeks. "Darling, we shall never meet again," she said, and kissed him on the mouth. Trembling with pride the waiter picked up her glass and struck off its foot against the edge of the table. "No one else shall ever drink from this glass," he said. "I shall keep it as a souvenir of you—I shall take it home. Thank you, madam; thank you!"

Leaving the lieutenant standing, with lipstick on both his pallid cheeks, we were hustled out to the plane. It was brand-new and gleaming, and the seats were upholstered in red leather. My typewriter was already in the baggage rack, and the angry man assured me that all my other stuff was in too. Three propellers sprang thunderously to life and the aircraft turned and taxied over the grayish-yellow runway. Smoke from a smokebox floated close along the ground before the wind, and a few gray men wearing wooden clogs were languidly filling in some bomb-craters at the edge of the airfield.

There were only six passengers. The airfield vanished beneath us and Berlin vanished behind us: a scarred marvel full of despair and strength. The film star fell asleep as soon as we were air-borne. My eyes smarted from lack of sleep and my head felt utterly empty. It was terrible to be flying in a shiny new aircraft over a country at war, with the passport of a neutral country in my pocket and with the sense of being entirely useless. I never even smiled to think how delighted my people at home must have been to hear I'd been locked up. My early release was no doubt a bitter disappointment to them. So long as I was in my cell they at least knew where I was and what I was doing. Now I didn't know this myself, nor where I was bound and why. I fell asleep, too.

2

The sun was setting red over yellow plains and black rivers when we started to come down. We had flown direct and shared a luxurious lunch basket, which also contained two golden-necked bottles of champagne. The film star was pale under her make-up, and clutched her head faintly moaning. She chewed at her foie-gras sandwich without being able to get it down, and at last took a couple of heroin tablets from a little gold box, which she also handed to me. The giant talked to her tenderly in a low, persuasive voice. Soon her eyes became unnaturally bright and they changed from blue to gray. Even in this wretched state she was an enchanting woman.

The three other passengers were in civilian clothes, and

changed languages carelessly as they spoke. They had nothing to say to me, but I heard one of them respectfully addressed as Prince. I was evidently in very exalted company, but this didn't particularly disconcert me. Once, in the happy days when I still had a little money, I belonged to the Cannes Jockey Club. My aunt still lived in Lugano, and I knew that she could get me a visa and a ticket for the United States at any time.

My aunt assured me that in the States I could always get a well-paid job as butler to some millionaire, being well-turned-out and mannerly; but so far I had preferred being a newspaperman in drowning Europe, though almost my only communications with the Swiss news agency that got me my press passport took the form of telegraphic distress signals for more money. The ever-helpful Ministry of Propaganda dispatched unasked all the hand-outs I should have been allowed to send, and although I might have wired these myself, I felt I could make better use of my telegram allowance.

Then one day I was suddenly arrested, and later as suddenly released; and to compensate me for the hardships I had undergone they told me that for once I might write what I liked. But I hadn't the remotest idea what it was I was to write about; I should find out when I got there, it seemed, and I was not to worry.

The situation seemed to me mildly absurd, but I consoled myself with the thought that those who had chosen me of all people for this job were making far bigger fools of themselves. I glanced up at the typewriter in the luggage rack; it was an American portable of the latest type, and I'd brought it with me merely to try and sell it in some country where typewriters were not to be had. I couldn't use it myself. Beside it on the rack lay the parcel with the black seals. It troubled me somehow: it was so heavy in proportion to its size.

The plane was coming in to land and the actress began arranging her features. She smiled at herself in the powder-box mirror, and her eyes changed color again from gray to a girlish blue. We touched down and rolled to a stop, while from the edge of the airfield two loudly hooting, shining black limousines drove forward. Vivacious gentlemen with white teeth embraced us all, pressed our hands, and kissed our cheeks with their silky mustaches. In a moment we were on our way at sixty miles an hour along an asphalt highway, past thatched farmhouses and fields of millet. Snow-white geese hissed angrily by the roadside, and in the fields of ripening grain red poppies glowed in competition with the setting sun.

Half an hour later a wrought-iron gate opened before us and we drove into a park enclosed by a high wall. On the farther side of an artificial lake stood a summer palace, light and beautiful in the modern style. It seemed deserted save for one manservant in black. Our exuberant hosts urged us to hurry and choose our rooms, have a bath and change, as we were an hour late already. They moved as naturally and casually about the house as if it were a hotel, taking bottles and cigarettes from the cupboards and bickering among themselves in a language I didn't know.

"Our dear allies," explained the big man dryly, and he guided me to a long corridor with guest rooms on either side. After opening a few doors I chose a spacious corner room with a fine view in two directions over the park. The entire floor was covered with a magnificent Oriental carpet, and the counterpane was of blue silk. On the wall between the windows hung a few Picasso etchings in narrow frames. I had a quick bath and got into evening clothes. On my way back to the hall I noticed that the furnishings included nothing fragile or easily damaged.

I was the first. My hosts rose with shouts of delight and gave me a drink. It was a clear, fiery apricot liqueur. That was how it began. Of that evening and the following days I remember nothing but a confused whirl of music, tail coats, evening gowns, medals and orders, smashed glasses, and screams and yells in at least ten different languages. I have a dim recollection of a horse race at which I sat beside an unutterably lovely and brilliant-eyed lady who held my hand tightly, as we had no other language in common.

I also have a blurred picture of a great ballroom where officers shot out the lights with pistols. A gypsy girl danced on one of the tables with her clothes reduced to rags. She shrieked hideously when she cut her foot on a bit of broken glass. We were also taken to symphony concerts, to the opera, and the theater—or so it says on the printed program of festivities, which I read afterwards. I'm not certain whether I was present at all these functions; I may have been asleep. Now and then during this week of gaiety I came across the film star. I believe we kissed once, but I'm not sure. I kissed so many, being ignorant of their language. Perhaps they kissed me because they took me for an ally; or perhaps on the other hand because they didn't.

I was dazed, battered by color, noise, changing scenes, and appalling heat. It was strange that I was so often able to keep on my legs, for at every party I remember guests being led discreetly away to lie down in small adjoining rooms. At some point it was borne in upon me that the climax of the celebrations still lay ahead, and was to take the form of a visit by an exalted personage from the allied country. So eminent and powerful was he that his name was never mentioned; it was merely whispered that he was one of those who stood nearest to the leader. He had promised to spend the weekend with us at the summer palace.

The object of the visit was to strengthen friendly relations between the two nations—of late regrettably impaired—and the task had been entrusted to him in order to dispel the rumor that he had fallen into disfavor. Newspapermen of many nations had been invited to this week of culture and festival, but I was the only one quartered in the summer palace, to which no other journalists were to be admitted. This was as baffling to me as everything else.

As the week went on I gathered further details, from scraps of conversation and surmise. Saturday night was to be the great night, and therefore the pace slackened slightly during Friday. No doubt it was for this reason that on Saturday morning I actually woke in my own room; the one allotted to me when I arrived. I may have slept there on some previous night as well, though I was not quite sure of this. At any rate I found myself there now, and in a fairly sober state. Gentle sunshine filtered into my room through the leaves of the trees outside. The windows stood open, the room was full of birdsong and the scent of flowers, and in bed beside me lay a woman, sound asleep. I had no idea who she was, and supposed she must have mistaken the room the night before. Without waking her I went into the marble bathroom and let cold water pour from every available tap over my sick head and quaking body. Then I soaked myself in scalding water, wondering whether I dared shave. In all the other places I'd wakened up in there had always been a servant at hand to shave me, lead me to a bathroom, find me a clean shirt and see that my suit was pressed, while in a borrowed dressing gown I recalled myself to life with dry martinis or champagne, in company with other members of the house party.

I was still lying in the bath, plunged in blurred thought, when the lady who had slept in my bed came in. "Oh!" said she on seeing me, and arranged her clothes, looking at me closely as if trying to remember something. "I was just wondering—" she went on, but left her sentence unfinished. Her irregular features were swollen with sleep, and looked woebegone. To be on the safe side I looked only at her face. Apologetically she asked, "I wonder if you can tell me where my frock is? I can't very well get out of here without it."

I couldn't remember seeing any frock, but I realized only too clearly that I should have to climb out of the bath and help her look for it; nevertheless I remained where I was in some embarrassment, wondering how a gentleman gets out of a bath in the presence of a lady who is a complete stranger to him. It's true that we had slept in the same bed, but that was neither here nor there.

"How ghastly I must look," she lamented, and rubbed her face with both hands. Then she looked at me again; her face cleared and her eyes sparkled vivaciously. "But we know each other!" she cried gayly. "Do forgive me; it's so difficult to tell men apart without their clothes. You're Schmidt. That's it—you were going to Lapland. How do you come to be here?"

Only now did I recognize the film actress without her make-up: the one I had drunk vermouth with at Tempelhof airport. I liked her better like this, and no longer hesitated to let my eyes stray from her face, having seen more of her in her films than was visible now. I replied that Schmidt must have reached Lapland long ago, and that I was merely a neutral journalist.

"Ah, now I remember!" she exclaimed. "I came into your room last night looking for something, and now for the life of me I can't remember what it was. I have an idea it was very important, too."

"Your parcel," I suggested. "It was left with my luggage. You know, that heavy thing with the black seals."

"That's it!" she cried, brightening. "His Excellency's coming tonight and before that I have to hand it over." She rubbed her aching forehead in irritation. "If only I could remember who it is I have to give it to."

I got out of the bath and tied a towel round me. She passed into the bedroom in front of me without giving a thought to what she had or hadn't got on. Her limbs were straight and she was beautiful in a childish sort of way, and very agreeable to look at. On the floor at the foot of the bed stood an opened champagne bottle, half full. I picked it up and looked at her inquiringly. She shook her curly head and shrugged her white shoulders. "I don't know," she said. "Perhaps I brought it with me."

The champagne was flat, but having already lost the habit of morning coffee and adopted the customs of the allies, I poured some out into a tumbler which we shared. My watch had stopped, but I somehow knew that it was Saturday, and so did she. That was why she had come for the parcel. We found it safely stowed away in the cupboard between my suitcase and typewriter, but her dress was nowhere to be seen.

I pulled the silk coverlet from the bed and threw it round her. "They'll think it's a dressing gown," I told her consolingly, and helped her to tuck the heavy parcel under her arm, for she needed both hands to hold the bedspread together. I kissed her warmly and she gazed into space over my shoulder. "It's frightful to be a German at a time like this," she said as I released her. "It's very kind of you to kiss me in spite of my being German."

Her presence was going to my head and I assured her that I would do it again any time.

"I can't open the door," she complained, clutching the coverlet with both hands; so I opened it for her and went with her along the corridor to her own door, which I also opened. A servant in black met us on the way and bowed low, though he looked past us into the distance. Not until I returned to my own room did I discover that I was still dressed simply in a bath towel.

The flat champagne helped me to shave and dress. The room was still full of birdsong and the scent of flowers. The black-clad servant knocked on the door, said good morning in French and brought me a cup of hot soup on a heavy silver salver. He asked whether I would like anything else to eat, and told me that His Excellency was expected at six P.M., when the prince, our host, hoped to find all his guests assembled in evening dress in the reception hall. Dinner would be at seven. In reply to my question he told me that it was now three in the afternoon and that the day was Saturday.

I put on my light flannel suit with the brown stripe. My head felt full of dough and my knees sagged. I longed more than anything to go for a walk in the fresh air, but I was terrified of falling into the hands of my hospitable hosts if I left my room. As I was knotting my tie the film star came back. She was now wearing a red silk dressing gown embroidered with loping silver wolves. Drops of water were running down her bare legs.

"Would you like a heroin tablet?" she asked kindly. "It helps."

"I'd rather have a walk," I replied. There was ineffable charm, maidenliness, and timidity about her face without its make-up. "Will you marry me?" I inquired. "I imagine not, but there's no harm in asking."

"Do you mean that?" she whispered, and she gave me a startled look as if I'd unexpectedly touched her at her tenderest spot, and pleased her, though she ought not to have been pleased. "No," she said, stiffening. "They'd never let me leave here with you. It would only cause you trouble." But her blue eyes rested on me like those of a child who has been given an unbelievably lovely Christmas present. "No, no," she said again, shaking her soft curls. "But you can love me if you like. It makes no difference. And I'm married already, though I don't always remember it. With an oakleaf in diamonds; didn't you know? They wanted it. Propaganda. It was all the same to him; he prefers boys. You must have heard that?"

Abstractedly she slipped a heroin tablet into her mouth and swallowed it with a jerk of her slender neck. "If you like," she said sadly. "It's such a little thing. But lock the door first."

She must have forgotten that there was no key in any of the doors, so that none of the rooms could be locked: evidently a deliberate precaution. Or perhaps she remembered, but wanted to be friendly. I cooled a little, and glanced round the room. "Whoever listens in must have fun," I remarked. "I wonder if they make recordings?"

"No," she said simply. "I don't think they've put in any microphones yet; nothing important has happened. They may do it tonight when we're all downstairs."

She put her arms round my neck and kissed me lightly on the corner of my mouth. "You're the kindest person I've met for a long time," she said. "Perhaps that's why I strayed into your bed. A human being is a very lonely thing. But there'll be an end to it all soon. I'll be seeing you, fellow-human."

When she had gone I crept into the corridor and began seeking a way out. I lost myself in galleries and rooms, but now the whole place was alive with servants and I could ask my way. In the great banqueting hall a big horseshoe table was being laid for dinner, and in the entrance hall a wrinkled gardener was at work with numbers of assistants, surrounded by masses of flowers in baskets. I went outside, unhindered, walked round the artificial lake and crossed the park to the gate. No guards were to be seen. Before me stretched a dusty road. My knees still felt weak as I stepped out into the blazing sunshine. The festivities were over; now followed reality—the reality for which preparations had been made throughout the week, and no doubt long before that.

3

I strolled a little way along the road, and from either side of it, poppies shot fires into my drowsy eyes. The poppy-glow hurt my eyes, and the world around me lay horribly desolate under the burning rays of the sun. I passed a couple of thatched cottages, but not a sound came from them. Where the road crossed the main highway there was a clump of trees and bushes, and in among them were parked two light armored cars, camouflaged with leafy branches, but there were no soldiers to be seen. Nevertheless I felt that hidden eyes were spying on every step I took.

I walked on and on. My shirt stuck to my back and sweat poured down my chest. I entered a thatched cottage to ask for something to drink, but there was not a soul about. I passed a cart that had been overturned into a ditch. All was quiet. There was nothing but ripening wheat and the smell of dry earth. Evidently the whole region had been evacuated for the occasion. The walk did me good: my knees stopped trembling and my steps were surer. I was sweating out the alcohol through every pore, and a buzzing cloud of flies now followed me.

In the roadside ditch I came upon the body of an old

Jew. His gray beard bristled upwards and his eyes stared blankly at the blue sky. His sallow face was speckled with dried blood. He had probably been killed as casually and indifferently as one swats a teasing fly. I looked at my watch and saw that I must turn back if I was to be changed and ready by the time His Excellency arrived.

No one stopped me. No guards were to be seen. No one came to ask for my papers. The impending visit was after all to a friendly disposed country, to an ally, and therefore no security measures were necessary. Yet I had a feeling that the earth, the fields, the grain were all petrified in hate-filled expectancy, under the broiling sun. The sweat streamed off me, spoiling my neat flannel suit, but my soul shivered. I'd given up wondering why I had been chosen as witness. It was perhaps because I was the stupidest and most superfluous of all the correspondents, or because I drank when I could get anything to drink and borrowed money when anyone would lend it. I talked mostly about horses and cars and knew nothing of politics. A harmless type, if ever there was one, to admit into a country at war. Or that was what everyone thought; and no doubt those who had interrogated me in prison had gained the same impression.

When I returned, two pretty, smiling girls were decorating the entrance gates with garlands of flowers. They laughed coquettishly, with flashing white teeth. Two pretty, dark-haired girls. I passed the lake, wherein the white summer palace was reflected, radiant, dreamlike. In the hall I was met by a swooning fragrance; on each side of the entrance were cascades of pink flowers. One of the hosts was already awaiting me, in tail coat and decorations. His blue chin was freshly shaven and he smiled with a glint of his gold tooth.

"We've been wondering where you were," he remarked,

to hasten me. "It's time to change. Perhaps you'd be kind enough to translate His Excellency's speech into French, at dinner. You'd be doing us a great service. We want as few outsiders here as possible. We're quite on our own here, you understand; it makes everything freer and more informal."

His strained smile included me in this distinguished company, and I realized that a great honor was being done me. I was just going when he asked cautiously, "Of course you've no firearms about you?"

I assured him that I was not in the habit of carrying weapons.

"My question was a mere formality," he said. "We assume that our guests are unarmed. Naturally we can't search anyone; the party's too select, and every guest is vouched for. Still—" He looked a little uncomfortable. "But we have time for a drink," he added quickly, and led me into the service room. "You're a newspaperman—an intelligent man. You must know—this is entirely confidential, of course—that we're putting out indirect peace-feelers. Our great hope is to achieve peace on tolerable terms. That's why *he's* coming. They've smelled a rat and they want to bring a little pressure to bear. They would like to occupy the country, or at least part of it, and if anything were to happen to him while he was here it would give them a wonderful pretext. That's why it's best that no one should carry arms; we're a hot-blooded nation."

He gave a curious smile, still holding me by the arm. "On the other hand," he continued, stressing every word, "in the eyes of the allies it would be a token of our good will if something did happen. It might ease our relations with them. Occupation is a serious matter—very serious. But at a pinch it can be borne. Germany will lose the war

anyhow in the end. So you see, this situation this evening
is complicated. Keep your eyes open."

I saw he was trying to give me a hint, though why I
couldn't make out. Of course he had authority to say this
to me, or he would have held his tongue. But why—and
why to me? I drank a glass or two of fruit juice with him;
it was the first soft drink I'd had for a week. I simply
couldn't bother my head about what he'd said. We were
all in a net which was already so tangled that no one
could free himself, so why puzzle one's brains for nothing?
The evening had not even begun.

A young man with the face of a spoiled boy now came
into the service room. "You know the Prince, our host,"
said my companion by way of introduction. The youth
offered me two fingers in indifferent greeting and poured
out some of the famous apricot liqueur from a polished
decanter. "Bottoms up," he said carelessly. "You'll feel
better." The strong liqueur swept through me like fire,
but I couldn't refuse to drink at my host's behest; he might
have been offended. I put my hand on the doorhandle to
steady myself, and he looked at me with a sly, cruel smile.
"This evening you shall meet my wife," he said. "My wife
is something very special. Worth looking at. Keep your
eyes open."

As the drink scorched my stomach I reflected in impotent rage that it would be no thanks to him if I managed
to keep my eyes open until the evening. Besides, I was
getting tired of all these injunctions to do so. He went, and
I made for my room feeling muzzy again, and weak at the
knees. I wandered endlessly through dark corridors, still
dazzled by the sunlight, and in some anxiety, as I still had
to have a bath and change. At last I hit the right passage
and the right room, but when I opened the door I hardly
recognized it. The floor was littered with empty boxes,

and on the table were amplifiers and tape-recorders, which two men in brown were just assembling. One of them had earphones on. The big man whom I already knew met me in the doorway and hustled me out again.

"You're not wanted here," he barked. "Get out—we're in a hurry." He was ferocious; his face was covered with thin white scars, such as glass splinters might have made. I hadn't noticed them until now.

The valves of the apparatus on the table began to glow and the room was filled with cracklings and muffled echoes. I was overcome by a horrid feeling of unreality.

"But this is my room," I protested. "Where are all my things? I've got to change. I'm in a hurry too."

I forced my way in again, and peered under the bed and in the wardrobe, but my belongings had vanished.

"This room suits us best," said the big man, and he shoved me out again with all his weight. "We need space. It was selfish of you to choose the best room in the house; you've only yourself to thank for this. We've thrown your things out into the corridor. You'll find them there, unless someone has tidied them away."

He thrust me out with finality, and I made no resistance. My one thought was that the time was dangerously near six and that I had to get into a white tie before His Excellency arrived. There could be no question of appearing in my light, sweat-soaked flannel suit. Somehow I had to find my clothes and an unoccupied room.

The long corridor was now in a commotion. Doors banged, valets and maids rushed up and down the red carpet, half-dressed people popped out of their doors shouting impatiently in different languages. Bells buzzed continuously, and on the indicator board at the end of the passage fresh numbers kept bobbing up. I saw no one I knew. The servants I managed to waylay didn't under-

stand what I said, and simply shook their heads and hur-
ried on. I even tried the floor above and by now was
almost beside myself. At last I met a servant in black
whom I remembered seeing before and who I knew spoke
French. He was carrying an evening dress over his arms;
something wonderfully light and gauzy. I asked him feverishly about my things, but he knew nothing, and merely
eyed my light suit and dusty shoes with disfavor.

"If your luggage was put in the corridor, sir, it must
have been taken to some other room. Perhaps you should
ask some of the other guests. If I might suggest it, sir,
you'd better change at once or you'll be late."

This was as crazy as everything else. For a week I had
reveled with the rest; my head felt like a lump of dough
and hadn't a clear thought in it. I had to find my evening
clothes; that was all that mattered. Here was I, the only
independent witness to these momentous events, losing
precious time dashing about the house like a maniac,
looking into one room after another, knocking at doors,
opening them, slamming them again. In every room someone was dressing. Women screamed, men swore. In one
room alone all was quiet; but there a young man was lying
peacefully asleep in bed, with an equally young woman
beside him. There was no sign of my luggage.

The only person who showed any willingness to help
was an ugly little woman who was already dressed. She
came out of her room, stood with her back against the
door and questioned me closely as to what had happened.
Her German and French were inadequate and she kept
asking the same thing over and over again; while I didn't
grasp half of what she said, and merely saw that she was
showing a lively sympathy in my troubles. At last we both
stood shrieking at the tops of our voices, in the belief that

we should understand one another better if we talked louder. But we didn't. I gave up. It was hopeless.

At this point a furious man in evening dress rushed up with a great clinking of medals. "Hush!" he shouted. "His Excellency is on his way. Everyone to the hall. Hurry!" To me he said angrily, "What are you doing here? Why haven't you changed?" I replied with equal heat that someone had thrown my things out of my room and I couldn't find them. He insisted that this was no excuse; I must change instantly. I couldn't translate His Excellency's speech in a flannel suit, still less could I sit down to dinner so dressed. He squeezed my arm till it hurt, and I realized that he was as nervous as I was. I went with him to the landing and thence to a little gallery from which one could look down over the reception hall. About thirty guests were already assembled, men and women, all in evening dress. Not a single uniform was to be seen, in spite of its being wartime. The smell of the flowers reached us even here. A rigid silence reigned.

A very pale young man carrying an attaché case was already standing on the balcony. He wore some kind of decoration with a purple ribbon on his lapel. My companion released me, and went over and clapped this man on the shoulder.

"You've got the attaché case," he said. "That's something. Everything else is in as big a mess as it can be."

The young man wiped his moist hands on the silk lining of his tails. I remained there alone with him. I was suddenly weary of the whole thing; I didn't care how I was dressed—what did it matter? I could just as easily look on from up here. I lit a cigarette and threw the match down into the hall.

"Would you look after this case a moment?" asked the

pallid man. "There's someone missing from down there; I've got to find her. God, this is hell!"

He handed me the case, which was unexpectedly heavy, and I stood with it in my hand looking down. The prince was standing nearest the door, staring in displeasure at a watch in his hand: the distinguished guest was late. Suddenly he flung the watch on the floor and shouted, "Music! We're not buried yet." At once a dance band struck up, somewhere behind a bank of flowers, and the cheerful music wrought an instant change. I pulled greedily at my cigarette; it stung my mouth as I stood looking down on the bare arms and backs of the ladies. "Dance!" shouted the prince, kicking the watch over the slippery floor. Instantly laughter broke out like a hurricane, the guests grouped themselves in couples and the dancing began, wildly, feverishly. The dreary period of hang-over was past, the reveling was resumed and the guest of honor was missed by no one.

The pale man returned, dragging with him the film actress who was vainly attempting to hook up her dress at the side. Her eyes were bright and the pupils were black dots. She was quite drunk with heroin.

"You'll ruin everything!" the young man said furiously. "Go down at once and dance. Do your job." He took the case from me and I knelt to help her with the hooks. Her waist was bare and warm beneath the frock. I wondered how she kept her stockings up.

"Come down with me and dance, fellow-human," she pleaded. "I can't see a thing; I shall fall downstairs." But I couldn't go with her; I had no evening clothes. The pale man stared at me and began cursing softly, almost inaudibly. The actress went down the stairs holding firmly to the bannisters, and disappeared at the turn behind a

fine piece of antique marble sculpture. Just then a three-
note chord from a motor horn sounded above the music,
the laughter and the shouts. The dancing stopped; but
only slowly, and still laughing, did the beautiful people
below move back to their places along the walls. The
prince advanced to the door.

His Excellency entered alone. He was a fat man with
graying hair. From up in the balcony he looked small and
harmless, yet when he appeared the laughter died and the
flowers lost their scent.

4

The prince shook hands with him, and bade
him welcome with an air of confidence. He expressed his
pleasure at having the good fortune to spend a pleasant
and informal evening in the company of a statesman who
was one of Europe's—indeed the world's—great architects
of the future. He then led his guest over to a table and
with his own hands presented a gift of welcome: a heavy
gold tray, with a wine-flagon and goblets also of gold. His
Excellency weighed the tray in his hand and in an instant
was all good humor. "I like this sort of thing," he remarked simply. The prince then presented the guests to
him in order of precedence; he clasped the hands of the
men cordially in his own soft one, and kissed the prettiest
women on the cheek.

The pallid man beside me leaned over the balustrade
and stared down at the scene. He had set down the attaché
case at his feet, and now gripped the rail before him with
both hands. I offered him a cigarette, but he never looked
up. Below, servants in black were handing round cham-

pagne, and every time a cork popped, the distinguished guest started slightly. He had put his arm round the waist of the actress, to support her. "We know each other already," he explained to the prince; then scolded her mildly: "Drunk again?"

The prince raised his glass, and at the same time pinched the actress's arm surreptitiously, but so sharply that she gave a little scream and dropped her own glass. It smashed to pieces on the floor. She seemed suddenly to have recollected something, and freeing herself she looked up at the balcony as if seeking help. Then she waved. Instinctively I waved back; but her wave was not for me. The pale man beside me sighed heavily, shook his head and turned his back to me. He opened the case and poked at something inside; then having shut it noiselessly he strolled downstairs and propped it against the wall at the turn. Then with equal composure he came back, smiling crookedly and swearing to himself.

"What are you up to?" I asked suspiciously.

"Give me a cigarette," was all he said.

The prince now walked with his guest to the foot of the stairs, where they passed from my line of vision; but His Excellency unexpectedly reappeared and went back to the gold tray to weigh it in his hand once more. It was massive enough and he smiled contentedly. His dress suit was tight and uncomfortable. For many years he must have been more accustomed to wearing uniform and boots.

At that moment came a flash and a crash from the stairs. The tall windows were shattered, the blast hurled me against the wall and clouds of plaster dust settled on my hair. The pale man had been prudently standing behind a pillar. He glanced at me, smiled wanly and threw away his cigarette. "Au revoir," he said, and went quickly downstairs, jumping nimbly over the part that had collapsed.

All that was left of the wonderful sculpture at the turn was a torso; yet even now the surface of the marble glowed with the imperishable beauty of the human form.

I was momentarily deafened; I gasped for air and rubbed the lime dust from my eyes. Below, in the hall, most people had crouched down and shielded their heads with their arms. The distinguished guest carefully replaced the tray on the table and looked searchingly from face to face. It was at that moment that the pallid young man ran down the stairs, and the prince drew a pistol and shot him point blank in the head. He fell instantly, but at the same moment many of the guests drew their own weapons and fired shot after shot at the body on the floor. The women held their ears and shrieked between bangs.

The guest of honor laughed a little and turned an ironical eye on the prince. When the firing had ceased he went over to the dead body and turned the limp head upwards with the toe of his patent leather shoe.

"*Schade*," he said. "The boy's dead, and of course the responsibility for this act lies with him alone."

"There are the bomb fragments," suggested the prince. "They might give us a clue."

"Quite unnecessary," said his guest dryly. "I know already. Let's continue with the program; luck's still with me."

Accompanied by the prince he began mounting the stairs. At the turn he walked round the gap and passed his soft hand over the flat marble belly of the statue. "*Schade*," he said again. "But there are an unpleasant number of firearms about. Perhaps you'd be good enough to have them all collected and put in a safe place—your own included, if you'll forgive me. It was most thoughtless of you to shoot him, Prince."

His tone was one of mild reproach. As he drew near to

where I stood he pretended not to see me. Behind him came two men supporting a gentleman with a gray mustache who had been accidentally shot in the foot during the general firing.

I suddenly found that I was desperately hungry. For days I hadn't been in a condition to eat a proper meal, and now I felt as if I had a gaping void inside me. I had to find my clothes or I shouldn't be able to go down to dinner. Once more I started going from room to room in search of my luggage, but now I did it methodically instead of dashing at random about the corridors.

At last I came to a room where on the arm of a chair silver wolves pursued one another over red silk. I paused to wipe the sweat from my forehead. From somewhere far below came the sound of frenzied dance music. Then I heard a clattering in the bathroom and the big man came from it with his hands full of toilet things. "Oh, it's you," he said, tossing bottles and jars with a crash into an open suitcase. "This room will be free in a minute; you can have it if you like. I've had your things moved in here." He swept the dressing table clear with one movement. Pots of face cream, bottles of scent and nail polish clattered into the suitcase. Then he bundled the dressing gown together, crammed it over the rest and pressed down the lid of the case with his knee.

I found my belongings. My dress suit had been pressed and was hanging in the wardrobe. Shirt, collar, white tie, socks, and shoes were laid out. It only remained for me to put them on.

"Why couldn't you have told me at once?" I said angrily.

"I was in a hurry." His grin was almost friendly. "Forgive me." He bowed, and the thin scars lay like a white net over his irritable face. He shoved open the door with his elbow, carried out his luggage and kicked the door shut behind him. I could think of nothing but my clothes and my raging hunger. Dashing into the bathroom I turned on the tap. The bath smelled pleasantly of bath salts. The mirror showed me that my hair was white with lime dust.

As I washed and dressed I could hear the fevered beat of music from below, muffled by many walls; it both stunned and electrified. Beside the bed, hidden by a corner of the counterpane, I found an opened bottle of brandy. I poured some into a tumbler and swallowed it, and my hunger was deadened. The music thudded at my temples as I went downstairs.

A carpet had been laid on the stairs, the broken glass had been swept up, and drawn curtains waved gently before the shattered windows. The guests were dancing the conga in a winding column through the rooms with their hands on each other's hips, led by the prince. One after another tailed on with screams and laughter. The big man was standing looking on by the door. Suddenly he put out his hand and snatched the film star from the line. "Come here," he said. "You're tight." She smilingly resisted him and called out some meaningless remark, and the man dancing behind her with his hands on her hips protested too. But the big man drew her easily to him by her bare arm and led her away. As they went upstairs she looked round; her dimming eyes found me and with her free hand she waved, calling "Good-bye, fellow-human!" She was enchantingly beautiful. A flower of brilliants fastened her blue dress in the hollow between her little breasts.

In the banqueting hall the dancers, with twistings and turnings and loud cries, moved round the splendidly decorated horseshoe table. The guest of honor stood somewhat apart with a tall glass in his hand, smiling at the prettiest of the ladies. Beside him, leaning on a stick and talking to him in French, was an old gentleman with a gray mustache and a bandaged, slippered foot. His Excellency nodded absently now and then; he did not understand French. I passed quickly through the billowing curtains into the fiery splendor of the sunset; its last rays illuminated the terrace outside, and the palace was reflected like a glowing dream in the still surface of the lake.

I heard a thin cry, a swishing sound—as when a bird takes flight—and then a horrible thud. Turning, I saw the the blue dress lying across the stone balustrade that bordered the terrace: the actress had fallen on her back, in a twisted position, with her head on one side and her legs on the other. Her spine had snapped like a twig.

I looked up. The big man was standing far above, on a balcony just under the roof, looking down. "Is that you?" he called, smiling. "Imagine it! She tripped and fell over the rail. She was tipsy. Wait a moment; I'll come down."

I took her head and shoulders in my arms. She was heavy and quite limp. Perhaps she oughtn't to have been moved, but I lifted her from the balustrade and laid her on the stone paving of the terrace. She moaned softly and opened her lovely blue eyes. "Is it you?" she whispered; she tried to move, but couldn't. Her back was broken. "My bag, those tablets," she said. "Nothing more then." A jeweled evening bag lay open on the flagstones; I found the little gold box and slipped a couple of heroin tablets into her mouth, but she couldn't swallow them. The hooks of her dress had been torn open down the side, and her skin gleamed through.

I lifted her curly head on my arm and kissed her quickly on the mouth; I couldn't help her in any other way. Her lips tasted bitter from the drug. "You should have loved me while there was time," she whispered with an effort, and she tried to smile. "Now my body can't feel anything. But kiss me again, if you don't mind doing it. It's good to have someone near." She swallowed and swallowed, and carefully I put two more tablets between her lips.

The big man strolled up to us and stopped. He lifted her silk-clad leg on the toe of his boot; it fell limply back when he drew his foot away. Thoughtfully he lit a cigarette. The sun went down; darkness came suddenly, and the flame of his match lit up the face crisscrossed with thin scars. Somewhere in the garden a row of powerful lamps were switched on, and the whole façade of the palace was flooded in bluish light.

I embraced her limp body and kissed her lips once more. She was heart-rendingly lovely. Then she lost consciousness. At this moment there came to us the sound of hooves and harness bells. Three gypsies in bright colors rode on shaggy ponies past the lake and into the ring of blue light. They reined in and looked about them. Then they rode on up the steps and in through the main entrance, between billowing, floating curtains.

I laid her down on the paving. "You've murdered her," I said to the big man, and brushed the dust from my knees.

"What of it?" he returned, again lifting her foot carelessly. "What's it got to do with you?"

He was right. What had it to do with me? My job was simply to interpret His Excellency's after-dinner speech. I looked once more at her pale face in the floodlights. Then I went in.

5

The gypsies were riding round the banqueting table on their ponies. They performed amazing circus tricks, while the guests bombarded them with plates and glasses. A fat woman rocked on her chair, lost her balance and tumbled over backwards. Her neighbor rose, seized her arms and began dragging her across the floor. Next a quite unsober gentleman flung himself on his stomach, grasped her ankles and was dragged along too. Medals tinkled on him like Christmas tree decorations. The servants dared not bring in their dishes, and when a guest wanted anything to eat he took his plate and went to the service room to fetch it. Not many were eating. Wine spread in little pools over the dazzling white tablecloth. Women demolished the floral decorations and scattered the flowers round them. His Excellency smiled pensively and stroked his chin with his soft hand as he watched them.

But this was not the sort of thing that had been going on all the week. This was something new; I felt it in my bones, I saw it in the distorted faces round me. This was lunacy, an orgy beyond all reason. There was something behind it—some purpose which escaped me. It was useless to puzzle over it, and so I swallowed champagne and burning liqueurs by turns, until I was well and truly drunk.

The princess was sitting between the prince and the chief guest. She was young and dark. She laughed aloud when His Excellency, somewhat fuddled, pulled her dress down and kissed her shoulders. The prince too roared with laughter. Then he got up and chased away the gypsies; dance music began again and reeling couples clung fast to one another. Women's gowns were ripped to pieces. And still the curtains waved in front of the broken windows, and the night wind blew into the room.

I remember little after that. I suppose I fell asleep. At any rate I woke in a strange bed, with someone standing under the shower in the adjoining bathroom. Then the big man appeared; he shook me unmercifully and handed me a medicine glass saying, "Drink this." It may have been vinegar. At any rate I sobered up enough to go with him. The corridor of the floor above was lit only by a dim red light, and men were standing outside a closed door, listening gravely, among them the prince. His willful, boyish face was twitching, but as far as I could see he was perfectly sober. From behind the door came a thick laugh; then a long silence, until all at once I was startled by a cry of distress. A woman was calling for help. The door burst open and the princess ran out; her beautiful evening gown hung in shreds and she tried to hide her naked breast with her hands. Calmly the big man drew a pistol from his hip pocket and handed it to the prince.

"Your turn now, sir," he said. "Try your luck."

The distinguished guest appeared in the doorway and steadied himself against the jamb. He was in shirt sleeves, and his tipsy expression verged on the imbecile. His lardy, hairless chest could be seen through the opening of his dress shirt. He had no time to speak. The prince raised the pistol and shot him between the eyes, and the heavy body toppled heavily onto its back. The princess clung sobbing to her husband, and after a moment's silence the big man stepped over the threshold, bent down and felt His Excellency's head. Straightening up with a cheerful smile he said,

"Yes, he's dead. Congratulations, sir."

The prince drew himself up. "You may report to your superiors that he attempted to violate my wife—under my own roof, as a guest in my own house. I shot him in defense of my wife's honor; these gentlemen are all witnesses." He looked straight at me and I nodded readily. I was still pretty drunk. One of the men opened his gold cigarette case, officiously handed it to the prince and then gave him a light. The prince pulled at the cigarette and his hands shook. "God!" he said. "We could have done it with our bare hands. But of course it's tidier this way."

The big man thrust his arm under mine and began leading me back. I was as helpless as a child in his iron grip.

"You've earned a drink," he said. "Don't you think so?"

I made no answer. I could still see her dying face in the blue floodlight. My companion took me down to the service room, where he tore the wing from a roast bird, dipped it in congealed sauce and began gnawing at it. I took two glasses which looked only slightly used, and filled them from a bottle snatched up at random. "Here's to your death!" I cried.

"Arrh!" he said. "Why think of things like that? Tomorrow you'll be flying home. You're free to leave, and you're free to write exactly what you like. There'll be no censor trouble. Believe it or not, you may write what you please."

So that was it.

"You're alive," he went on. "At this hour millions are dying for a new Europe. *You've* got nothing to complain of."

I drank. "One day you'll be hanged," I said. "It's a consoling thought. Indeed, it's the only thought that does console me."

He laughed and looked at me with a sort of detached appraisal, as if I were a noxious insect that he wouldn't bother to destroy. "You neutrals, you're all neurotics," he said. "Foreigners. You don't understand Germany and never will—any more than these people here." He waved contemptuously towards the banqueting hall. "You're simply an unessential piece in a vast jigsaw puzzle, which only a superior brain can comprehend. You'll never grasp the whole of it, nor shall I. But I serve it, because I know that tomorrow's world will be ours."

"One day the puzzle will get too complicated," I returned, and I tossed back more of the fiery liqueur. "One day it'll get so involved that no brain will be able to deal with it. Even now it may be in such a muddle that none of these events have any purpose or meaning. You'd do well to think of that." I drank some more, and choked. Tears came into my eyes. Her skin had been so warm and smooth when I did up the hooks of her dress.

"Expensive stuff, this," he remarked, knocking the neck off a tall bottle of wine against the edge of the table. "It's good when one's thirsty. I'm always thirsty." He poured the sparkling wine straight into his mouth, and I saw that his teeth were yellow but faultless.

During the night I rose and drew back the curtains from my window. The night sky was full of stars, and the moon was setting beyond the park, crisscrossed with blue veins. Through my muzziness I was aware of the scent of trampled flowers and sour wine. My sick senses were suddenly intolerably keen. It was a moment of stabbing beauty, and it was worth all that had gone before. I still carry a vivid memory of that veined moon, and the scent of flowers and wine.

Next day he accompanied me to the airfield and never

let me out of his sight until I had boarded the plane for Switzerland. That day newspapers all over the world carried front page headlines announcing His Excellency's fatal heart attack, brought on by exhaustion, during his good-will visit to the allied country.

The seats in the aircraft were shabby, and the fuselage was patched with metal plates of different colors. But the propellers glittered in the sunshine as we circled the airfield and headed for the west. I refused to be a piece of the crazy jigsaw puzzle any longer; I took my typewriter on my knees, and in the eternal sunshine of ten thousand feet, far above the motionless sea of cloud, I composed the telegram to be sent off as soon as I set foot on Swiss soil. With two fingers I laboriously tapped out something like this:

Your correspondent, who has recently returned to Switzerland, confirms that His Excellency died as the result of a heart attack shortly after his arrival at the summer palace. Exhausted by his journey he had to take to his bed immediately, but before medical assistance could be obtained from the capital a further attack occurred which proved fatal. Your correspondent was present at the deathbed and read the bulletin issued jointly by the most eminent physicians in the country. Any rumors suggesting that the death was due to other causes may therefore be regarded as entirely groundless.

As a result of this fatality, all the festivities planned in connection with His Excellency's visit have been cancelled. Please wire money.

Even though for some reason I may have been intended to tell the truth, or as much of the truth as I saw, I was resolved not to be their tool. I read through what I had written and corrected the typing errors. I then crossed out the last sentence; for once I would not be petty.

In Zürich I pawned the typewriter and took the train for Lugano and my aunt.